LARRY D. SWEAZY

"This new series
takes us into the
heart of our nation
and the hearts of
the people who were
carving it out."
—Nuvo.net

JAN

ESCAPE
FROM
HANGTOWN

A LUCAS FUME WESTERN

BERKLEY

$7.99 U.S.
$9.99 CAN

S EAN

ISBN 978-0-425-26933-6

50799

PRAISE FOR

VENGEANCE AT SUNDOWN

"With *Vengeance at Sundown*, author Larry D. Sweazy has once again created a destined-to-be-classic that surpasses genre and cracks along strong and true with fistfuls of action and precise, vibrant language. Readers won't soon forget saddling up with bold hero Lucas Fume on this hell-for-leather ride down the vengeance trail."

—Matthew P. Mayo, Spur Award–winning author of *Double Cross Ranch*

"As an amalgamation of genres—Western, detective, mystery, historical realism—this new series takes us into the heart of our nation and the hearts of the people who were carving it out from under the lives of the original inhabitants whose bad luck it was to be in the path of Manifest Destiny. It's our unpretty story that keeps repeating itself." —Nuvo.com

THE GILA WARS

"Sweazy writes the most realistic and exciting accounts of the Rangers, bar none . . . The reader feels as if he is right there, fighting the dust, heat, flies, and fear, riding into the thick of battle . . . gut-wrenching . . . completely true to life."

—*Roundup Magazine*

THE COYOTE TRACKER

"A masterful page-turner full of suspense and surprises. It demonstrates the skill that has won Sweazy an appreciative following and numerous awards and recognition."

—Buddies in the Saddle

"A great entry in what has become one of the more solid Westerns still coming out. This harkens back to the old writers of the Old West . . . It's the Western that Erle Stanley Gardner never wrote." —Bookgasm

continued . . .

THE COUGAR'S PREY

"[A] gem among gems. Sweazy is a superb storyteller, and this quick-moving yarn is cut from tightly woven cloth. He breathes life into the frontier, and readers are immersed in the sights, sounds, and ever-present threat of death lurking at every corner." —Phil Dunlap, author of *Cotton's Inferno*

"Larry D. Sweazy once again spins a fine historical adventure full of compelling characters and gritty action."
—James Reasoner, Spur Award–nominee and author of *Redemption: Trackdown*

THE BADGER'S REVENGE

"A richly layered story that offers twists and turns that dare the reader to speculate who is guilty and why."
—Matthew P. Mayo, author of *Speaking Ill of the Dead*

"[A] fine entry to a great Western series . . . Wherever he goes, I'm on board, through thick and thin." —Bookgasm

THE SCORPION TRAIL

"Larry D. Sweazy's Josiah Wolfe books promise to stand among the great Western series. Think *The Rifleman* in the deft hands of a Larry McMurtry or a Cormac McCarthy."
—Loren D. Estleman, Spur Award–winning author of *The Confessions of Al Capone*

"Larry D. Sweazy takes you on a fierce ride . . . This crisp, well-written story returns you to the West as it really was."
—Cotton Smith, author of *Sorrel Moon* and past president of Western Writers of America

ESCAPE FROM HANGTOWN

LARRY D. SWEAZY

B
BERKLEY BOOKS, NEW YORK

BERKLEY

An imprint of Penguin Random House LLC
375 Hudson Street, New York, New York 10014

ESCAPE FROM HANGTOWN

A Berkley Book / published by arrangement with the author

ISBN: 978-0-425-26933-6

PUBLISHING HISTORY
Berkley mass-market edition / June 2015

PRINTED IN THE UNITED STATES OF AMERICA

10 9 8 7 6 5 4 3 2 1

Cover art by Bruce Emmett.
Cover design by Diana Kolsky.
Interior text design by Kelly Lipovich.

Penguin
Random
House

To Faith Black.

*Your hard work and dedication to the story
will always be greatly appreciated.*

ACKNOWLEDGMENTS

Every novel I write stands on the shoulders of authors who I've read, met, or who have inspired me along the way. When I mentioned to Loren D. Estleman in passing that I hadn't read any of Donald Hamilton's Matt Helm novels, it wasn't long before the first book in that series, *Death of a Citizen*, showed up in my mailbox. It was a great gift, and an apt start to the research I was immersing myself in for the Lucas Fume books. I had already decided that Lucas would be an ex-spy in a post–Civil War world, so the comparison of the characters had a similar seed since Matt Helm was an ex-spy in a post–World War II world. The early Helm books turned out to be amazing resources, and exceedingly well-written. I am now a fan, and will always be eternally grateful to Mr. Estleman's thoughtful generosity.

This book wouldn't be possible without the tenacity and support of my longtime agent, Cherry Weiner. Faith Black, my editor, and the Berkley production team have been invaluable. A special thank-you goes to Bruce Emmett for going the extra mile with my excellent covers. Finally, there's Rose, my wife, my partner, my best friend, who struggles right along with me through each book. Poor girl didn't know what she was getting herself into. Thank you again and again and again . . .

PART I

Welcome to
No Man's Land

But a silence vastly deep, oh deeper
    than all these ties
Now, through the menacing miles,
    brooding between us lies.

        —CLAUDE MCKAY, FROM "ABSENCE"

ONE

LUCAS FUME STOOD ON THE REAR PLATFORM of the train car, staring out over land so flat that it looked like a giant cast-iron skillet had fallen from the sky and smashed everything underneath it.

The wide-open view, the long-reaching vista was a far cry from the mountains and hills of his childhood home in Tennessee. That life, that green, lush landscape was just a memory now, and Lucas was certain that he would never return to it, never travel east again, across the Mississippi River, or back to what was once a perfect existence. Not out of fear, but out of self-preservation. He didn't want to look back, be held by the chains of the past. Grief had become an unlikely bedfellow of recent, and it had, as far as he was concerned, warmed him for far too long. There was nothing left for him in Tennessee. Everything that he had ever loved was either dead and buried, or sold off; every bind cut by choice or by fate.

There was a constant wind that blew across the Kansas plains. It cut and turned and whistled, rising and falling over the grasses, making the millions of pointed blade tips in the vast lea look like waves of an ocean. Such a body of water he had never seen, nor could he imagine, even though at the moment he felt like the captain of a small ship. Trees were sparse, and towns even more so. The sky had free roam, deep and blue as a happy eye, reaching overhead forever. Clouds came and went so fast that it was hard to tell if they offered a threat or not.

Lucas was still uncertain of what the next second would bring after years spent unjustly locked up in a prison cell.

The law of the land had allowed him to move about as he wished, but his footing was not as confident as it once was. There were still elements in the world that sought to do him harm, inflict revenge on him for his past deeds. Just because he was free of all criminal charges didn't mean that he didn't have to concern himself with retribution. Freedom by decree only went so far, at least in the world in which he had previously traveled.

Lucas never forgot that he had enemies, or that it was prudent to take an extra second to look over his shoulder to make sure he wasn't being followed—or watched.

And it was that desire—the desire to be able to see in all directions—that had brought him to where he was standing. On a railcar, detached from any visible train, sitting in the middle of a meadow that went on vacantly as far as the eye could see. It was like he had been left behind, left to forage for himself in a prebuilt pioneer shack—though one of many comforts—but that was hardly the case. The railcar belonged to him, or the lease of it, for the time being, and he wasn't alone. Fending for himself only came at his pleasure, by his own choice. His loss of ties back East had left him a very wealthy man. It was a position to which he had once been accustomed, raised in, taken for granted, then lost to the war, the loss finalized by treachery, trickery, and ultimately, a betrayal so deep that it took the life of his one true love, and nearly his own.

If he had learned only one thing from that event, it was this: Comforts could be taken from you at any moment. Comforts and love.

Lucas would never take either for granted again—one, comfort, could be bought, while the other, love, was best left to the poets. Love was the furthest thing from his mind. He doubted that he would ever venture down that path again.

Birds and animals were strange and new, too, in this foreign country—the territories of the West. He had seen three buffalo on a recent hunt, thin at the ribs, and so straggly and sorrowful looking that he hadn't been able to bring himself to shoot one of them. The steaks would have been a pleasure for their taste, but nothing more. There was no worry of food.

The railcar was staffed with a cook, Hobart "Hobie" Lawton, a hired man from a fine St. Louis hotel who had come highly recommended. So far, the cook had not been a disappointment. Lucas had already gained a tight waist on his pants, and had been forced to have a new set of trousers tailored in Abilene. His dinners were a far cry from the roach-filled gruel that the prison kitchen had served him. Still, it had taken more time than he would have ever imagined for his appetite to return.

From where he stood, Lucas thought the open field would be a fine place to stop, put down roots, but he knew that idea was just folly. The isolation would be too much to bear, and the winters too difficult to endure. He would have to move on soon, before the summer season offered a change—but for now, he enjoyed the long view before him, and waited.

Winter was a distant concern, and he was hardly alone. He enjoyed a comfortable isolation, and intended to make it as safe as possible.

A gunshot cracked off to Lucas's right, reminding him of that very thing. He didn't flinch, just sighed, looked over to the field to his right, and took in the sight of Zeke Henry, holding a smoking rifle, looking at it curiously, balancing it in his big skillet-sized hand without offering any readable judgment on his face.

"You haven't made up your mind, yet?" Lucas called out. He made his way down the platform, off the steps, and onto the hard, unforgiving Kansas ground.

Zeke, well over six feet tall, and black as a mature thundercloud, shook his head. With a few more arms to offer as limbs, he would have made for one of the larger trees around. As it was, the Negro was of normal composition for his height, everything in perfect proportion, along with a smile that would light any dark room with his flawless ivory teeth. Zeke had been a houseboy once, and the air of that position had never left him.

Zeke looked away from the rifle, let it fall to his side. "Ain't shore, Mistuh Lucas. Negro with a gun ain't encouraged less you be in the Tenth Cavalry Regiment. I never was no soldier, though I could ride with those fellas in that troop, and be just fine, I suppose."

Lucas stopped next to Zeke, and glanced over to the table that they stood in front of. It was loaded with weapons. Six-shooters, rifles, derringers of all makes and sizes, along with a few knives, both to carry in plain sight and to conceal. It was a wide array of firearms, old and new, from the personal armory that Lucas had amassed before leaving St. Louis. He had wanted to be prepared for anything that came their way.

The West was a mysterious land, with only the stories that had traveled back East over the years to navigate by. This was Lucas's first venture deep into the territories, his first journey into the new land. He wanted to be as prepared as possible, and was still taking pains, and making the best plans he knew how.

"That's why we're here," Lucas said. "So you can find one that fits you the best, that you're comfortable with."

"Ain't necessary," Zeke said. He put the rifle, a Springfield 1870, down onto the table, and shook his head.

"You don't like this one?"

"No, suh, it ain't that. Any would do. But you knows I'd just as well be on my own. I'd rather not carry a gun at all, if it all be the same to you."

"Trouble's coming for you, Zeke, you know that. A gun's as necessary as a good horse. Especially here."

"I does know that I be an object of capture, but you a free

man now. Me, I'll never be such. It is the hand I was dealt. You knows that. We got this great big country, and I hope to be a flea, and disappear down into the fur of the dog. Ain't that what all this grass look like to you? I ain't never seen such a thing." Zeke shook his head in wonder, but there was melancholy in his voice.

"They'll find you. You've got a price on your head."

"Don't want to spend my life runnin' if it all be the same to you. It'd been best if I'd turned myself in back in St. Louis. Then you be free to explore this land free of any trials due to me." Zeke shifted his shoulders, broad and straight as a two-by-six piece of lumber, like the shirt he was wearing was uncomfortable. He had been outfitted head to toe, boots to hat, in a new wardrobe himself, setting any doubters straight that he was not a convict on the run. With the bowler hat, fine linen shirt, maroon waistcoat with trousers to match, he passed more as a suave Negro carpetbagger than an escaped convict.

"They would've hung you on the spot, Zeke."

"I can't outrun the touch of Judgment Day. It'll catch up with me no matter how many guns I carries, or how much you wishes it to be untrue. Fate is fate. I be a marked man for all my comin' days."

"You have done nothing wrong."

"Say you." Zeke picked up another rifle, a new model Winchester. He settled the butt of it into his shoulder, fired, pulled the lever down, fired again, and again, until all of the cartridges were gone. A nod of approval came as he placed the rifle back on the table.

"That rifle's going to change the world," Lucas said.

"Just means you can kill a man faster, Mistuh Lucas, ain't nothin' new gonna come from that. Just more blood. Always gonna be new ways for mans to make war on himself and those that disagree with his ideas. Sad that we bring that fight to this land. It look so pure that I feel like I shouldn't be standin' on it."

"That Winchester just might be the blessing we've all

been hoping for," Lucas said, eyeing the horizon. "Get the war with the Indians over quicker."

"Or, it may well be another curse." Zeke followed Lucas's gaze, and settled on the point, on the image, that Lucas had suddenly focused on. "Somebody's a comin'." He looked down to the table, and reached for another fully loaded Winchester.

"There'll be no need for any weapons, Zeke," Lucas said. "I'm expecting company for dinner."

Zeke let his hand slip off the rifle, but he didn't let it fall too far away. "I hope you're expectin' a lot of visitors then, Mistuh Lucas."

Lucas followed Zeke's gaze, and the contented look on his face fell away. Before he could say another word, a thunderous gunshot rang out, echoing across the flat land quickly and unexpectedly.

The bullet pinged off of one of the iron wheels of the railcar, and was followed by another foreign, unexpected sound. A chorus of whoops and hollers: an Indian call to charge and attack.

"Cheyenne," Lucas said, reaching for the closest loaded rifle, another Springfield.

Zeke stood staring at the oncoming tide of Indians and horses, caught in a moment of fear, or awe, it was hard to tell which. "I 'spect I'll need that rifle now."

"You'll need as many as you can carry," Lucas said, firing the Springfield, backing up as fast as he could, dodging back and forth, trying to make himself as difficult a target as possible.

A flaming arrow arched through the air, descended rapidly, and stabbed into the ground with a resounding thud. The flame didn't extinguish, just wavered in the wind.

Luckily there was little for the arrow to use for tinder. The grass was beat down from Lucas's and Zeke's presence, and moist from a recent rain. It sat there like a candle in the daylight—only it offered no comfort to Lucas—just fear. He glanced back to the railcar, and broke into a run. "Come on, Zeke, let's go. Let's go."

But Zeke Henry didn't move, didn't act like he'd heard a word. He just stood there big and tall as a cottonwood tree, almost like he hoped one of the arrows, or bullets, would hit him just so he could see how it felt—or put an end to the hopeless wandering that lay before him.

TWO

MOST DAYS, CELIA BARLOW SAT ON THE SANA-
torium's veranda staring blankly into the distance. Words
had been lost to her for longer than seemed possible. At least
words that could roll off her tongue and slip from her mouth.
It was like her tongue and throat had been glued shut,
clamped tight, the ability to mutter something intelligible,
to speak, had been a skill she had never possessed. But she
was aware of far more than most people around her thought
she was. The doctors and nursemaids talked like she wasn't
there, like she couldn't comprehend anything they said, or
didn't say. She understood silent implications as well as any
loud argument.

The reality that she would never be what she once was,
that she wouldn't heal, that there was no ending for her other
than to just slip away one night into the sweet hands of death,
was not lost on her. Celia prayed for death to come and take
her away almost every minute of every hour.

She was also aware of patterns and schedules, and could
recognize faces, voices, and certain touches. It had been in

accordance to the time of day for her to be wheeled out in a chair, covered with a blanket, and left to drool on herself, as she looked out over the green valley, unable to swat at mosquitoes or flies, or scratch the tip of her nose, no matter the severity of the annoyance. Along with the ability to speak, she had also lost the ability to move. If she screamed, no one heard her. If she wanted to run, no one could catch her. She was trapped, a prisoner inside her own skin. Death was her only escape. And so far, it had been her hale physical health that had kept her alive and firmly planted in front of a path that she could not traverse, no matter the intensity of her desire to do so.

It was, however, at that moment that two shadows appeared, one on each side of her. There were no voices, no warning. One of the two men, who she had never seen before, stepped in front of her, and looked down at her like she was nothing more than a piece of meat. He smelled unfamiliar, of whiskey and tobacco, and it wasn't until she was being lifted into the air that Celia thought to be afraid.

But who would she call out to? The nurse who had scowled in disgust when she fouled herself? Or the doctor who poked and probed her like she was a pincushion with no feeling? Just because she couldn't scream didn't mean she didn't feel pain.

Celia thought she was either being kidnapped or rescued. Either way, she would be free of the walls that had held her prisoner for so long, free of the mush shoved down her throat to keep her alive, and the horrid-tasting medicines that did nothing but make her sleepier, and more immobile than she already was.

For all she knew, Death himself had answered her silent pleas, had come to visit her, and this was her voyage, deeper into the darkness, a final punishment. Punishment for the misdeed that had brought so much pain upon her, and her family, already.

If she would have been in her right mind, in her right body, she might have questioned the two men, asked them where they were taking her. But knowing full well that she couldn't, she relaxed her mind, and prayed. *Please, let it be soon. Please, this is no way to live. It was only true love that I surrendered to. How could that have been so wrong?*

The senator stood at the window of the hotel, looking down the long street that ended at the Capitol building. He was as tall as a doorway, and thin as a rail. A long, well-groomed beard, gray like a winter sky, announced his age and stature from a distance. But it was his eyes that were his most distinguished feature. They were deep blue, black in the lack of light, hard like steel, and full of ambition, even though such a thing should have run its course long ago.

The hotel room was as lush and fine as the man's clothes; it was a massive lion's den, appointed in all the latest fashions. He had stayed in the suite on every visit to Washington since he had been elected. Now, it matched his personality, and was decorated and furnished just for him, for his unusual size.

Lancaster Barlow had been compared to Lincoln in height, but that was all. Barlow was not a homely man, but one the ladies still found attractive—though he was most often suspicious of their motives. Nor was he a great orator, though he could legislate with the best of men, write laws for man and his misdeeds, and wrangle votes with favors, and promises, like the best of senators were expected to do. Being a small-town litigator was the only skill that he had shared with the sixteenth president. But Lancaster Barlow had never enjoyed the practice of law, not like Lincoln had. People and their petty problems bored him. He had always aspired to something grander, bigger. Leaving his mark on the world meant far more to him than solving a crisis of debt—or murder. Being a lawyer had only been a means to an end: It had transported him to Washington, and the title that came with it meant more to him than almost anything else in his life.

Sadly, the opportunity to climb higher in political office was lost, too. His causes and reputation had taken a beating recently, and Barlow was old enough to know that he did not have the time, nor the treasury, to repair both. It would have to be one or the other. Cause or reputation. He was still trying to decide which to pursue.

A knock came from the door, startling him out of his thoughts. "Yes," he said.

The door opened and a nervous looking man with glasses hurried inside the room, and closed the door behind him. "Sorry to bother you, Senator, but if you do not leave now, you will be late for the afternoon session, and I have news to report before you leave, sir."

"Yes, Paulsen, I was just gathering my thoughts about the Hills Regulation." It was a lie, of course. Barlow could have cared less about the latest attempt to encourage mining in his home state. His concerns for Tennessee were far and few between. "What news? Business or personal?"

"Both, sir."

"Business first."

"Are you sure, sir?"

"Of course. We are in Washington. Business is of the utmost, don't you agree?"

Leland Paulsen sighed, and nodded. "The notes will be in the carriage." The man wore round, rimmed glasses, and was just a little taller than most twelve-year-old boys—but there was no question that he was of an elder age. He was bald, with only a few stray graying hairs circling his head. Thin mutton-chop sideburns struggled down his cheeks like a dirty gray waterfall. He had been Barlow's secretary of affairs since the senator had arrived in Washington, some twenty-odd years prior. There was a small quarters set aside for the man in the front of the suite.

"I expected such," Barlow said, perusing Paulsen from head to toe. "Is there a problem, man?"

"Yes, sir. A reporter just left. He was asking questions about your son."

Barlow stiffened. "What type of questions?"

"Whether you were aware of his business dealings with the railroads."

"It is old news, Paulsen. I hope you sent the scallywag on his way with a swift kick in the ass. Election season is heating up early. I suspect I will have to face such nonsense if I seek to keep this office—which I no doubt will."

"He was a persistent man," Paulsen said.

"Roaches. The press is full of roaches, snakes, and traitors. I don't have time for this drivel." Barlow headed to the coatrack to retrieve his hat and cane. "My son is in prison for actions all of his own doing, and that is as it should be. I hope you told this reporter that that is my view. My son deserved the punishment he received."

"I did, sir. But he questioned your involvement. He seemed to believe that your son couldn't have maintained the contracts he held without your help, and that your hands, so to speak, were the ones that stirred the pot and still need washing."

Barlow cast Paulsen a hard look at the mention of hands. His son had been relieved of his hands, cut off, leaving stumps at the wrist in an attempt of his own to complete an alibi, and propagate a story that ultimately had sent an innocent man to prison for his son's false murder. It was a sad state of affairs, but Lancaster Barlow silently held his son in high regard for his commitment to the plan, and the execution of the deed.

Paulsen flinched at the look. "I'm sorry, sir, to have brought up such a sensitive subject."

Barlow shrugged. "I broke no laws, I can assure you of that, Paulsen. There is no need to pussyfoot around about my son's fate. He did it to himself, or had it done. So be it. That action cannot be changed, and now he lives with his choices like we all do."

"It is not me who has to be satisfied with an answer, Senator Barlow."

"You speak as if there is an inquiry being planned into this matter, Paulsen. Tell me, is this the news I should really be concerned about?"

Paulsen nodded. "The Speaker of the House is in the

process of ordering a public investigation to your link in the matter, sir."

"In the process?"

"Yes, from a reliable source. I understand the news will break a week before the filing deadline for the next election. Theobold Gladstone will take the lead in the investigation. It seems a matter of revenge, a public flogging, if you will."

"Gladstone will do anything to see me escorted out of this city, or thrown into some brig, along with my son. But he will only go so far. I have made it known to him that I am aware of his unfortunate proclivities, and will be just as glad to air them through my own channels."

"I am just doing my job, sir."

"I appreciate the intelligence, Paulsen. Your networks are intact and functioning at the highest order. I'm glad to see that my investments are proving their worth and paying the expected dividends." Barlow turned his lip up, and began to pace the length of the room. "These new Republicans are despicable in their quest for power. I shouldn't be surprised, though I admired them more as Whigs. I would most likely do the same thing if I were in their shoes." Senator Lancaster Barlow smiled then, stopped in front of Paulsen, and extended his hand straight out so that it rested on the short man's shoulder. "You have proven to be a fine secretary. I am in your debt for the gain of this information."

"I'm afraid," Paulsen said, hesitantly, "that I have more news, sir. The personal side of the equation that I spoke of when I entered the room. I think you should sit down."

"I take all my news standing up, Paulsen. You know that."

"It is very bad news, sir."

"Has there been a death?" Part of him would have been relieved if it was the news he thought it might be—hoped it might be—but would never say so out loud.

"No, sir. I believe it may be worse than death itself. A wire just came in. It is fresh news."

"Tell me, man, of what do you speak? I am old and tired, wary of heart attacks and excitement. You have brought enough for me to consider on this day. My reputation is at stake, and now I know what must be done, where my focus must lie. I am grateful for that. Be on with it, time is ticking."

"I was afraid to tell you, sir, but I must. It is your daughter, Senator Barlow. She has vanished."

THREE

THE SECOND FLAMING ARROW HIT THE RAIL-
car square in the middle. Fire hurried up the wood-paneled
exterior like it was on a short fuse. More fire-tainted arrows
rained onto the ground and into the railcar, pointed and sure
in their target, coloring the once perfect sky with black
smoke and fear.

Before long, the railcar would be nothing but firewood
for a giant bonfire; there was no water to save it, nor was
there time to expend such energy, under attack from the
raiding Cheyenne.

The second fire-borne arrow had struck at the heart of
the car, but others were piercing the roof at each end, ensuring total destruction of the elaborate abode.

Hobie Lawton ran out onto the platform where Lucas had
stood just minutes before, and stopped dead in his tracks.
"Redskins. Damned if I knew it weren't redskins. Not even
a month into the journey, and we draw heathens to our doorstep. Damn, if I didn't know I should've stayed in St. Louis
where it was safe from such nonsense."

A gunshot crackled out across the wide meadow, and the

bullet sliced into the door frame, inches from Hobie's head. He looked upward, shocked at the closeness, then stepped back inside the burning railcar, out of harm's way.

Lucas hadn't really been listening to Hobie's rant. The man always seemed to be bellyaching about something: the weather, the sway of the train, the speed of the train, the lack of ingredients to cook with, anything to hear himself talking. But Lucas *was* annoyed at his lack of action. "Would you grab a gun and help out, Hobie?" Lucas yelled.

Hobie, a man of normal height, and middle age, stuck his head out of the door and shrugged. "Don't see how it's gonna do any damn good. No, sir, don't see it at all. Injuns got us two to one. I got half a head of hair. Be an ugly scalp on a belt, for sure, but they'll take it and be proud of it."

"Damn it, Hobie!" Lucas hollered out. "Get a gun!"

More arrows thudded into the railcar, and it was starting to burn in earnest. Flames crawled up the side of the car, just under the windows, in short, steady leaps, advancing to the roof, which was starting to blaze on its own with assured determination from the other arrows.

Zeke had woken up from his stupor, and now recognized the danger that they all were in. He scooped up as many of the rifles as he could, then knocked the table over to use for cover. He crouched behind it the best he could, aimed the Winchester '73, and returned fire.

It was only a matter of seconds before an arrow sliced into the wood table, and it began to burn, too.

The black smoke fully engulfed the encampment, if it could have been called that, encouraging the attacking braves to scream and yell with delight. They were sure of their success, and Lucas couldn't blame them.

Hobie disappeared back inside the railcar, opened the first window, jammed a rifle barrel out of it, and began to fire at the distant raiders.

Between Hobie and Zeke offering cover, Lucas had time to grab up a couple of single-action Army Colts, and the loaded ammunition belts that went with them. He crouched as close to the ground as he could, firing as he went, and hurried up onto the platform.

A quick glance over his shoulder told him that there were at least six in the raiding party; Dog Soldiers wearing wolf skins on their heads, faces painted red with white stripes flowing from their noses onto their chins and cheeks, feathers tied to their black hair, and their buckskins adorned with bone jewelry.

Lucas had been warned by the train's engineer that it would be dangerous to unhook in Kansas, be left out in the open, but he had felt the risk was worth it, that he could handle anything that came his way. Now, he wasn't so sure. He had been overconfident, and not nearly as prepared as he thought he was. An uncertain tremble was growing in his belly.

Hobie continued to fire, and the smell of gun smoke mixed with the burning railcar caused Lucas's eyes to water and his lungs to complain. It was an unlikely and unexpected return to the battlefield, a place Lucas had hoped to never return again. He had hoped that the life of fighting, of killing to stay alive, was behind him, but he should have known better.

It was a different kind of fight that he had put himself into.

This was not a war between the states, but a war against a people whose land and life were being altered by the advancement of progress, of the opening of new territory for white men to inhabit and make their own. Lucas had no choice but to fight back. He had put himself squarely in that war, setting up the railcar, almost like bait, offering the Cheyenne an easy target. He saw that now. He should have listened to the engineer, but his pride and his desire for solitude had been stronger than common sense might have offered. He had needed some time to gather himself before moving on.

The Cheyenne rounded a rise about twenty yards straight out from the railcar, then joined together and leapt from their horses, almost in unison. The horses trailed off quickly behind them, out of sight, while the Indians took up prone positions, flat on the ground, and began to fire their single-shot rifles in unison.

"Zeke," Lucas yelled out, "there's only four of them under the ridge . . ."

Thunder cracked from behind them, and lead tore into the ground just at the big Negro's feet, nicking his bootheel, before Lucas could shout another word of warning.

The shot was like rousing a sleeping giant. Zeke spun around with the Winchester, zeroed in on his targets, and started firing.

It was an astonishing sight to see the Winchester rifle in action, and even more gratifying to see Zeke's skills matched with it. They were either latent, natural, or the Negro had been holding out about his comfort with a firearm.

Zeke's first shot hit the closest Dog Soldier square in the forehead, sending him spiraling out of sight. The other attacker didn't have time to react. The second shot sent him stumbling backward.

A slow smile eased across Lucas's face—but it didn't last long. The encroaching fire forced him off the platform with Hobie on his heels.

Flames jumped five feet into the air, and the whole of the roof was engulfed in hungry flames. The interior was starting to surrender to the rage of the fire, too.

There was plenty of tinder to offer as fuel inside the railcar. The walls were lined with mahogany paneling, and the floors were covered with Oriental carpets. Velvet draperies hung at the windows, and there was enough furniture inside to offer kindling for several fires, if the need had ever come. Other than clothes, there were very few personal effects at risk. Lucas had had little time to amass material wealth beyond what had come with the car when he had taken it on as his own. Anything that was inside the railcar was most certainly lost.

Hobie had armed himself with a Henry rifle. It was a lever-action rifle with a breech-loading tubular magazine, and fired copper rimfire cartridges. It was his own personal weapon, an 1860 model that he had carried through the War of Northern Aggression, and beyond. Used correctly, the rifle could fire twenty-eight rounds a minute. But Hobie was more adept with a spatula and skillet than the rifle. He'd been a battlefield cook. He was nearsighted, and was prone to leaving his spectacles lying next to the stove, claiming he could see to cut a carrot without them just fine. Which was true. But shooting at a great distance, even with a rifle such as the Henry, was a problem for him.

Hobie had nearly shot all of the rounds loaded in the Henry before the fire had forced him out of the railcar.

Zeke and Lucas fired at the remaining Cheyenne, staying low to the ground, hanging back behind the burning table. It wouldn't be long before it, like the railcar, started to give into the fire. As it was, the table still offered cover.

Lucas looked over his shoulder, and saw Hobie running straight for them, firing as he came. About halfway between the platform and the table, the Henry jammed, and without thinking, obviously, Hobie came to a stop.

"Keep running!" Lucas screamed. But he was too late. A gunshot rang out, and lead hit Hobie directly in the chest. He stumbled backward, and looked more resigned than surprised. Another shot followed in a blink, and caught him square in the belly, sending the cook spiraling to the ground with a groan and a thud. A cloud of dust wafted over him for a brief second, then joined the smoke, becoming one with the cloud.

Zeke stood up and unloaded the fully loaded Winchester in a series of trigger pulls, lever cranks, and presses. The smoke surrounded the Negro like he had conjured it to hide in. The reports of the gunfire echoed across the lea—and were not immediately answered back.

Lucas peered over the burning table, and watched as two Cheyenne ran off, gathered up their horses, and beat hoof as fast as they could, north, away from them. "I think we ran them off."

"They'll be back," Zeke said. He hurried to Hobie, and Lucas followed, though it was easy to see, even amidst the smoke and fire, that there was no saving the man.

They made no attempt to put out the fire. There was no close source of water, other than a thin stream that cut through the meadow about a hundred yards to the south of them. The railcar burned itself out. There was nothing left of it but a smoldering skeleton: iron frame on iron wheels, with some black timbers sticking up like charred toothpicks.

Nothing of value to either man had survived the fire. All that remained were the weapons that Zeke was trying out before the attack came. Nearly half of the ammunition had been used up in the attack.

Zeke had taken the chore of digging a grave for Hobie without being asked or told. Lucas had just wandered off, a Colt Army dangling from his right hand.

The ground was dry, easy to dig with big hands and the butt of a rifle. The shuffle of dirt sounded like the soles of shoes scraping across slate. There was music in the consistency of the digging, but it offered no joy. Death seemed to follow Lucas Fume wherever he went, and the thought of losing another man because of his escapades touched him deeply, in a dark black place in his soul. One that he avoided as often as possible.

The air still smelled of fire and soot, and the iron frame of the railcar was still hot to the touch. Blue sky had returned, and the perfection of the summer day seemed to have already forgotten, or ignored, the fight that had taken place.

Lucas overlooked Zeke and the task at hand as best he could, and made his way to the center of the railcar.

The railcar had belonged to John Barlow, the man who had faked his own death in order to see Lucas thrown into prison. The ploy had not worked—at least forever like Barlow, who had changed his name and identity to Lanford Grips, had hoped.

Lucas had survived countless attempts on his life, and had escaped the prison with Zeke. All that ugliness had been cleared up in St. Louis. But at a cost. First, Zeke Henry was still a wanted man—wanted for the brutal beating and rape of John Barlow's sister, Celia. And then there was the loss of Charlotte Brogan, a woman Lucas had known, and loved, since he was a boy. She had died in his arms in St. Louis. He couldn't save her. And now, any semblance of her presence was gone, burned to ashes and tossed to the wind.

Lucas had slept in her bed, in her quarters of the railcar, trying to inhale her smell for as long as it would last, trying to feel something other than guilt and shame. He had failed. Failed miserably, and could hardly find it in himself to take another step, to move on. He wished he could trade places with Hobie Lawton. Unfortunately, Lucas was going to be forced to live out his days with regret following him everywhere he went.

FOUR

"GONNA BE DARK SOON," ZEKE SAID. HE walked steadily with three gun belts thrown over his shoulder, and two wrapped around his waist. Each had a Colt of some make in it. He carried the Winchester rifle, barrel down. Metal against metal clanked with each giant step he took, even when he walked slow, so Lucas could keep pace with him.

Lucas had on one gun belt, and carried Hobie's Henry rifle. It was the only keepsake he had allowed himself. "We need to get as far away from there as possible."

"They'll find us if they want."

"You buried the rest of those guns with Hobie?"

Zeke nodded. "Ain't no Indian gonna look for them there from what I knows. Death is a repellent like no other."

It was a small comfort for Lucas knowing those guns wouldn't be used to kill anyone else, and he hoped Zeke was right. The Negro seemed to have a working knowledge of Indian ways that they had never discussed before. For now, Lucas decided to leave that conversation to another time. Truth be told, there was a lot about Zeke Henry that he didn't know.

The ground was flat along the bank of the small stream that they navigated, doing their best not to leave a visible trail. Mosquitoes and flies buzzed about, glad for their presence, their offer of new blood. The insects seemed drunk with the prospect of flesh to eat, immune to fear, maniacal in their attacks. Lucas swatted at the swarms but it did no good. They hovered over his head in a cloud. "There's no escaping creatures who want to see us dead, or do us harm," he said, frustrated.

"You expected it to be different here, Mistuh Lucas?"

Lucas shrugged. "I had hoped for a new start for both of us."

"You maybe. No such thing for me. Not now or in the future."

"What if we could do something to free you? There has to be something I can do, that we can do."

They continued walking, skirting the water, fighting off the marauding insects the best they could, listening for Cheyenne, or any other Indian, at every breath. It was a new skill to develop, but old in its very prospect. Lucas had fought in the war, but rarely as a soldier. Instead, he worked mostly as a spy, gathering intelligence, crossing enemy lines at will, donning getups and identities that allowed him such currency. But those skills were old, used up. Not forgotten. Just atrophied from too many years spent locked inside a prison cell.

"What's done can't be undone. You knows that, Mistuh Lucas."

"She's not dead," Lucas said.

"Might as well be. Can't talk. Can't walk. Can't do nothin' to tell the truth of matters."

There was a quiver in Zeke's voice that Lucas had heard before. He remained quiet, said nothing more. What he had said was enough. The subject of Zeke's crime always put the Negro deeper in the funk he already walked in.

The only sounds that followed them were the constant wind, the buzz of insects, an occasional bird offering a song, and the shuffle of their feet in the mud and gravel along the bank of the stream. Lucas had no clue where they were going, where they were. He just knew that they couldn't stay near the railcar, and wait for another train to pass by and rescue them. It was too dangerous to stay there. The Cheyenne would come back; there was no doubt about that.

As much as both men were held in grief and regret, they both had carried the will to live, the appetite to put one foot in front of the other.

There had to be a town somewhere up the railroad line, a destination to walk to. Leavenworth was the next big train stop, a town of nearly thirty thousand people, so there had to be outliers close by, farms and such that would offer them direction and, hopefully, safety.

The land might have seemed desolate and lonely, but the Cheyenne and the Kiowa, and the other Plains Indians, were angry for a reason. Not only had the white man come into their territory and spoiled their hunting grounds, they had stayed. And now they were claiming the land as their own—a concept foreign to the Indians as much as the English that rolled off the white man's tongue. Eleven railroad lines crisscrossed Kansas, and thousands of people poured into, or across, the state every week. The desolation and emptiness that Lucas had found himself in wouldn't last long.

Lucas stopped, and stepped into ankle-deep water. His stomach growled with hunger, and at that moment, he would have given anything to hear Hobie bellyaching about the weather. "We best start looking for a place to camp. Doesn't look like there's going to be any place to stop any time soon," he said.

Zeke nodded in agreement. "You ever think we shoulda stayed in Libertyville? Just found a life with them folks?"

Lucas looked at Zeke oddly. "You want to go back?"

"They ain't there now. Moved on. Just askin', that's all. Far Jackson ain't a bad man to follow."

It was Lucas's time to shake his head. He wasn't following anyone, and he knew his presence, and Zeke's, had brought the people of Libertyville a lot of trouble, and would only bring them more: raging prison guards with an axe to grind, and a quarry to catch. Carl the Hammer, who was dead now, would have just been replaced by someone else. The Klan would have seen to that. "We're safer here," he said.

"Hobie Lawton might argue that fact with you. But if you says so."

"I do." Lucas forged ahead then, deciding against stopping to camp. He wasn't comfortable. There was still a little light left in the day, enough to find someplace safer—if that were possible.

He picked up his pace so he could put a little distance between him and Zeke. The question of safety had brought up another memory, another sorrow. How could he not think of Avadine, the Scottish woman who had nursed him to health, saw to it that his strength had returned, and welcomed him into her bed? And what had he done for her in return? He had left her. Ran out at the first chance he had, chased by men with guns, leaving her standing alone in the growing gloom of night, surviving fire and assault, her heart broken for all the world to see. He hoped never to see Avadine, or that look in a woman's eyes, ever again. She was hopeless, enraged, full of hate and love at the same time.

Just at the onset of dusk, Lucas spied a spiral of smoke in the distance. He eased up his pace to allow Zeke to catch up with him. It didn't take long for the clatter and clank of the guns to slide up next to him.

"Figured that something would come along this close to the crick," Lucas said.

"Yup," Zeke said.

They both stood there looking at the chimney smoke, and the little house, if it could be called that, from which it came.

"Never seen the like," Lucas said.

"Me, neither. I spent most of my life in them Tennessee hills. Never seen so much brown and open spaces in my life," Zeke said. "Or a house not made of wood."

"Not a lot of trees out this way."

"Was good for you."

Lucas shrugged. It was true. The lack of trees in the West had made him, and his family, very wealthy. They had owned a few million acres of woodlands in Minnesota. Timber cut and floated down the Mississippi, and used as railroad ties, used to build the railroad lines west. But he owned nothing now. He had money in the bank, the clothes on his back, and the gun in his hand, and that was it—for what good any of it did him.

The way Lucas saw it, he had lost ten times more than he'd gained. His childhood home, his family dead and buried, and Charlotte Brogan killed, because of all the wealth, all of the money and its potential. Add in the betrayal of the one man he thought he could always trust, and he would have traded pasts with Zeke Henry in a heartbeat.

"I hope they're used to strangers around here," Lucas said.

Zeke eyed Lucas like he wanted to say something, but restrained himself.

Lucas struck out again, and headed straight for the sod house.

The sky was gray and the curtain of darkness was falling quickly. The day had slipped by, leaving Lucas and Zeke in a very familiar situation—on their own with little resources other than their skills and wits. And even those were rusty, dulled by recent events. Still, there was enough light and will left in them to make it to the house.

The closer they got, Lucas could see another building beyond the house. It was set inside a fence, bore large double doors, and windows with wood sashes and that was all. Low moos of settling cows told him that it was a barn. Something that he wouldn't have guessed at first sight. Nothing was what it appeared to be in this new land. At least, not to Lucas.

Zeke caught up, walked beside Lucas, doing nothing to hold back the clink and clank of the guns he carried. They weren't trying to sneak up on anybody.

A thin copse of cottonwoods stood about fifty yards from the front door of the house. Lucas thought nothing of it, and started to skirt the trees, avoiding the shadows that fell off of them.

"You both just stop right there," a man said, stepping out

from behind one of the taller trees. The trunk was just wide enough to hide him, but there was no mistaking the aim of the rifle in his hands.

Lucas and Zeke did what they were told, and automatically put their hands into the air.

"We mean you no harm, mister," Lucas said.

The man stepped fully out from behind the tree, certain in his hold of the gun. On second look, it was a shotgun, not a rifle. He was about the same height as Lucas, which meant that Zeke towered over him. He seemed fit and clean. His clothes were typical of a man who farmed or tended a herd of animals: simple trousers, a linen shirt, sturdy boots, and a faded wide-brimmed felt hat that had soaked up its fair share of sweat.

"I think you all just need to put down all those weapons. Lord, what'd you do, rob an armory?" the man said.

Lucas unclasped his gun belt and eased it to the ground. Zeke followed suit, putting the gun belts and rifle he carried in a pile at his feet.

"Nothing of the sort," Lucas said. "We were attacked by Cheyenne earlier today. We were trying these out when they rode in. Killed our cook, and burned the railcar to the ground, leaving us no choice but to move on with what we have left."

"Thought we saw a stem of smoke east of here," the man said. His face looked to place him about forty, weathered and cut with worry lines, but it was hard to say for sure. A man's age was hard to judge under stressful circumstances and bad light. His eyes, though, were curious, and a tad fearful.

There was no question in Lucas's mind that they could outwit the man, disarm him in an instant, if the need arose.

"You was out there by yourself?" the man asked.

Lucas nodded.

"Kind of foolhardy, don't you think?" He looked up at Zeke like he was trying to see to the top of a tree. Zeke didn't respond, just stared back at the man. "Even with a big Negro at your side. Not sure I believe what you're a tellin' me is the truth."

Lucas started to defend himself, but a light caught his eye. A lantern swayed and steadied out of the house, then headed toward them.

The gaze caught the man's attention, and he looked over his shoulder, sighed out loud, then faced Lucas. "Tell me you don't mean us any harm, mister. We've had enough trouble recently."

Lucas offered his hand to the man. "My name is Lucas Fume, and this here is my friend Zeke . . . um, just Zeke. We're on our way west, out of St. Louis, and I swear to you, we came upon trouble with the Cheyenne. We don't mean to bring you any problems. We just seek a safe place to spend the night, then we'll be gone in the morning. You have all I have to offer, my word. I promise, we'll be gone in the morning."

The lantern grew closer, and Lucas could tell it was a woman carrying the light. Or a girl, he couldn't see her clearly.

"I'm Rutherford Tullet," the man said, taking Lucas's hand. "Most folks just call me Roy. The one comin' is my daughter, Victoria." He unclasped his hand from Lucas's, and turned to watch her come to them.

The soft light from the lantern mixed with the passing of twilight made Victoria Tullet's face distant, but distinct— her jaw and cheeks perfectly cut, like they had been sculpted by a lovelorn artist. She wore a simple blue gingham dress, and her chestnut locks almost vanished in the darkness. There was no mistaking that Victoria was a young woman, one that would garner a hearty drove of suitors—if they were in town, or near a place where men gathered.

"Is everything all right, Pa?" she said, coming to a stop next to Roy Tullet.

"I think so. They say they was attacked by Cheyenne earlier in the day."

"The smoke?"

Roy Tullet nodded. Lucas stared at her, trying to decide what it was about her that bothered him. She had an air about her that he couldn't place, but his instinct rubbed him wrong, warned him not to trust her.

Victoria noticed, and stared directly back into his eyes.

It was an icy, *mind your manners* stare. Lucas obliged quickly.

"Well," Victoria said, "I guess we have no choice but to show them some hospitality, don't we, Pa?"

"I suppose not," Roy Tullet said.

"Thank you, ma'am, we appreciate it," Lucas said, extending his hand to Victoria.

She didn't respond right away. When she did raise her hand, Lucas found himself looking directly into the short barrel of a Remington derringer.

FIVE

FOR WHATEVER THE REASON, THE MEN HAD
put a burlap hood over Celia's head. She had lost her most
valued entry into the conscious, more alive world: her eyes.

At first, the pitch-blackness ignited a panic deep inside
of her. She could feel the birth of a scream in the pit of her
stomach. It catapulted all of the way up her throat with the
force of rushing vomit, then stopped suddenly, like it hit a
brick wall, at the tip of her tongue. The only thing that escaped her mouth was a whispering breath that even she had
to struggle to hear.

After that, Celia regulated herself. *You have nothing to
fear,* she told herself. *Perhaps, death is like this. But with
hope. Darkness without knowledge. An end to thought, feeling, and frustration. A final end to everything that hurts.
That would be pleasant.* Calmness returned to her, and she
surrendered to the situation the best she could, pictured her
body relaxing, melting into whatever plank she was lying
on. Outside, there was no twinge of muscle, no sign that she
was even awake. She was sure of it. Her body was dead, but
her mind was alive.

The only viable sense left to Celia's disposal was her hearing. The men who had carted her away from the sanatorium had remained quiet, communicating with grunts and groans, and she suspected, hand signals, once they had put the hood over her head.

She was certain that she was on a wagon being carried away at great speed. There were two horses, fairly large and well behaved. The driver only had to urge them on, not whip them up to speed. For that she was grateful. The striking of a poor, dumb animal had always bothered her, seemed inappropriate, harsh, and sad. Her attraction to gentleness was formed at an early age at the sight of many beatings, both animal and human. Sometimes, she still had nightmares when she heard the slaves screaming, ones that had tried to run away, and had been returned. The field foreman had a taste for pain. She could see his face, all twisted up in pleasure, raising a whip, and cracking it hard. Funny thing was, she couldn't remember his name now.

Night sounds surrounded her. Crickets and frogs sawed and croaked lazily, the urgency of spring gone from the calendar and the loins of all that sought to reproduce. Celia had been barren, unable to bear a child before the incident that had left her in the state she was in. There were blessings in pain and loss, she saw that now.

The air was cool on her hands, but the rest of her was warm, covered with a heavy blanket. Most likely hidden, like she was a load of milled flour or wheat, on the way to market.

The horses ran at a fast pace, pulling them farther and farther away from all of the ordinary things Celia had come to know. If she was afraid, she would have been concerned about eating, where her next meal was going to come from, whether she would be bathed, and made as comfortable as possible. Her care had been physically well managed, but emotionally neglectful. She had been fussed over, her position as a United States senator's daughter known and respected by most everyone who had come into contact with her, even though they thought her no smarter than a peach or a cucumber—or able to feel physical or emotional pain. But she was no longer afraid. Celia had accepted her fate. To that end, she awaited the next adventure, her next destination.

Oddly, she felt more alive than she had in years.

Lucas restrained the urge to pull a gun on Victoria Tullet. He had felt confident that he and Zeke could take her father, Roy, if need be, but the truth was Lucas had pretty much lost all of the fight he had in him for the day. He withdrew his offer of a handshake, and said, "Well, I don't suppose the hospitality around these parts comes with rules that I understand."

Zeke stood at Lucas's side and remained quiet. In the past, the Negro had been adept at following Lucas's lead, paying close attention without looking interested, then jumping in when the need arose. Lucas hoped that was still the case.

"For all we know, kind sir, you could be agents come to see us harm," Victoria said.

The glow of the lantern attempted to soften her features, but her face was drawn tight, and she offered no suggestion of tenderness, or relenting her position. The derringer remained pointed at Lucas's head.

"I don't enjoy the threat, ma'am," Lucas said. "I can assure you that the events of the day I have spoken of are true. How is it that we could be agents of harm? Here? This looks like pleasant enough country, and we are not on the side of the Cheyenne, I can guarantee you that."

Victoria smirked, and looked to Roy, who was about the same height as her. In that moment, Lucas could see no resemblance between the two. There was no doubt that Roy Tullet was older than Victoria, by about twenty years according to the gray that was showing itself in his whiskers and sideburns. His nose was bulbous, while hers was thin, almost birdlike. The most striking difference, though, was in their eyes. His were brown, and hers were blue. There were similarities, however. Both Tullets were of equal height.

About the same as Lucas, making her a little taller than most women, but not unnaturally so. And they carried themselves in a similar manner: confident, sure, hard as an iron nail. Most likely, come daylight, Lucas would see more similarities between the two. For now, he trusted his gut, and it told him to tread carefully.

The smirk faded from Victoria's thin lips, and she broke eye contact with Roy. "I don't suspect that you're loyal to the redskins. We both saw the smoke, know their ways better than we should. But they aren't the only worry we have here."

Roy Tullet cleared his throat. "I think you should put the gun down, Victoria."

She cast him a hard glance, but made no indication that she was going to obey him any time soon.

"Tell me, how I can be a threat?" Lucas said. "We walked straight up to your father, guns openly displayed, offering no violence in our nature or voices. Only a request for safe lodging, and then we will be on our way, first thing in the morning. I promise you that."

"You always travel with a Negro at your side?" Victoria asked.

"I travel with this Negro. We're partners," Lucas said, looking up to Zeke.

"Partners," the young woman said with disbelief. "Your tongue is about as Confederate as I've heard in a long while. What would cause a man such as you to take up with one such as him?" Her disbelief folded into disdain without showing a crease.

"It's a long story," Lucas said. "If we're too much trouble, we can just be on our way." He looked to the sky, took in the sight of the three-quarter moon, and nodded. "There'll be enough light to navigate by. Surely the road will be safe from Cheyenne at night, and there'll be a place for us along the way."

Roy shook his head, then reached over, put his hand on Victoria's wrist, and forced it down. "You'll do no such thing, Mr. Fume. You'll have to forgive my daughter. We had raiders come in the other night, and she's still a bit on edge from their visit and the ruckus they raised."

"Raiders of what kind?"

Roy exhaled, and settled back to himself once Victoria's arm was at her side. Her finger, however, had not left the trigger. "This is stock country. And there are growing enterprises who wish to control all of the land, forcing simple homesteaders like us to move on, forgo our claims. It's a common story, but with the cattle business booming, and the transfer of head back East, and Abilene so close, the proximity of these grazing lands made them far more valuable than anyone ever thought. Add in the closeness to the stream there, well, there's water to control, too. Our spot is desirable, necessary for the growth of enterprise. We're homesteaders in the way of progress."

"So," said Lucas, "you're being intimidated. Forced out."

"Something like that," Victoria said. "Only I'd call it revenge. That's what I'd call it. Plain and simple revenge."

"I'm afraid you've stepped into a hornet's nest, Mr. Fume. Until recently, Victoria was engaged to be married to Kingsley Nash, the largest landowner in this part of the state. But that relationship has come to an obvious sour end."

"And Kingsley aims to take what he was after all along," Victoria interjected.

"Your land?" Lucas said.

"Exactly," she answered.

"But we're not moving an inch," Roy said. "This is our home. Our land. We've made great sacrifices to stay here, and our journey hasn't been easy. I intend to die an old man here."

Lucas nodded. "We know nothing about any of this. I can assure you of that."

"I'm sorry," Victoria Tullet said. "I have plenty of reasons to not trust a word any man says, including you, Mr. Fume."

SIX

LANCASTER BARLOW SAT UNCOMFORTABLY in the back of the carriage, and took in the sight of the United States Capitol Building. The domed marvel had been completed less than ten years prior, just after the end of The War Between the States, the polite term used in the city.

Construction on the Capitol had continued through the conflict to signal to the masses that government was still at work, growing, that the Union was sound. On the surface, it was a beautiful building, with its grand fresco, *Apotheosis of Washington*, staring down on to the great hall. But that hall could present some of the most viable ugliness that the senator had ever encountered—but would not dare to ever express openly.

"You will have some time in Cincinnati, sir," Paulsen said.

"Have you wired ahead, letting them know I am en route?"

Paulsen nodded. "Of course. The necessary lodging arrangements have been made, and a return scheduled. All of your needs have been provided for."

"For the next day, or open-ended?"

"Open-ended, sir."

"That is probably best." Barlow didn't look at Paulsen, didn't acknowledge his presence with eye contact, but continued to stare out at the landscape of the city as it passed by. He silently wished he had been born of the city, that he didn't have to leave. But that fate was sealed when he had brought children into the world. Now, even at a time when they should have been grown and no longer in need of his presence, he still had to look after them, tend to their needs. Except one. One was dead and buried, a nun returned home from China, his oldest; the only child that he had truly loved—and even she had been a great disappointment, giving her heart to an invisible being, and following that love halfway across the world.

"There are three search parties out in the area, sir," Paulsen said. "If there is word of Miss Celia, you are to be notified at once, and I have alerted the houseman of your home to be ready for your arrival if you should need an extended stay."

Barlow sighed, lowered his head, and shook it. "I fear this will not turn out well, Paulsen."

"I hope it is all a mistake, sir, a failure in communication and placement."

"How do you misplace a person who cannot fend for herself? At the most basic level, that is why she is there."

"There are no guards at the sanatorium, sir."

"Then you have failed, Paulsen. You have put my daughter in a facility unable to protect her from those who seek to do her harm."

"I knew of no threat, sir." There was fear in Paulsen's voice. He looked perplexed, aghast, and angry.

"There are always threats, Paulsen. You should know that by now."

"It won't happen again, sir."

"No, it won't."

No word came on the journey. Stops in Pittsburgh and Cincinnati proved fruitless, and painfully silent. As the train rolled into Nashville, Lancaster Barlow could only hope that the situation that had brought him home had come to a satisfactory conclusion, allowing him to turn right around and return to Washington.

He disembarked the private railcar into the grayness of dusk. The city, and the surroundings looked drained of color, like there wasn't, or never had been, any life there at all. It was a world of shadows and gloom: blacks, grays, and dirty whites in every direction he looked.

The ground was moist like it had rained recently, and the puddles reflected the murky sky. His footsteps echoed, and there was a semblance of winter about him, a chill in the air, even though that season was far away in time, and usually mild in its arrival and stay. Whatever day it was, whatever season it was, there was no doubt that it was a sad one.

Barlow's elbows and fingers ached and bowed, reacting to arthritic pain and stiffness that always seemed to flare up on his return to the city. There were many reasons why he wished to never return to Nashville, and his physical discomfort was only a minor one.

"Mr. Barlow," a man called out, walking toward him.

The senator recognized the man immediately. It was Sheriff Curtis Keane, come to greet him.

Barlow stopped and waited for the lawman, stoic in his travel cloak, free of luggage or attachments. Arrangements had been made by Paulsen for the porter to deliver his necessaries to the Maxwell House, a magnificent five-story structure at the corner of Cherry and Church streets, and owned by one of the senator's greatest supporters, John Overton.

"I take it you had a comfortable journey, Senator," Sheriff Keane said. He was nearing middle age, and spoke in rising and falling baritone notes. He squinted at the end of certain words, and made no effort to look Barlow directly in the eye. There was a smell of old tobacco about him.

"Tell me news, Keane. That is all I wish to know. No journey like this could ever be considered comfortable." There was no mistaking the admonishment. If he had a whip, he would have slapped the man's hairy knuckles.

"I have no news, sir. The trail has grown cold. Almost

like the girl was picked up by a giant bird and carted away into the mists of time. There is absolutely no sign of her."

Barlow stepped in so he was toe-to-toe with the sheriff. "Do you realize the severity of this situation? My daughter is an invalid. She cannot care for herself, she cannot speak, she cannot defend herself, and she is out in the world without any safety at all."

"I understand that, sir, and you have to know that I have put every man on this I have to spare. There has been no word, either, no demand of ransom, no communication at all."

"So you do not think this is a kidnapping?"

"I don't know what it is, sir."

Barlow had to stop himself from speaking another word. If someone would have come up behind him and pushed him, he would have snapped in half, he was so tense. "That is unacceptable, Sheriff."

"I am not a magician, sir. I cannot just make things—especially people—reappear when they vanish."

"You are right. I apologize," Barlow said.

"I understand your dilemma, Senator. Truly, I do. I wish this episode were over, that you could return to Washington satisfied with the conclusion. But I'll need more time, and unfortunately, more information and resources, to see that that happens."

Barlow nodded. "I have little to offer as far as information goes, but I think I know where to start asking questions."

"And where is that?"

"At the prison. I need you to take me to see my son."

SEVEN

LUCAS FOLLOWED ROY TULLET TOWARD THE house. Zeke followed, quiet and plodding. Victoria brought up the rear, the lantern in one hand, the derringer in the other.

The barrel of Victoria's pocket gun was pointed to the ground, but Lucas still couldn't help but feel captive, certain that if he made a run for it, he'd be shot square between the shoulder blades.

Roy stopped about ten yards from the front door of the sod house, and turned to face Lucas and Zeke. "The Negro's gonna have to sleep in the barn."

Lucas cocked his head. "Really?"

"Folks wouldn't look kindly on a black man staying in a house with a white woman. I figured you would know such a thing."

"But there's room for me?" Lucas asked.

"Of course. We'll put a pallet by the stove for you. Probably not the kind of accommodations that you're accustomed to, according to the way you're dressed in duds that ain't had time to fray, or lose the crease from the tailor's shop, but Victoria can cook a fair meal, and the quilts are soft, filled with plenty of down."

Lucas glanced over to Zeke, who showed no emotion at all. "If it's the same to you, I'll stay in the barn with my friend. I'm sure I'll be just as comfortable there—unless you want me inside so you can keep an eye on me."

Roy Tullet shrugged. "You're free to come and go as you please, Mr. Fume. I ain't got no cause to hold you, unless there's something you're not telling me."

Lucas shook his head.

Victoria pushed by Lucas so close he could feel the heat from the lantern on his forearm. "I think that's a bad idea, Pa," she said, coming to a stop next to Tullet.

"These men have done nothing wrong," he said. "Now, show some respect, and put away that gun. We'll feed them, and see them off in the morning. If they decide to leave before then, that's their choice. Do I make myself clear, Victoria?"

Lucas expected to hear a frustrated "Yes, Pa," but the young woman offered nothing but a glare directed at Lucas, and a spin toward the door. Before anyone could say another word, Victoria disappeared inside the house, and slammed the door so hard it echoed across the flat land like an unexpected clap of thunder.

"You'll have to forgive my daughter," Roy said. "She's a bit high-strung, and more than a little on edge since her breakup with Kingsley Nash. She always did believe in fairy tales, that happy endings were hers for the takin', but this situation has harmed her in a way that I've never seen before. Add that to the threat of Indians that you two are a grim reminder of, the lack of female companionship, others to confide in and learn from, and well, she's about to come unstitched with loneliness and fear."

"I'm sure it's been hard on her," Lucas offered. "We'll be off as soon as the sun rises, and our presence will be one less thing to agitate her."

"You sure you won't reconsider and come inside?" Roy asked.

Lucas shook his head. "The barn'll be just fine. Given some of the places I've slept in my life, I'm sure it'll be like a palace."

The barn was small—three stalls, and an open corner to store tack. One horse, an old swaybacked mare, hardly noticed when Lucas and Zeke entered. It smelled like the stall hadn't been cleaned for a day or two.

"Not a lot to run a place on," Lucas said, setting the lantern and blankets down that Roy Tullet had provided.

Zeke eased down the collection of gun belts and guns next to the blankets. "I'd been fine out here by myselves, Mistuh Lucas."

The glow of the lantern didn't extend far beyond Zeke, but his big shadow fell against the wall, making him look like a giant.

"I doubt I'd be alive if you hadn't taken me to Libertyville and hid me there," Lucas said. "You showed me a kindness in a way I'd not been shown before. Or if I had been, I was too arrogant to notice it."

Zeke looked at Lucas oddly, like he didn't understand a word that had been said.

"Negroes got cause to hate me," Lucas said. "You included. You could have left me by the river after we escaped from that prison. You had no investment in my freedom then."

"It was the right thing to do," Zeke said.

"Exactly. Now, enough of that." Lucas leaned down and started to unfurl the blankets to make a bed, but he stopped about midway through. "One other thing, Zeke."

"Yes, suh, what's that?"

"I'm no sir or mister. Let's just leave that formal stuff behind us, all right?"

Zeke took a deep breath, then smiled slowly. "I can do that."

"Good, I was hoping you would say that."

It didn't take long for them to get settled, with the lantern on low.

Zeke was lying on his back, staring at the ceiling. Lucas was sitting up on the pile of blankets that he'd made into an acceptable bed, listening to the comfort of night sounds. Distant crickets. An occasional bird or owl that he had never heard before, and couldn't put a name or face to, but sounded familiar, like maybe they had relatives out East. The swayback mare shuffled about, settling in for the night. All of it took his mind off the events of the day. At least until Zeke brought it up.

"Who was you waitin' on, mistuh, um, sorry, Lucas?"

"I figured we needed some time to get our footing out here," he said. "I wanted to avoid Abilene, and I'm not sure what lies west for us. Could be possibilities in Fort Collins, or even farther west. We got no ties, and only have the wind as our traveling companion. I was waiting on news, that's all. I was expecting a rider to bring me news of a query I sent out before we left."

"You know folks out this way?"

"I had a network of acquaintances before I was sent to prison."

"From the war, and such?"

Lucas nodded. "A lot of them fellas headed west afterward in search of a new life, new opportunities."

"Or to get away from what they done lost, and couldn't get back."

"True. But, yes, there are friends out here. Even if it doesn't seem like it at the moment."

"I sure does feel bad about what happened to grouchy ol' Hobie," Zeke said.

"No worse than I do," Lucas answered.

Silence fell back between the two men, and the night sounds returned. Lucas knew how guilt felt, and the death of Hobie Lawton only added to the load he carried with him. He wondered if every man that had crossed the Mississippi River to start a new life had as much trouble leaving the memories and losses that occurred at home, back East, as he was having.

Violence, blood, and death had followed him like a curse, coming much sooner than he had ever anticipated, or hoped, on this trip.

The thought of the dead cook made Lucas incredibly sad and tired. He was about to settle down on the bedding when a knock came from outside the barn door.

"You men decent in there?" It was Victoria Tullet.

"Yes, ma'am," Lucas called out, standing up. Zeke followed, and they stood shoulder to shoulder.

Victoria walked into the barn carrying a blue enamel Dutch oven. Even with the lid on, the smell of a thick, hearty stew reached out and reminded Lucas that he hadn't had a meal in quite a while.

He was happy to see Victoria, even if he didn't entirely trust her intentions—or words.

"Pa said I should bring you boys some dinner to make up for some of my meanness."

"Nobody thought you were mean," Lucas said.

She stared at him, and forced a slight smile. The dim light from the lantern made her sharp features softer, more genial. She was a fine-looking woman, and she reminded Lucas of a spirited horse, perfect in every way but demeanor. A horse could be broke, but it had been his experience that a woman couldn't be, or shouldn't be reeled in any more than they wanted to be. That was a trial, at the moment, that he had no inclination or interest in attempting. He knew nothing of this man, Kingsley Nash, but it looked as if he had failed to improve the girl's attitude. Just the opposite. The man had thrown straw onto a raging fire.

"That sure do smell good, miss," Zeke offered.

Victoria stopped midway to them. "You know, boy, where we come from, a Negro doesn't speak until he's spoken to."

"And where is that?" Lucas intervened, and stepped forward in front of Zeke.

"Georgia. Out Dallas way if you need specifics," Victoria answered.

For some reason, Lucas didn't believe her. He had spent plenty of time in Georgia during the war. Dallas was on the line of Sherman's march, and there had been plenty of intelligence to gather, enemy lines to cross, and messages to intercept and decode. Victoria Tullet did not have the deep, rolling tongue of a high-born woman from that state. Her accent was weak, almost nonexistent, like it had been watered down, the South wrung out of it like a wet rag.

To Lucas's ear, Victoria Tullet's voice sounded like she hailed from the north: New York or Washington, somewhere cold in the winter. But he wasn't going to push the issue. Not with the promise of food at stake. That, and he knew for certain that that little pocket gun was stuffed somewhere inside her petticoats, close at hand, if she decided there was a need to reach in and pull it out.

EIGHT

DARKNESS HAD FALLEN OVER NASHVILLE,
and the ride to the prison was taken in obscurity. There were
no parades to celebrate the senator's return home, no digni-
taries to glad-hand, no babies to kiss. It was something for
Lancaster Barlow to be relieved about. Being seen entering
the Tennessee State Prison, at any time, was bad for his
reputation. The trial that had placed his son behind bars had
brought enough negative attention to him, and his family
life—and name—as it was.

The stone building stood strong, even in the thick gloom
of a rainy night. Fire had recently gutted a good part of the
interior, and sections of the prison were already being
rebuilt. Still, the façade stood intact for all the world to see.

The carriage pulled to the back of the building, away
from the main road, allowing for Barlow to enter through a
delivery door.

He was dressed in black, shrouded by a cloak with the
collar pulled up high, and his hat pulled down as far as it
would go. A guard holding a torch let him inside, then closed
the heavy wood door behind him and locked it. There was

no way out. Barlow tried not to think about that, as he breathed in air that still held ash in the dust, along with the cremated remains of prisoners burned alive. If it happened to them, it could happen to him.

The guard was a short, thin man with a permanent scowl attached to his leathery face. There was no pleasure in his work, and the flickering flame of the torch made him look even more sinister than he might really have been.

"This your first visit, Senator?" the guard asked as they made their way down a long corridor.

"Yes." Barlow was in no mood for casual conversation with a stranger. Their footsteps and voices echoed into the darkness of the hall.

"He's a sly one, that son of yours. Got the whole crew of guards bringin' him fresh vegetables and favors just for the askin'."

"He's always been talented that way."

"Keeps to himself, mostly. Got a cell mate who acts as his monkey. Gets things for him. Does things for him. Odd, never seen the like of that."

The senator grunted as they continued to walk forward, but offered nothing more. He had pleaded with the judge not to put his son away alone, that there had to be an allowance made for his condition. After some serious lawyering and wrangling, an agreement was made, and another prisoner was to be put in the cell with John Barlow.

The long hall narrowed, and the two men passed through another door that opened up into a cavernous two-story section of the prison. It held a row of cells on the bottom, and a row on top, with a walkway overlooking a long set of grimy windows that barely reflected the light from the torch.

The old section of the prison was like walking inside a deep cavern drilled into the earth, dark and cool, thick with the smell of human shit and urine. There was no other light, no other torches lit. Night had been forced on the inmates, and most of them slept, or remained quiet in their cells.

Barlow felt a hundred sets of eyes staring at him, but he couldn't see them. Didn't want to.

"He's down here at the end," the guard said, keeping his pace steady.

The senator was not interested in his surroundings, didn't care to allow his eyes to adjust, but they did on their own accord.

The stone floor was moist, and there were rats about, just at the edge of the light, who seemed immune to the presence of humans. Somehow, they knew they were safe outside the cells. Barlow wasn't sure about inside. From what he saw, most of the men were emaciated, desperate for meat, a decent meal, in need of a bath and shave, of some decent care. But he had to remind himself that they were criminals who deserved nothing, deserved what they got. That judgment included his son—whether he liked it or not.

The guard stopped. They were at the end of the row of cells, and the light of the torch bounced off another stone wall, wrapping them in the soft glow of orange light.

"A visitor to see you, Barlow," the guard said.

The senator stood next to the guard, and peered inside the cell. At first, he saw nothing. Then the form of a man moved, stood up from a cot.

"Ain't no cause for visitors here," a voice said. It wasn't the voice of a Barlow, of his son. There was a country slip on the tongue, hardly discernible to the ear of an educated and proper man.

"Where is my son?" Lancaster Barlow said. "You may be his keeper of physical things. But you don't speak for him."

"Ah, Father," another voice said. "And what do I owe the pleasure of your company at such a late hour?"

"Come here, John, where I can see you. We need to speak."

"Fetch knows everything," John Barlow said.

"I don't care what this man knows, it is you to whom I wish to speak, and I will. The journey here was long, and the matter is urgent, but hardly any other man's concern. Especially men here."

"You are among friends, Father." It was still just a voice. The form, the man who the senator assumed was Fetch, stood pat, like a statue, or a dog ordered to stay.

The senator glanced over to the guard. "Don't go anywhere."

"No worry, sir." The man smiled, and tapped a sidearm with his free hand, a fully loaded six-shooter that allowed the senator to relax, if only slightly.

Lancaster Barlow stepped up to the iron bars of the cell, and pressed his face in. "You come here this instant, you petulant little fool. Your sister has gone missing, and I need to know what you've gone and done this time."

Shadows danced off the back wall of the cell, and the senator could see inside, see the man who acted as his son's servant and aide. Fetch was expectedly thin with long gray hair, like a mop thrown atop his skull, and withered in the face. He was an old, decrepit man, more akin to a grape left out in the sun far too long than a human.

"Celia?" Another form appeared, rising up from the lower bunk. There were two beds, one over the other, bolted into the wall.

"You only have one sister that lives. Of course, Celia."

"What do you mean *gone missing*?" John Barlow said, stepping fully into the torchlight. The time in prison looked like it had been hard on him. His clothes were little more than rags hung over a thinning frame. Not that John had ever been a big man, but he had been healthy at one time, back in the war, running a small group of spies for the Confederate cause. His face was sunk in, and in the light the madness that had landed him in prison was fully apparent: neither of his hands that he had been born with were attached to his wrists. They had been severed, cut off in a maniacal attempt to prove himself dead. It was a trick, a plan, a plot, to rid the world of Lucas Fume. All in the name of love and greed. Love for a woman who was now dead, and greed for a business that had been sold to the highest bidder, Harrington Fetterman and the Union Pacific Railroad. Leaving John Barlow with nothing. Nothing but time and darkness to hide in.

"Gone. Absconded. Vanished. Your sister is gone. Like she never existed. Someone, or two someones from the report of the footprints found, waltzed right in and carried her away," Lancaster Barlow said.

John Barlow pressed his face against the bars, and his father stepped back. The foul smell of his son's unwashed skin nearly made him vomit.

"And you won't pay the ransom?"

Lancaster Barlow shook his head. "There's been no demand. No communication from anyone. I would happily pay whatever amount I need to get her back safely where she belongs."

"And you think I would have had something to do with such a thing? From in here? Why, Father? Why on earth would I harm Celia?"

"Revenge has always been one of your greatest motivators."

"You think that I would do that to her?"

"No, to me," the senator said. "I failed you. Like always, I didn't do enough for you. I am sorry. Truly."

"Don't grovel, Father. It is unbecoming of a man of your position and stature. Besides, I don't believe you."

"You don't believe that Celia has been taken from us?"

John Barlow stepped away from the bars, and glanced over to Fetch, who was huddled in the dark corner. "Oh, I believe that she has been kidnapped, but you know me better than you let on, Father. You know I would not harm Celia. That is your weakness, not mine. Not knowing when to stop, what the limitations of the human body are. No, Father. I think you came here because, in truth, you know that I am the only person in the world who can help you."

NINE

THERE WAS NO WAY TO TELL WHAT TIME IT was. The sun could have risen and fallen again and again for all Celia knew. The movements of the sun, moon, and stars were her only calendar, her only clock, other than the routine of the sanatorium. Now, with the burlap fastened over her face, she had lost sight of the sky, of the season, of the kind of day or night that it promised to be, or where she was, for that matter.

Her stomach told her that it was well past the time of her feeding. If it could be called that. She could not chew any more than she could scream. The nourishment she received had to be smashed up like a thick stew, or soups, that would slide down her throat without any effort on her part. Her menu was limited, and it consisted mostly of potatoes, mashed with some butter and cream mixed in. Sometimes, there was a flavor of meat, of beef or pork, in her meal, but it was distant. Sadly, her taste buds remained alive, not paralyzed like the rest of her body.

The grand injury, the one that encompassed her entire body, had taken time to adjust to. Her body, limp and useless, had protested, but now with her muscles gone, atrophied and wasted away, the worst part of eating came afterward, when she couldn't clean herself, or alert anyone that she needed attending to. There had been times when she'd had to lay in her own filth for hours at a time, or overnight. The sense of smell had not left her, either.

In all cases, when she ate, and dealt with the result, Celia relied heavily on her memories of meals past, and on her imagination to take her away from whatever the unpleasantness of living presented her.

But now, in this situation, captured by strangers, she couldn't bring herself to conjure a magical exit from her own reality. There were no memories of holiday meals that would offer her relief from this situation. No goose or ill-fated turkey to taste, or remember the taste of. No stewed cymlings, pattypan squashes cooked in bacon drippings, potted partridge, or roasted woodcock to transport her back in time to a place of comfort and flavor. It was a parlor trick anyway, and rarely worked, but the effort of it passed the time, the drudgery of the daily chore of breathing, of living inside the shell of herself.

Celia was stuck on her back in an unknown wagon, hungry and dirty, anxious to breathe fresh air, and at least, have her eyes set free. Sleep was impossible. She feared she wouldn't wake up, that she would be killed, or tossed to the side of the road, left for any animal to wander by and take a bite of her flesh for their own pleasure and survival. If that were to come, she wanted to face it awake, not drift off into a blackness never knowing what had happened to her. She had faced everything else, there was no way she was not going to be present for her own death.

Almost as if she commanded it, the team of horses slowed, and the wagon finally came to a stop. Even through the burlap she could smell fresh straw, could tell that they had entered a livery or barn of some type.

Both men scooted off the seat behind Celia's head. One man tended to the horses right away, while the other's footsteps hurried off in the distance, vanishing like he had never existed in the first place.

The man that remained rubbed on one of the horses, whispered to it that it had done a fine job bringing them home. The words were slightly muffled, dense through the burlap, but the senses that remained with Celia had become more heightened than they'd ever been. She could hear better, smell better, see more clearly than ever before. Which was a shame, since she had no way of sharing her perceptions with anyone.

She liked it that the man was gentle with the horse, appreciated its effort. She hoped she would receive the same degree of tenderness as the beast when the time came for her to be touched.

It wasn't long before the horses were unhitched from their driving gear, and led off, leaving Celia alone in the silence of a foreign place. She had anticipated a reckoning, or a final end to her journey. But none came, at least not right away. She calmed herself, and without intent, slipped into a shallow sleep. Not one deep enough for dreams, just a nap, a place where she hovered between the waking and sleeping worlds. It was a place of comfort for her.

Voices and footsteps woke her, brought Celia back to the reality that she existed in.

"We're gonna move you now," a male voice said. He was the one she had smelled first, whiskey and tobacco. It was the first sentence either man had spoken to her since she'd been taken. There was no way to answer the man, to say thank you, or protest, but in her mind, she relaxed her body. *Take me to wherever you will.*

And they did. She sensed movement, heard the struggle of her dead weight, or the awkwardness of her limp body, of carrying her gently or roughly, she didn't know which.

The burlap hood remained intact over her head, but the smell of the barn quickly faded behind them.

Sounds of the night seeped into her ears, and there was a moistness to the air. Crickets sawed dew-coated legs, playing warbling love songs. Virginia bats, goatsuckers to those from the old country, tweeted overhead, offering sharp cries as they dove in rounding waves, feeding on the newly hatched insects that abounded on the cusp of evening and night. There were wavering insect buzzes close to her ears, and of all the things that Celia feared, it was a bug bite that troubled her the most. The itch could be maddening.

They weren't outside for long. The clunk of boots crossed over a threshold, landing heavily on wood plank floors. She was happy to be inside. Happier when she heard a door shut behind her, and three locks slide into place.

In another moment, the movement stopped and she was settled down, onto a bed or a board. Comfort was lost to her, as were the strong smells of the barn, of nature. Her own odors returned to her, and she strained to listen, but heard nothing except the two men walking away, disappearing out a door, their presence replaced only by the tick of a nearby clock. The sound of it calmed Celia, made her feel as if she were safe. Hopefully, she had been brought to a place where order and timeliness mattered.

Another set of footsteps came toward her, entered into the room. She could tell that there were walls and a ceiling from the echo. It was a large room, and the echo was dulled by upholstery and draperies. She was sure of it.

Celia's breathing sped up, and she found herself suddenly afraid. *Please, kill me quickly.*

The footsteps were gentler on the floor, the person smaller, cleaner. Celia was sure it was a woman. She brought the sweet fragrance of summer with her; a plot of gardenias, clean air washed by a slow rain, something distant, foreign air that she could not place or identify.

Next came a slight tug on the burlap, and then it was slowly pulled away, causing Celia's eyes to flicker and flutter in the newfound light, even though it was dim, offered up by several hurricane lamps scattered about the room.

A blurry image hovered over her face, sweet brown eyes looking down on her. "Hello, missy," the Chinese girl said. "My name is Little Ling, and I am here to take care of you."

TEN

LUCAS WAS AWAKENED THE NEXT MORNING
by the sound of a persistent axe meeting a target of wood.
There was little slice into the object; the bit was dull, making
the sound distant and futile—like the sleep that he had
fought during the night.

Restlessness was not an uncommon foe to Lucas, but the
loss of Hobie Lawton had affected him far more than he had
considered it might, even though he hardly knew the man. He
had failed at a simple responsibility. Hobie was a hired man,
and it had been a very long time since Lucas Fume had had
to hold the welfare of anyone other than himself in his hands.

A long, long time, he thought as he pulled himself up from
the straw bed. His back ached, and his shoulder was sore
from lying on ground without much padding. The pain of
loss and the lack of comfort made him feel like an old man.

Zeke was still sleeping, butted up against the inside wall
of the stall, his back as big as a dam, turned away from the
world. Who knew where Zeke's dreams took him? The Negro
hardly spoke of his past, much less his fears and hopes.

The swayback mare was gone, the barn empty, which

kind of surprised Lucas. He had heard nothing through the night, and he was certain that he had spent more time awake than asleep. Maybe there had been more winks in the tossing and turning than he thought.

Lucas eased out of the barn to relieve himself as quietly as he could.

Morning had broken shortly before the beat of the axe drew him out of the bed. The sun had already started to poke up over the horizon, and the easy blue sky offered a calmness that was hard to misinterpret. Thin clouds moved along at a slower than normal pace, reflecting the minimal wind that pushed across the open field, and up to the barn. Lucas noticed the change right away, even though he hadn't been in Kansas all that long.

The constancy of the dull axe continued, and after finishing his business, Lucas walked around to the other side of the barn to investigate.

He had expected to find Roy Tullet chopping wood for the breakfast fire, but it was Victoria who was swinging the tool handily.

"I expected to find your father here," Lucas said.

Victoria stopped mid-swing, let the head of the axe drop to the ground, and then leaned on the handle as confidently as any man Lucas had ever seen at the chore. She didn't seem surprised to see him, or bothered by his presence.

Sweat caused Victoria's chestnut hair to glisten in the soft morning light, casting a glow around her face that caused her to look ethereal, otherworldly—but there was no sweetness about her, no angelic stature in the surrounding light. Her face was hard, set with determination, or anger, Lucas couldn't tell which.

"This stump is going to get the best of me yet," she said.

"Looks tough."

"There's a reason folks call it ironwood. Pa's been trying to get rid of it since we took this land as our own."

"Where's he at?"

"Town. Got up before the sun, and headed in. Said he had some business to tend to."

Victoria stared at Lucas, almost like she was looking right through him. Her manner had bothered him the night before, and his opinion of her had not improved. He broke eye contact with the young woman, glanced up and down her body from head to toe—not to size her up in any way. He was looking for the bulge of the pocket gun, but didn't see one. That didn't allow him to relax, though. He was certain there was a gun about somewhere close.

"And what kind of business would that be?" Lucas asked.

Victoria shrugged her shoulders. "He didn't say. Hardly ever does. Comes and goes as he pleases. Always has, always will. We're both past the age of answering to one another."

"He's not worried about leaving you here alone with the Cheyenne and Kiowa raiding about?"

"I'm not alone now, am I?"

"I suppose not."

"I expect you'll want some coffee?"

Lucas shrugged. "We don't want to be a bother."

"I wasn't offering any to the other one with you," Victoria said.

Her tone made Lucas more uncomfortable than he already was. "Well, I'll just go rouse Zeke, and we'll be on our way. We've overstayed our welcome as it is. The sooner we get into Leavenworth, the better."

"Oh, you won't be going anywhere soon."

"Really, and why's that?"

Victoria Tullet flicked her head to the west, drawing Lucas's attention to a rising cloud of dust. A crowd of horses were headed his way, toward the small homestead.

For a second, Lucas thought to turn and alert Zeke, but as he had suspected, there had been a pocket gun stuffed somewhere inside the woman's dress—and she had produced it, then pointed it directly at him.

"What makes you think I can't take that little gun away from you, Miss Tullet, discard it, and turn you across my knee? Seems like you need a lesson in manners. You shouldn't point a gun at someone unless you intend to use it."

The gun didn't waver. "You'd do yourself a great favor,

kind sir, not to underestimate my shooting skills just because I wear a skirt. I'm not afraid to pull the trigger, nor would I regret killing a man such as you, given the cause. Pa said not to let you leave until he returned, even if it meant putting a hole in your lung or your head, whichever one I could get to first. So, I aim to do as I was told. Are you willing to take the chance that I'm just a squeamish woman, Mr. Fume, or would you like to stand there until these riders show themselves, and we see what's what?"

Lucas put his hands up. "I apologize if I have offended you. I meant no disrespect."

"I've known men like you before, Lucas Fume," Victoria sneered. "Nice hair, the scruff of a beard, a twinkling eye, fancy duds, and the charm of a thief. You think a woman should fall over herself for you. You smelled like trouble from the first sight of you. You and that boy you travel with, and something tells me I'm right, otherwise Pa would be by himself."

Lucas eyed the approaching plume, and began to get nervous. He knew then that he had made another serious mistake, one that might well have put Zeke at as much risk as Hobie Lawton: He had used his own name, and Zeke's first name upon introducing himself. It concerned him that his senses were so dull, that prison, and what had come after, had affected him so deeply. They should have holed up in St. Louis, taken some time to recover—but that's not what had happened. Lucas had been in a hurry to ride west, to put things as right as he could.

He glanced over his shoulder to the barn, thinking he might call out to Zeke to run again, but he thought better of it. The riders were close now. He could see six horses all with their heads down, running as fast as they could.

The look on Victoria Tullet's face warned him off of doing anything that might provoke her. It would only take a quick flinch, and the pressure she held on the trigger would be enough to do him in. He believed her fully. She would pull the trigger without regret, if he gave her cause.

The riders broke onto the land like they were a posse that had found its quarry.

Roy Tullet led the way, looking very much like he must have ten or twelve years before, riding into camp with reinforcements, readying for battle: He was proud, tall in the saddle, invincible. It was easy to tell a former soldier, either by age, the loss of a limb, or by the carriage of his frame. It was the first and the former that had told Lucas that Tullet had fought in the War of Northern Aggression. Problem was, he didn't know which side the man had fought for.

All six of the men were armed, though Tullet had no weapons in hand, just the reins of his horse, the swayback mare, who looked like all of her energy had been extinguished in the ride back from wherever they came.

The other men carried rifles, wore handguns on their hips, and had full complements of cartridges in their gun belts.

Tullet rode in, stopped, quickly found purchase with the ground, and headed straight to Victoria. He eased his right hand to the Colt he wore on his own hip. "You all right?"

Victoria nodded, then looked over her shoulder, taking her eyes off of Lucas to sneer at another man. "You had to bring him?"

"Now, Victoria, we got more problems now than we had before. Mr. Nash has more to offer in a circumstance like this than any other man around."

Lucas eyed the man he assumed to be Kingsley Nash.

Nash sat high in the saddle of a pure black gelding, looking very much like gentry, a haughty landowner with the air of power so thick it kept the mosquitoes at bay. He was dressed properly, fresh from a tailor, not a catalog, and the horse looked to be of high breeding.

"I assure you," Lucas said, "there is no need for all of this. I would appreciate it greatly if the guns drawn were taken off my head. I am not guilty of anything."

Roy Tullet dug into his back pocket, produced a piece of paper, a wanted bill, and unfurled it for Lucas to see. He sighed at the sight of it.

The paper held a poorly rendered likeness of Zeke, and pronounced him an escaped convict on the run, dangerous, wanted for the beating and rape of a woman in Tennessee.

It wasn't the shock of the paper that set Lucas back. He had expected that there would be such a thing. What bothered him was that it had circulated so fast. He had hoped that he and Zeke would have some time to set things straight, time to get their feet under them. It didn't look like that would be possible now, if at all.

"That has nothing to do with me," Lucas said.

Victoria Tullet's face was tight with confident righteousness. "I knew there was something out of the ordinary with you two."

The other riders had surrounded Lucas, and sat pat on their horses. Only Kingsley Nash made an effort to come to the ground. He eased his medium frame off the black gelding, and walked over to Roy and Victoria, head cocked in the air, with no weapon on his person—at least in sight.

Nash was nearly a head taller than Victoria, and about the same age as Lucas—in his early thirties. Old enough, like Roy Tullet, to have seen war and battle, but that wasn't certain. The man looked like a cross between a snake oil salesman and a carpetbagger, Lucas couldn't tell which. Either way, he didn't like him, and would have been glad to put his fists to the man, though now wasn't the time for that.

"You have done the right thing, Rutherford, coming for me and the boys," Kingsley Nash said. He wore a black mustache on his lip. It was misshapen, like a leech had crawled under his nose and fallen asleep. Lucas wondered if the man was deformed in some way—it looked like he was trying to hide something with the growth of hair.

"He's in the barn," Victoria said.

"You can put the gun down, darlin'," Nash said to her. "Fume's not going anywhere, and neither is his friend."

Victoria ignored the command, and looked to Lucas. "I should've shot you both when I had the chance."

Nash smiled, then turned to the closest rider, and flicked his head. "Search the barn, but don't shoot unless he runs. The bill says he's worth more alive than dead."

The rider, who wore dusty old Union boots, nodded,

dismounted, and sent two more of the riders to the other side of the small building. All of the exits were covered.

Lucas knew that it was best not to say a word. There was nothing he could offer Zeke at the moment.

Nash, and the Tullets, watched as the other riders followed suit and went to the door of the barn, guns drawn. "Come out with your hands up," the man with the Union boots hollered out.

He was met with silence, and called again. When no sign of movement came, he motioned for the two men next to him to go inside. They did, operating like they had conducted the same kind of invasion a hundred times before.

It didn't take long for the first man to come back. He had a disappointed look on his face. "Barn's empty, boss. Ain't nothin' in there except for mice and horseshit."

ELEVEN

"TIE HIM UP, AND PUT HIM IN THE ROOT CEL- lar," Kingsley Nash demanded.

Lucas was trapped. If he ran, Victoria Tullet would have her opportunity to shoot him, as would the others. Not that he didn't think that that wouldn't happen, but at the moment, he seemed to have some value alive to them, just like Zeke did.

Surrendering without a fight was never easy for him, but Lucas saw no way out of the situation he'd found himself in, so he hoisted his hands up over his head. "I'm all yours."

"Where's the Negro?" Roy Tullet asked.

Lucas shrugged. "He was asleep when I came out of the barn. Must've heard the commotion, then set out for his own safety."

"He won't get far," Kingsley Nash offered. "Not too many places to hide between here and Leavenworth. Besides, a man as big and dark as he is stands out. If we don't find him, the Cheyenne will be glad to take a black scalp."

"Go on, Fume," Roy Tullet said with a poke of the barrel of a gun to Lucas's back. "Head over to the root cellar."

Rage began to build in the pit of Lucas's stomach. He

was confident that he could spin around and disarm Roy Tullet, a man he now considered a traitor, and pistol-whip him in the process, but it was a bad plan. Or reaction. Neither would do him, or Zeke, any good.

Lucas was directed toward a mound behind the sod house. Movement behind him told him that three horses had taken to the hoof in search of Zeke. That left one hired man along with Kingsley Nash and Roy Tullet. The hired man, the one wearing Union boots, was inside the barn, most likely searching for, or collecting, the weapons that had been left behind—depending on what Zeke had taken with him. Lucas knew the big man well enough to know that he hadn't run off unarmed.

Nash stayed put, hovered over Victoria. His weapon, a long-barreled Walker Colt, more for show than anything else, was drawn as backup for Roy.

Tullet quickly circled around Lucas, and opened the cellar door. "Go on, now. You do anything stupid, and your head's gonna get blown clean off."

"I got that," Lucas said, stepping down into the darkness of the cellar. "I hate to tell you, but I've been in worse places than this."

"I bet you have. Now go on, and don't try to escape. The way I see it, it won't be long before we catch your friend. Once we're sure you can't help him, or that there's no law lookin' for you, too, you'll be free to go."

"I wouldn't think of such a thing as escaping," Lucas said, as he stepped down onto the dirt floor. "You mean that there isn't a reward on my head? I can guarantee you that there's not."

"We'll see, won't we?" Roy Tullet offered nothing more than that. He let the door slam shut, then locked it tight with a chain.

Damn it, Lucas thought, *what the hell have I gone and gotten myself into now?*

Light filtered down through the slats of the door, allowing air to circulate into the cellar. Still, it was dank, nothing more than a grave a man could stand up in.

If there was food stored in the cellar, Lucas couldn't see it. He hadn't explored the whole of the place, didn't want to venture too far away from the strips of sunlight that dripped down inside.

The darkness seemed to go on for a little ways, but it could have just been an illusion. At the moment, his curiosity was not in control. He wanted to stay close to the door, listen to the comings and goings of the men above. But all he could hear was the distant song of a lark of some kind singing away the day. If a mate was answering, it was too far away for Lucas to detect.

He settled in, butt on the ground, his back against the cool dirt wall. It didn't take long for spiders to start a trail over his boots, uninterested in his presence, in biting him. Lucas feared nodding off, feared losing his vigilance. Just like he knew little of the animal life in the West, he knew little of what could do him harm under the ground. He suspected there were poisonous snakes about, but it was just an assumption. Surely, there were mice, and possibly rats, just like there had been in the prison cell in Tennessee. That place had been infested with vermin. He shivered at the thought.

Further incarceration was a plight he had hoped to avoid for the rest of his life, and now he was back under lock and key, his freedom in someone else's control. Anger bubbled inside him, and Lucas wanted to scream out, but he restrained from drawing any undue attention to himself.

Who knew what Tullet or Nash had in mind for him? They weren't obligated by a badge on their chest, no matter what had been said. The only law that seemed to matter to either of them were the words on the wanted bill. "Worth more alive than dead," *Nash had said of Zeke.*

"Damn you, Barlow," Lucas seethed, as he smacked the back of his head against the dirt wall. "Goddamn you."

Even the most meaningful memories faded with time, but there was nothing in the world that could make Lucas forget John Barlow, or the betrayal the man had plotted against him.

There were as many cobwebs in Lucas's mind as there were in the root cellar, but forced to remain locked up, he found he had no choice but to reflect on what had gotten him into the situation in which he now found himself.

Lucas had known John Barlow since he was a boy in Tennessee. They traveled in the same social circles. Lucas's father was a landowner, intent on owning as much as possible, while John Barlow's father was a lawyer, who had ambitions of his own. Paired with similar interests and time, Lucas and John quickly became friends. So much so, it seemed they were always together—or more accurately, John Barlow was always with Lucas, always at the grand house in Seven Oaks. Lucas could only remember being at John's modest house once or twice, but it had never occurred to him that there was anything the matter with that at the time. Lucas was just glad for the company.

He was an only child, and had spent a lot of time alone. Not that he minded, but Seven Oaks was a big place, covering several hundred acres, and the house seemed just as big to a small boy. Before John came along, Lucas would sneak into the kitchen and spend as much time at Mattie Pol's feet as possible. She was a good mammie, and looked after him the best she could. Lucas's mother was distant, socially active, away from the house more than she was there, taking up one cause or another. His father traveled frequently, too, amassing a fortune, buying up tracts of woodland in Minnesota— tracts that would become extremely valuable after the war with the building of the railroad.

Lucas and John spent days together roaming the woods, playing, imagining different lives, different worlds—skills that would come in handy when The War Between the States came along, and both of them, young men by then, operated as Confederate spies.

John's father had followed his ambitions, and ended up in Washington, but would not become a senator until afterward, until Tennessee rejoined the Union and representation for its citizens was required. But business being business, contacts had been made, and positions taken. John

Barlow was a natural leader, able to get people to do his bidding easily with his charm, imagination, and strategic planning skills. It was no surprise that he managed to lead a group of men in the covert activities of winning the war for the South.

Lucas was more of a dreamer then, a follower, prone to fits of fancy. His mother worried that Lucas would throw away his birthright, his place in the world, and run off with a troop of thespians, becoming an embarrassment to the family. Truth was, she feared he'd turn out like a Booth even before John Wilkes took up the gun and killed the president. But it was his skill of mimicry, of transforming himself with a wardrobe, or a gait, that made him valuable to John Barlow. Lucas became a top spy, and learned even more survival skills during that time, making him and John quite a team.

But there was always one thing that stood between them, that became a rub, a chasm that separated them as they got older, and that was the presence of Charlotte Brogan—the woman they both loved. The woman who had recently died in Lucas's arms.

John Barlow's betrayal had caused Lucas to lose everything that he had once loved, and now, his only comfort was knowing that the man who had taken so much from him existed in a cell, locked away for the rest of his life.

The fact that they were both prisoners, a thousand miles apart, was not lost on Lucas. It did nothing to ease his pain, calm his sad memories, or vanquish his regrets.

TWELVE

THE WATER WAS PERFECTLY WARM, ALLOW-
ing Celia to relax more than she had in a long time. Soaking
in a bath had been a pleasure of the past, when she was *alive*,
able to take care of herself, able to express herself completely and easily. It had been so easy then, as a girl, as a
young woman. Not now. She considered herself dead. Half
dead, at least. Broken. Trapped inside an unmovable shell;
imprisoned with no prospect of happiness—or escape.
Death was her only hope. Or had been until she had been
spirited away from the sanatorium at the hands of strangers.
Now, she wasn't so sure.

At the present moment, she existed, situated in the water
so that she was in no threat of drowning; naked, and warm—
perfectly warm—she felt a glimmer of hope.

"You need food," Little Ling said, staring down at Celia.
The Chinese girl's sleeves were rolled up, and she was engaged in washing every inch of Celia's body. There was no
embarrassment, no shame, no nothing. It just seemed a
normal chore for the girl. She was gentle, took her time, said
little—but there was a sadness in her yellow face, in her

slight brown eyes, that at the time glistened, like they were rimmed with tears.

"You look like your sister," Little Ling said with a whisper.

You knew my sister? For some reason, the announcement of such a thing surprised Celia—until she looked closer. Of course, she knew my sister. She is the little Celestial girl, now a woman in her own right, who had accompanied Mary Catherine home from China, who had tended to her as she lay dying in our parlor, and was taken in by John. She had disappeared with him, lost in a peril that seemed like an unimaginable plot, but was wholly true, part of her own story, her own tragedy.

A million questions exploded inside Celia's mind, but, of course, she couldn't ask them. She couldn't do anything but lie there in the bath, comforted more by Little Ling's presence than she ever thought possible.

Lancaster Barlow exited the prison as quickly as he could. "Take me back to the Maxwell House," he instructed the carriage driver with a hard, frustrated tone.

Sheriff Keane had arranged for a cab to transport Barlow to the prison, opting to return back to his office, and continue the search for Celia Barlow.

The driver was an unknown man, typically dressed in regular work clothes, which was neither here nor there to the senator. There was nothing of note about the man. He was just a means to an end, a way to and from the hotel, hardly anything to be concerned about.

"As you wish, sir," the driver answered as he opened the door, and stood back for the senator to enter. The harsh tone didn't seem to bother him. The driver had a thin, nondescript face, freshly shaved, clean of any facial hair at all, making it difficult to consider his age, if one was prone to such an exercise. Lancaster Barlow was not—unless there was need to know more about a benefactor, or an enemy. He barely had any concern about such a common man.

Barlow stepped inside the empty carriage, and eased into

the seat, expecting the driver to close the door and get on with the journey. But that didn't happen. Instead, the driver peered inside, and said, "I was given a note to give to you, sir." He offered a piece of paper to Barlow.

"And by whom were you given this note?" the senator asked, not making any effort to retrieve the paper from the man's hands.

The driver shrugged his shoulders. "A man, it seemed, in a hood and cloak, his face not completely visible, which was not alarming on a night like this." It was gloomy out, foggy and gray, presenting the street as a den of shadows more akin to London than Nashville.

"A man approached the carriage outside a prison in a hood and cloak, and you were not alarmed?" Barlow demanded. It didn't matter to him that he had no power over the man, no credibility with him. It was just one more thing to be angry and frustrated about.

"I have seen plenty of odd things as a driver, sir, and that was not one of them. There were people coming and going from the delivery entrance, just like you. Commerce at a prison carries on at all hours of the day and night. That, I am accustomed to knowing. So, no, again, I was not alarmed."

"Were you given coin to deliver this message?"

Barlow continued to demand more information than was his right, but that did not occur to him. However, the look on the driver's face said as much. "That is none of your concern."

"Of course it is. I am here on a matter of extreme importance. Every moment matters more than the next," the senator ranted. "I am not certain who is friend or foe, or what is afoot. I demand you tell me your price to deliver this piece of paper."

"That is none of your business, sir." With that, the driver tossed the note at Barlow, slammed the door, and rocked the carriage heavily as he climbed up on the seat.

"Well!" Barlow exclaimed, so exasperated the tips of his fingers tingled.

"Yaw! Yaw!" the driver yelled out, then flipped the reins, setting the vehicle into quick motion.

They sped off at such a rate that it nearly knocked Barlow to the floor. He lost his grip on the note, and it slipped away, out of sight. Panic set in, and he scrambled to reach forward, nearly falling headfirst.

The carriage lurched, groaned, and rocked heartily from the high rate of speed it was traveling, but Barlow was able to scoop up the note, and right himself. He pushed back as far into the plush seat as he could, arching his back for safety more than comfort.

It was difficult to see clearly out the window. Everything was a blur, and the night had so fully enveloped the world that even the shadows that were so prevalent outside the prison had retreated from sight. Still, the senator's vision had adjusted enough to see the note. He opened it, and pulled it close to his eyes to make sure he could read it.

The note was written in clear script: LEAVE NASH-VILLE BY MIDNIGHT, OR YOU WILL NEVER SEE YOUR DAUGHTER ALIVE AGAIN.

There was no demand for money, no amount of ransom given, like he had expected. Just a dire warning for him to leave town, and nothing more.

"Preposterous!" he said aloud. "Where is she? Where in the hell is she?" he demanded of the note. But, of course, there was no answer, just the rush of wind pushing inside the carriage through the window, tugging at the note, trying to release it from his grasp.

"Driver! Stop! Stop, I tell you. Stop, this instant!" Barlow demanded.

But no answer came. The driver was as deaf as the note.

Barlow pounded on the ceiling of the carriage with his free hand. "Stop! Stop, now! We must stop!"

The carriage continued speeding on through the night.

The horses' hooves echoed behind them, rushing into the carriage on the wind. Clack, clack, clack, like a quick tempo of drums, never wavering in their beat.

A hard swerve nearly sent Barlow flying to the other side of the coach, and in the tumble, he felt the first seed of fear, a consideration rising in his mind that could not be true.

He pounded the ceiling again, and again received no answer, so he stuck his head out the window, looked high above him, planning on chastising the driver for being so reckless.

But his fear proved to be true. There was no one in the driver's seat.

The carriage barreled down the street directly into the heart of the city, wholly out of control, with nothing but the Cumberland River standing in the way of stopping it.

Lancaster Barlow screamed at the top of his lungs, in abject terror, but there was no one near enough to hear him, to save him.

THIRTEEN

THE ROOT CELLAR WAS FULLY ENGULFED IN darkness. The light of the day that cut through the door slats had slowly faded away, leaving Lucas in a place of blackness that rivaled the solitary hole in the Tennessee State Prison. Even with his eyes wide open, it was like they were closed, like he could see nothing but the backs of his eyelids.

He hadn't moved from his spot on the floor, back against the cool wall, under the door so he could hear what was going on in the world above. Any desire to explore was minimal. He feared becoming lost in the dark if the cellar was larger than normal. So he sat, ears tuned, without much concern of becoming sessile, permanently rooted to the floor or the wall, if such a thing were possible.

No one had brought him food or water, and it had been hours, just before dark, since he had heard any movement on the ground above: horses riding off in a rush.

Lucas had assumed that the Tullets had stayed behind, that they would at least treat him with the basic decency of a prisoner. But now he wasn't so sure. They may have left him there on his own, to die slowly, to just wither away and disappear.

Of course, he wouldn't give up so easily. He knew he could survive the night—but come daylight, effort without food and water, especially water, would start to be a challenge.

Lucas had pushed away the memories of John Barlow, Charlotte Brogan, and his previous life, the best he could. But now it was almost like the memories had become part of the darkness, so dense, so real, that he could taste them.

When he put his hands in front of his face, he couldn't see his fingers. He pinched himself every once in a while just to make sure he was still alive.

The air had started to turn cool, and finally, just when Lucas was about to surrender to the darkness and give in to sleep, the three-quarter moon started to rise into the sky. It traversed slowly overhead, casting a welcome glow of diffused light through the door slats.

He sighed, blinked, and saw the silhouette of his boot before him. It was starting to look like he wouldn't have to wait until morning to see what was what, climb up the ladder, and discover the potential for an escape.

The moonlight was dim, like a far-off candle, but it was improving by the second.

Heartened, Lucas stood up, and froze as soon as he was solidly on two feet. He'd heard something. A footstep, then another. And then it stopped.

It might have been the wind, or a coyote sniffing about, looking for a meal to steal. Lucas could sympathize: He was starving.

A rock clattered on the door, tossed there by some unseen someone. It wasn't a coyote, but could have been a predator of another kind.

Lucas eased up against the dirt wall of the cellar, and blended back into the darkness—even though he was hopeful that Zeke had returned to the homestead, set on seeing him free.

"Lucas," a man whispered. "I know you're down there. Are you all right?" The moonlight disappeared, and was replaced by a familiar shadow. It wasn't Zeke Henry come to rescue him. It was Joe Straut.

Every muscle in Lucas's tense body relaxed. "I'm all right."

"They got you locked in, but I can kick away the wood. Stand back."

"You sure you won't draw anyone's attention?"

"Place is dark, and all of them that rode in, rode out, along with that girl. Made toward town a few hours ago. I was just waitin' to see if they'd circle back, or were settin' a trap for Zeke to come back for you. Stand back, I think it's clear now. If not, I got a couple of extra Colts. We can shoot our way out if it comes to that."

Lucas nodded, relieved. "Go on."

Straut did what he said he was going to, and kicked in the door, then yanked what was left of it open. "Come on. I wouldn't dillydally if I was you."

"You don't have to tell me twice." Lucas scurried up the ladder, and nearly jumped onto solid ground. He came face to face with Joe Straut. "You're a sight for sore eyes," he said, offering the man a handshake.

Joe Straut shook Lucas's hand with a happy, tight grip. He was a recent acquaintance, a friendship acquisition from the incident that had freed Lucas from the lie perpetuated by John Barlow. Straut had originally been one of Barlow's men, a sergeant in his makeshift army of outlaws, only Straut wasn't an outlaw; he was just a soldier, like so many men, looking for a place in the world after the end of the war.

Barlow turned on Straut, was going to frame him for three murders that he didn't commit. Straut figured it out, and jumped sides. In the end, he helped Lucas prove his innocence, and send Barlow to jail—where he belonged.

"I was worried when I came upon the railcar and it was nothing but a pile of burned rubble and a frame left to rust in the rain and wind."

Lucas stood back from Straut, and eyed the water pump that stood just outside the barn. His throat was coarse with dryness, but he was glad to breathe fresh air. "Cheyenne attacked. At least, I think it was Cheyenne. Looked like Dog Soldiers," he said, looking beyond the barn to the rest of the property.

It was dark, uninhabited like Straut had said, only now, under the light of the moon, the sod house and everything around it looked abandoned, like no one had lived there in years. Lucas shook his head, a little confused, and walked to the pump.

Straut followed. He was a little taller than Lucas, hale and hearty, with a barrel chest, and square shoulders. Age, and the war, showed in the deep crevices on his face, and there were curls of gray hair in his beard. Lucas supposed the man was in his late forties, or early fifties, making him nearly old enough to be his father.

"Might've been Dogs," Straut said. "Hard to say one way or the other. I'm not well versed in all of the tribes, or their ways. Not like there's just one enemy like the old days. Wasn't too hard to tell a Union brigade, or a dirty liar, by the sole of their boots."

Lucas agreed with a nod. He pumped the water. It took longer to flow than he suspected it would, adding to his suspicion about Tullet's story. "It was my fault," he said, then cupped his hand under the faucet, and slurped a full cupped palm of water. It was a relief on this throat. The only relief he felt at the moment.

"What's that?" Straut asked.

"I set us up out in the middle of nowhere just asking for an attack. Hobie Lawton put his faith in me, and I failed him. He was a fool to believe in me. It cost him his life." There was a slight quiver in Lucas's voice, a hint of emotion that was obvious for the most hard-hearted man to ignore— which Joe Straut wasn't.

"I put my faith in you, and here I am." Straut hesitated, watched as Lucas took another drink, then wiped the dirt and dust from his face. "I was late. If I'd been on time, been there when you was expectin' me, well, things might've turned out just a little different with them redskins. You ain't to blame, Lucas. It was just one of them t'ings that happens out here."

"Maybe I should have stayed where I was, where I know the weather, the birds, the capabilities of those that are set on doing me harm. I know the ways East like the back of my hand, but here, it's like learning to swim in a lake that's not made of the same kind of water. You know what I mean?"

"I think I do," Straut said.

"You got any idea where Zeke took off to?"

Straut shook his head. "Can't say, really. There was other tracks to follow from the railcar. Three sets came in after you two headed out. Indians for sure, but who, or why they was there, is hard to say. They might trail after him, or they was just seein' what they could filch, which was hardly nothin' from what I could see."

"Just the clothes on our backs. Anything else of use, we buried with Hobie. Figured it'd be safe from any Indian there. That was Zeke's idea."

"Good idea, and he's most likely right. No Indian I know is gonna go diggin' in a grave."

"Not even for guns?"

Straut shook his head. "I doubt it."

"We have to find Zeke. There's a wanted bill out for him. A ten-thousand-dollar reward on his head makes him a target for just about anyone. White man or Indian."

"If they can read."

"Or divine a picture?"

"Good luck gettin' somebody to pay them. You know who's funding that reward?"

"Has to be Barlow's father."

"I wouldn't put it past the other one to be involved."

"John?"

"Whatever you want to call him. He was Lanford Grips to me for so long that I have a hard time with anything else. But I guess that name ain't the truth. But he's a fox, wily as hell. Hard to say what he can orchestrate from inside that prison cell."

"It's not as easy as you think."

"Not for you it wasn't. No offense."

"None taken." Lucas took another drink of water. "Ten thousand's only good if he's alive."

"We'll find him," Straut said. "I might not know much about this land, but a man like Zeke can't just disappear. We'll find him, or he'll find us. He's as lost as you are."

"I hope you're right."

"You'll see, I'm right. But I figured the senator would want him dead, keep him from talkin'."

"I thought so, too. They're up to something."

Straut smiled then, couldn't contain himself. "Well, Lucas, so are you. So are you."

Lucas narrowed his gaze at Straut. The moon stood over the man's head, emitting enough light for Lucas to be able to read Straut's face clearly, making no mistake about the truth behind his eyes. "It's done, then?"

"It is. Celia Barton is safe with Little Ling. At least for now. You know they're lookin' hard for her."

"They'll never find her."

"Nope," Straut said. "Not movin' about like they are."

PART II

Bound in Darkness

Evening and the flat land,
Rich and sombre and always silent . . .

—WILLA CATHER
FROM "PRAIRIE SPRING"

FOURTEEN

SLEEP HAD BEEN SO REFRESHING, SO DEEP
and completely restful, that Celia Barlow fought to stay in
the land of slumber. But no matter how hard she tried, there
was no way to return to the comforting darkness from which
she had just exited. And like any normal person after a good
night's sleep, she then sought to get out of bed, find a place
of private relief, then wash the night and previous day from
her face.

Except there was nothing normal about Celia's life. Not
now. The realization that she couldn't move, couldn't stand,
couldn't touch her own face with her own hands, was a
reality that she'd had to accept every morning, every time
she awoke to a new day.

The nightmare never ended . . . but something had
changed.

Something has changed, she thought, said to herself,
forcing her eyes to open wider. *Something has changed in
a good way.*

She felt comfortable.

There were no walls in the room she was in. At least not

walls like she understood them, made of wood and plaster, covered with horsehair wallpaper, faded and peeling, in odd designs that seemed mathematical, but equal to nothing she could ever calculate. These walls were off-white, made of a thin material, like canvas. They rippled in the wind, pushed in and out, like the room itself was breathing, alive. It occurred to her then that she was inside a tent. Odd, but lovely in a way. She'd never been inside a tent before, and hadn't expected to be, all things considered.

An easy breeze slipped in underneath the tent wall, and comforted her, caressed her face gently as it passed over her. Smells reached her nose shortly thereafter. Bacon fried in a nearby iron skillet. She could hear the sizzle, too, and the gentleness of the wood flame underneath it. People came and went. Horses and wagons passed close by, suggesting commerce of some kind was taking place within walking distance. *It must be a town, but where? Why am I in a tent near a town?*

The wall of the room glowed in the soft morning light, warming her, too, in a way that hadn't happened for a long, long time. She chilled easily. So easily that she had prayed for a fever to come and take her away.

The truth was, Celia didn't know where she was, or why, but oddly, she was just happy to be there.

"Good morning, missy," Little Ling said, coming into view, carrying a tray. A bowl sat steaming in the middle of the tray, offering a new smell, a new flavor to enjoy. It was familiar, though Celia couldn't place it.

Little Ling was dressed in a white buttoned-up tunic that looked to be made of silk. There was a pattern of big birds, cranes of some kind, dancing joyously, though obscured, almost like they were sewn of the same colored thread minus one hue of white. Her solid black hair was pulled back into a long tail, and she smelled like a garden of spring flowers: lilacs, brilliant purple blooms that only lasted a few weeks in the spring.

Celia smiled, but her face showed nothing.

The Celestial girl put the tray down next to the bed, then

situated her face so it was directly in view for Celia. "Did you sleep well, missy?" She leaned in even closer, like she was inspecting something.

Yes, I slept better than I have in ages. Did you drug me? Put something in my late-night tea so I would drift away to a nether land? But she couldn't say it aloud. She blinked.

"I take it that is very good," Little Ling said. "They say you not in there. But I think you are. Can you do that again?"

Do what?

"Blink."

Yes, of course. And she did, as deliberately as she could.

Little Ling pulled back, and smiled. "See, I knew you are in there. We gonna get along just fine, missy, you wait and see. Little Ling here now. You're not alone anymore. Okay?"

Yes. Yes. Yes. Oh, god, thank you. Yes.

"I have fresh baked biscuits for your breakfast, and I pour milk on it. That make it very, very easy to swallow. Do you like honey? I have treacle if no likey honey. But I don't know which to put on it."

In her mind, Celia nodded, and licked her lips. *Do you know how long it's been since I have had honey? Anything sweet? My mother put treacle on scones when I was just a girl.* She blinked again, deliberately. That's what she had smelled, a bit of her past, her innocence. Treacle. No wonder she didn't recognize it.

But Little Ling, whose sweet face hung over hers like a bright full moon, looked confused. "I don't know if that is yes or no. Let me see." She put her finger to her thin, almost invisible lip. "Can you blink one time for yes, and two time for no?"

Celia drew in a deep breath, felt the morning air fill her lungs. The Celestial smell of Little Ling and the food she had brought with her filled her nose even deeper. She blinked once.

"Yes?" Little Ling said, studying Celia. "Now you say no. Blinky two times."

With all of the might and intention she had, Celia blinked twice as quickly as she could, then waited for a reaction.

Little Ling pulled back, her face blank of any emotion,

and grabbed the simple white bowl. "Would you like honey?"

No. She blinked twice. She wanted treacle. She wanted to taste her childhood, feel the presence of her mother in some remote way.

Little Ling smiled. "Treacle it is." She grabbed a tiny little white porcelain pitcher, most likely made to use for cream, then poured a hearty helping of the liquid brown sugar over the mashed-up biscuit and milk. "We gonna get along just fine, missy. You and Little Ling are two peas in a pod, you wait and see," the girl said, as she set down the treacle, and began to stir the mixture into a smooth consistency.

Celia's vision immediately became blurry. If tears fell from her eyes, and rolled down her cheeks, she could not feel them, could not scream the gratitude she felt.

No one, not one single doctor or nurse, had ever asked her to blink, to communicate with them in any way, even though she had tried. They all had assumed she was unable, incapable of such a thing. Or, as she had thought many times, maybe they didn't want to know. If she could talk, then she might be able to tell the truth about what had really happened to her. *Thank you, Little Ling. Thank you for rescuing me.*

FIFTEEN

THE HORSE EASED INTO THE NIGHT. THE trail ahead was clearly visible by the light cast down from the almost-full moon overhead. There was no forest, no copses of trees, nothing tall like mountains or hills ahead of Lucas and Joe Straut, just an infinite flatness. Even the wind had vanished.

There was a loneliness to the openness of the plains that was more apparent to Lucas in the darkness. It seemed to go on forever, and it was empty, like there were no other people on earth, like all of the living creatures had departed from the land, and this blackness, only dented by the glow of the moon, was all that there was left of a vibrant world.

Lucas walked alongside Straut's horse, a paint gelding who seemed to tolerate strangers as easily as it did Straut. They kept an easy, methodical pace. Every once in a while, the horse would lean over and nudge Lucas gently with its long nose. The unexpected affection surprised Lucas with comfort. He breathed easier, walked lighter afterwards.

"How come you didn't try and bust out the cellar door?" Straut finally asked, after they'd been walking for an hour or so.

"Can't rightly say," Lucas answered. "I thought about it, and I would've tried something come daylight, I think, if you hadn't showed up. But I guess small spaces don't cause an immediate panic in me. I figured I was still alive. Zeke was out there somewhere, and you, too. I wasn't exactly expecting to be saved, but I was in no hurry to face the Cheyenne, or those Tullets any time soon, either. I figured I was better off where I was."

"You sure a part of you ain't still back in that cell?"

The directness of the question surprised Lucas. He didn't really know Joe Straut all that well, had only known him for a matter of months, truth be told. But the ex-sergeant had proven to be trustworthy in that short time, did what he said he would, and showed courage and valor when the need for it had come in St. Louis. Lucas trusted the man to a degree, and didn't take immediate offense to the query. It hit a nerve, though, it sure did. So much so that he hesitated to provide an answer straightaway. He looked to the dark ground and continued to step forward, walk on toward a town that he wasn't quite sure existed.

"I suppose that's possible," Lucas finally answered. "There's some security to be found in small places. You get to know the darkness, and the creatures that abound in it. There are few of them, so you learn their ways pretty quick. Or the ways of what is all around you. Routines develop quickly. Your body takes on a schedule. That hole felt familiar. You're right about that."

"I'd go mad," Straut said. "I'm sure of it. I'd just bug out completely and lose my mind."

"Maybe I did go mad in there," Lucas said. "The best parts of me are still back in that prison, lost in the darkness, and I'll never be the same. It's too soon to tell, I guess. Maybe that's my lot, madness. It might explain the unsettled feelings I have. The bad decisions I've made."

"I 'spect that's possible. Be a shame, though, from what I can see. Seems like you got a lot of life in you if you want to take it. Not many men I've ever known have the means to live like you do."

"I'm not sure I understand what those means are, Straut. Money? It doesn't keep death or illness away. The Cheyenne didn't care that we were dressed in fine clothes, had a full larder, or owned all the guns we thought we needed. Tell Hobie Lawton about the means I had. Or Charlotte Brogan. Her mentor, the late Rose O'Neal Greenhow, drowned because she wouldn't let her gold sink to the bottom of the ocean without her. And Charlotte died because she thought money could buy her the happiness that she thought was lost. She learned nothing from Mrs. Greenhow. Nothing. Even though she proclaimed to not live her life the same way, die the same way. Means don't matter, Straut. The more you have, the more you can lose."

"It's easier to have them means than to not have them if you ask me."

"I suppose you're right. I want to find Zeke. That's what I want more than anything at the moment. Nothing else that I've set in motion will matter if he's not alive to see it through."

"You think a lot of that Negro," Straut said. There was a hint of judgment in his voice, and it wasn't difficult to understand what side of the war the man had served on, and why.

"He showed me a kindness and sacrifice, gave me time to heal in Libertyville," Lucas said, ignoring the slight, if it existed at all. "There's a lot to be said for a man who'll do what he did. I owe him my life, and I aim to see to it that he has his freedom, just like he saw to it that I found mine."

"What then?"

Lucas shrugged. "That's up to him. He'll be able to come and go wherever he wants."

"Or stay locked up in his mind."

"We all have to figure out how to free ourselves, Straut. It's just easier for some of us than others."

Silence returned between the two men. Lucas was far more concerned about Zeke's safety than his own at the moment. If something had happened to the Negro, if fate had stepped in before all the pieces of Lucas's plan fell together, it would have been a tragedy. Zeke had no clue what

Lucas was up to, and from the way things stood, he might never know.

There was no choice but to stop sometime well past midnight. The whole of the night had fallen into a deep sleep. There wasn't a coyote yip to be heard, or one owl hoot echoing across the wide-open plain. Even the crickets had had enough pleasure and gave up the sawing of their legs in hopes of attracting a mate.

The air was cool; the temperature had dropped several degrees, offering a chill to Lucas. He craved a fire long before Joe Straut made the decision to give his horse, and the journey, a rest.

There was no one better spot than any other. They were left to the elements, to the ground without cover of rock formations or many trees. But they did luck out on a collection of cottonwoods, thin and tall, with a scattering of broken limbs underneath.

"I'll take first watch," Straut said, cupping a small flame with his big hands.

Lucas shook his head. "I don't think I can sleep. Go on, get settled."

"You sure?"

Lucas nodded. He was in no mood to argue, or pull rank. All he wanted to do was stop running, get his footing, then revive himself the following day, figure out where he was, and what he had to do to find Zeke Henry.

SIXTEEN

THE CARRIAGE CAREENED TOWARD THE
river, and no amount of screaming from Lancaster Barlow
would bring it to a stop. It was as if he were caught in the
middle of a tornado, or some great storm, being tossed about
like a doll crafted of yarn and cornstalks. He feared a bone
would break, or his neck would snap, leaving him alive and
feeble, unable to care for himself like Celia, or able to bring
forth the punishment deserved on the driver for leaving him
in such a frightening and dangerous situation.

There was no telling how fast the horses were running,
but jumping out of the interior was out of the question.
Surely, Barlow thought, *the beasts would stop before plung-
ing into a flowing river!*

The senator had never been so scared in his life. He was
certain that he was going to die, that his time on this earth
was measured in seconds, not years like he had thought as
he was leaving Washington. Oddly, he felt no regrets. Just
anger. Anger for the things that were left undone. Celia
would be cared for, if she was found, and John was locked

away in prison, but it was his own legacy that concerned him, his reputation in Washington, his ambitions left unfulfilled . . .

Just as Barlow was about to surrender to the ride, to settle back into the rollicking velvet-covered seat, and give his life over to the fates, he heard a familiar baritone voice, yelling distantly, but coming closer. "Whoa, whoa, there!" The voice belonged to Sheriff Keane, Barlow was sure of it.

Somehow, out of the depths of despair and danger, the lawman had come to rescue him. At least that's how it appeared at the moment.

It seemed like minutes, but it was only seconds, before the horses and carriage came to a full and complete stop.

Arming himself had not been a consideration for Lancaster Barlow, but as he sat and waited, barely able to control his breath, he thought better of being without means to protect himself. It was a mistake that wouldn't happen again.

The door to the carriage jerked open, and even in the dim light of the night, there was no mistaking Sheriff Curtis Keane's middle-aged face. "Are you all right, Senator Barlow?" he demanded.

"I think so," the senator answered, feeling about his legs, flexing his knees and elbows, to make sure nothing was broken. "Where the hell have you been? I could have been killed!" His heart was still beating rapidly, and every breath caught in his throat, still tinged with fear and anger.

"I beg your pardon?"

"What took you so long, man?"

"I'm sorry, sir, but I am not your personal bodyguard. Those services are beyond my duty."

Keane stepped back away from the door, and the senator quickly followed, pushing out of the carriage, landing solidly out on the ground.

The roar of the river took Barlow's breath away. The horses had stopped only a few feet from the rocky shore. If Keane hadn't come along when he did, they surely would have crashed into the cold water. The river looked like black quicksand, dangerous and unpredictable, eager to execute any living creature that dared to touch its waters. Barlow shivered again at the thought of his own death.

"I want you to find the man who abandoned these horses. It is attempted murder, I tell you. I want him charged and sentenced, put away for as many years as possible for putting my life at risk."

Keane stood a good five feet from the senator, stroking his chin, thinking furtively. He seemed unconcerned about the crime that had just been committed. "And what was this driver's name, sir?"

"How would I know that?"

"Perhaps you could have asked him. Struck up a conversation with the man."

"I am here on business. Do I need to remind you what is at stake?"

"I'm aware of your troubles, Senator Barlow. Have you considered that the man who was in charge of these beasts may have come to grief, instead of abandoning you? That is a great assumption on your part, that he just left you to your own devices."

"Come to grief? How?"

"Stabbed, sir. Stabbed in the back of the neck. His body is lying in the middle of the road some ways back. Your driver is dead, Senator Barlow. He was murdered as far as I can tell, and the ride you took, and survived, was only a matter of luck, if I am to presume, like you, that what I see is the truth of things."

Barlow's mouth went dry. He didn't know what to say. With an angry thrust, he pushed out the note that he received from the driver to the sheriff.

"What's that?" Keane said.

"The driver said he was approached by a man in a cloak and hood and given this note to deliver to me once I exited the prison from seeing my son."

The sheriff took the note and read it, then looked up at the senator. "Seems to me it was a serious threat. 'Leave Nashville before midnight, or you will never see your daughter alive again.'"

"Surely, you're not suggesting I do as it says?"

"Seems to me you've only got a matter of hours, sir, if what this says is the truth."

"Can you not protect me?"

"Not every minute of the day and night. That would be impossible. Besides, the way I see it, you're here on personal business. You could get a Pinkerton to look after you, but I've got my hands full. And besides, it ain't my job."

"But I've been threatened, man!"

Keane shrugged his shoulders. "I'd take that threat seriously, if I was you. Like I said, if that note is real."

"What in the Lord's name do you mean real, man? Of course, it's real. Are you suggesting that I wrote this note? That's the most preposterous thing I have ever heard."

Rage boiled up on Keane's face, and anger balled up in his fists. "I'm going to walk down the street and see if I can figure out who killed one of the fine citizens I was elected to protect. I failed to do my job for him. For all I know, you killed this man and wrote that note as an alibi. I know nothing of your character other than your elected title. Your son sits in prison in this very city for deeds committed that are so unscrupulous and heinous I cannot even begin to imagine how he must have been raised, and that says more of you than anything I could read in the newspapers, or see before my very eyes."

"Well, I've never been so insulted in my life," Lancaster Barlow bellowed.

"That's not an insult, sir, just the truth. I have a dead man and you, standing here with an unlikely story and nothing else to show for your time."

"I am not a killer. I am a United States senator."

Keane scuttled up toe to toe with Barlow and said, "I don't care what you are. Until I figure out what happened here, you are a suspect in the murder of this driver, and regardless of what that note warns you of, you will not leave Nashville until I am certain that you had absolutely nothing to do with the unfortunate end this man came to."

"I am a suspect in this man's murder?"

"That's what I said," the sheriff answered. "Unless you can prove otherwise."

Barlow stood speechless. He could offer nothing in his own defense except frustration and demands, which remained buttoned up inside his lips. Beyond the bizarre situation he now found himself in, he could tell that the sheriff was serious.

"Am I under arrest?" Barlow asked.

"Not at the moment. But that could change at any second. Why don't you just stay right here, and wait until I come back with a clearer notion of what's going on."

"I suppose I don't have any choice, do I?"

"No, sir, you do not."

And with that, Sheriff Curtis Keane turned and walked away, stalking curiously toward a lump in the middle of the dark road, leaving Senator Lancaster Barlow with the decision to stay put and do as he was told, or run off into the night, fleeing the situation like a frightened mouse, unsure of which way to turn, or where to go next.

SEVENTEEN

THE PULSE OF LEAVENWORTH IMMEDIATELY roused Lucas from his dark mood, and gave him the first glimmer of hope that he'd had since burying Hobie Lawton.

A ray of bright morning sun cut down the hard dirt street, and the smell of a new day caught his nose. Someone was frying bacon nearby, stalls in the nearest livery were being cleaned out, and yesterday's dust was being swept off the boardwalk by various shopkeepers who paid him little or no mind.

Most of the clapboard siding on the buildings that made up the main street of the town looked new, fresh cut, not weathered enough to suggest it'd stood the test of the seasons. There was no mistaking that Leavenworth was in the midst of expansion, a boom brought on by the demand of cattle, drawing new citizens and even more travelers that passed through every day seeking a new life, or running from their old one. Lucas fit fully into both categories, but he had no intention of staying in one place permanently. At least not at the moment. Leavenworth was just a stop along the way to somewhere else: destination unknown. He just wanted to gather himself, replenish his needs and Straut's, as far as that went, and get on with the mission on which he'd set himself since coming West: seeking Zeke Henry's freedom. It meant more to him now than ever.

"First things first, Straut," Lucas said, walking alongside the horse on which the ex-sergeant sat comfortably. "I'm going to need to obtain some currency, so I'll need to visit a bank and have a sum wired to this location. We can get our bearings then, and set out to find Zeke."

Straut looked a little bewildered as he glanced about his surroundings, trying to take it all in. "This town's bigger than I expected it to be. If Zeke's here, he'll be hard to find. Especially if he thinks he's bein' hunted."

"He knows how to hide real well, even for a man the size he is."

"Probably a good skill to foster, but I worry about those men who sent you down in that hole. I know those eyes. Commanded them myself. Ain't no end to their desire until they get what they want. Capture and reward will be the only satisfaction to their aim."

"I hope he's here," Lucas said, looking around, taking in the sights, too, just like Straut.

Leavenworth didn't compare to St. Louis, but it promised to last, to build up even more as time moved on. There seemed to be a saloon on every corner, and every kind of store a man could think of to put a sign in front of: haberdasheries, one mercantile after another, milliners, dry goods, and on and on, to meet the needs of the growing and transient population.

"There will be places he'll go, if he's here and not held tight in some Indian camp beyond the reach of the white man's eyes," Straut said. "Be easier if he's here in Leavenworth, even all things considered."

"There was something odd about those Tullets and the farm they claimed to keep."

"Didn't look too well tended did it?"

"No, it didn't," Lucas said. "My gut said not to trust either one of them. Something didn't add up. Like they weren't who they said they were. I've got some practical experience at that, at pretending to be someone else to further a cause. It felt like that. Especially after I was put in the hole."

"I suppose you'd know," Straut said. "There's a bank up on the next corner."

"Good. I'm ready for some breakfast. A bath and a shave would be welcome, too."

Lucas followed Straut's gaze, then walked confidently down the street right up to the bank. He was early, the door was locked, causing him to reconsider his options.

"I could go find another one," Straut said.

Lucas shook his head. "One's as good as the other. They'll all open around the same time, and wire my bank. Why don't you go see to your horse, and come back. I'm sure I'll be done by the time you get back."

"You sure?"

Lucas nodded. "I'm fine, Straut. I think I can look out for myself in a town like this."

"Sure, you can, but why don't you strap this on to make sure." Straut reached over to his saddlebag, pulled out a gun belt with a new model Colt fastened in the holster, and offered it to Lucas. "Make me feel better if you took it. I think them Tullets were minions. The real threat looked to be that Kingsley Nash fella. We want to avoid him and his like while we're here, but we need to be ready for them to show up anytime. I think that's more likely to happen, if I was to reckon on their plans."

Lucas took the gun belt, and wrapped it confidently around his waist. The leather belt was fully complemented with cartridges, and the holster hung a little low, making it feel a little off balance. Not a rig he would have picked on his own, but it made him feel better to have it. "Hopefully, we won't draw their attention. Looks easy to get lost in the mass of traffic that's here."

"Keep a look out." Straut nickered his horse, swung its head east, and trotted down the street in search of the nearest livery.

Lucas leaned against the wall of the bank, took a deep

breath, and watched all the coming and going that was bub-
bling up around him.

People walked by on the boardwalk in a hurry, some
dressed in their finest, others not so concerned about fashion
or local opinion, but like the wagons and their teamsters in
the street, they all looked to be late for some appointment
or another.

No one was going in the same direction. Leavenworth
was a chaos of sounds and movement, all rising together,
allowing Lucas to watch from underneath the shadow of the
bank's overhang, hoping that he was hidden from view of
those that sought to do him and Zeke harm. Hiding was part
of the plan that he hadn't counted on.

EIGHTEEN

A DISTANT CLOCK STRUCK NINE, AND A TALL,
thin man with wireframe glasses and white puffy hair walked
up to the door of the bank, unlocked it, and walked inside.
He didn't flip the CLOSED sign to OPEN, just left it as it was.

There was no mistaking the man's position, his station
in life, dressed as he was in a fine suit with a fresh, firm
collar on his shirt. The banker barely paid Lucas any mind.
He had just glanced at him quickly as he'd stepped inside
the bank.

Lucas waited, and watched as the traffic continued to trot
by in the street. The boardwalk vibrated with well-meaning
citizens lost in their own concerns as they passed by. To
them, Lucas was sure that he looked like nothing more than
a dusty cowboy, just off the trail, hoping for work, or waiting
out the dread of too much to drink. Nothing, of course, could
have been further from the truth.

The lock on the bank door clicked, and the sign flipped
in the window from CLOSED to OPEN. After collecting a few
disdainful stares, Lucas pushed himself off the wall, and
made his way inside the bank.

The interior of the bank was everything he expected it to be. It was one large room with offices off the back, trimmed in polished walnut, with the necessary fans, sconces, and lamps gilded with gold paint. There was an expectation of financial institutions no matter where they were located, and this one didn't disappoint, all the way down to the teller's cage that stood open and in wait of Lucas's transaction.

An elderly woman looked up, then down her nose, as she took in Lucas as he approached. Clearly a spinster, the teller seemed to be stiff with age and lacked any sense of happiness on her wrinkled face. It mattered little to Lucas. He only had one thing on his mind.

There was no sign of the banker who had entered the building earlier.

"I need a wire made," Lucas said, as he settled himself before the woman.

"You can't have that in here," she said, eyeing the holster on Lucas's hip.

"I don't intend to rob you."

"Doesn't matter. It's against the law. New ordinance was just passed this last week." The woman had a slight lisp. It sounded like she was trying to be haughty, but it wasn't working.

"I can take it off," Lucas said.

"It'll still be inside, won't it?"

"Look, I just arrived in town, I don't know all the rules. If I could just get you to wire a bank in St. Louis so I can make a transaction here, I'll be on my way, and happy to take my gun with me."

"I can see that you're not from around here," the woman said.

Footsteps approached from behind Lucas, and he angled his head backward so he could see who was coming.

"Is there a problem, Edith?" the banker with the puffy white hair asked in a refined voice.

"This man has a gun, Mr. Lemming. It's against the law to open carry in a bank," the woman, Edith, said.

"Well, that's true," Mr. Lemming offered, coming to a stop next to Lucas.

Lemming was thin as a rail, and a good head taller, causing Lucas to look up into the man's emotionless eyes.

"Is there business you need to tend to, sir?" Banker Lemming asked.

Lucas nodded. "There is. I need to have a thousand dollars wired from St. Louis to your bank, if that's possible?"

"A thousand dollars, you say?"

"I didn't stutter."

"And your name, sir?"

"Fume. Lucas Fume."

Lemming didn't flinch with any recognition. He didn't react at all. "I see, Mr. Fume." He paused, and looked to the teller. "Edith," he said, "I will handle this transaction."

"And what about that gun?" the woman demanded.

"Do you plan on robbing us, Mr. Fume?" Lemming asked.

"Of course not."

"There you have it, Edith. Come with me, Mr. Fume."

Lucas sighed and followed after the tall man. He had never been comfortable in the halls of institutions, whether they were government or financial. They all smelled of dust and legal documents that usually were slanted to taking rather than giving, and required more manners than they seemed to be worth. Truth be told, Lucas much preferred saloons. The odds were better. But roles had to be played. All Lucas wanted was his money. Enough money to establish his comfort, and see to it that he had everything he needed to continue his mission.

It only took a second to arrive at Lemming's office. It looked out on the busy street, and the sound of commerce reverberated against the window.

"There will be paperwork to fill out, of course." Lemming sat down at the desk, another walnut affair, the corners hand-carved with leaves and scrolls.

"I've done this before," Lucas said.

Lemming eyed him closely after he made the comment, as if the banker was trying to determine the truth of the statement. He offered no words, just slid a few papers to Lucas, who went right at filling them out. In a matter of minutes, he had completed the necessary requirements, and slid the paper back to Lemming, who then checked it carefully.

Satisfied, the banker stood up, walked to the wire machine, and began inputting the clicks and clacks that had become the modern voice of communication. Luckily, Lucas's ears were trained to check Lemming's ability to key as closely as his ability to write had been checked. Education, no matter the cost, was a powerful tool. His early years as a Confederate spy continued to pay off in ways he had never imagined they would. He had slaved over the dots and dashes of the code that was so clear to him now.

"It should only be a matter of minutes," Lemming said.

"That's fine."

Done with the wire, Lemming walked over to the window, and stared out, his back to Lucas. "If I may be so bold as to ask, sir, how did you come into such a sum of money?"

Lucas was surprised at the question, put off by the directness of it. He allowed no words to burst out of his mouth, but chewed on a good amount of thought as he watched the wire machine, hoping for it to start ticking. "Fortunes are won and lost in a variety of ways, sir," he finally said.

Lemming nodded, and continued to stare out the window. They were both waiting to be freed of each other's presence. Lucas was growing more uncomfortable by the second.

"This town changes by the day," Lemming said. "Are you just passing through?"

Small talk with a banker was hardly ever pleasant, but Lucas knew it was better to keep the man on his side than to give him reasons to be offended, so he pushed away his hesitation the best he could. "I'll be moving along soon. Just have to find a few things in town before doing so."

"And that will require capital?"

"Of course."

Lemming stood stiff, and let his words fall silent.

The steady beat of horses' hooves and rolling wagon

wheels quickly replaced the conversation. A clock ticked on the wall, adding to the concert of forward motion. Lucas began to tap his finger on the desk, joining in, staring at the wire key, willing it to come alive so he could be free to leave the stifling room.

Seconds later, the key did just that. It started tapping out its response, slowly, letter by letter, announcing to the banker that Lucas's bank account was solvent, and the requested money would arrive in a matter of days.

"Well," Lemming said, turning to Lucas, "we are in business, as long as you are willing to accept my terms."

Lucas stiffened. "Terms?"

"There is always a risk that a transfer will be interrupted, not delivered. If you are to make a withdrawal now, it will be in the form of credit. There's a price for my risk, sir."

Lucas didn't answer, just shrugged.

Lemming walked over to the desk and slid a contract toward Lucas.

He wanted out of the office as soon as he could, so he grabbed up the closest pen, signed the paper, and slid it back to Lemming.

A slight smile flickered across the banker's face, and Lucas suddenly felt like he had just made a deal with the devil.

NINETEEN

THERE WERE TIMES WHEN CELIA COULDN'T
tell when she was asleep or awake. She daydreamed in the
afternoon with more intensity than she could ever remember,
and at night she slipped away into the land of dreams and
night terrors, even though she guarded herself against them
as best she could.

Most times in her dreams, she was well able to stand and
speak like she always had before the doom that had been
set upon her had occurred.

In this dream—she wasn't sure whether it was day or
night in the real world—she was lost. Lost in the deep woods
that rose up behind the house of her childhood.

The woods were thick, and it was a small house, at least
in comparison to the homes of the Fumes and the Brogans
that had been built earlier in the century as an expression
of wealth, power, and standing in the community. Planta-
tion houses had their own beauty to most people, but not to
Celia. She liked simple houses. Like the one Celia's father
had bought with his attorney wages. It was a warm and

comfortable house. Not open and airy like those big houses. They were like mazes, with doors that led to hidden rooms. There were dusty secrets held prisoner in the dark alcoves and cellars of the Fume and Brogan houses. She hated cellars.

The woods were thick with itchy nettle, nearly as tall as her neck. How old was she? Fifteen, sixteen, not much more than her time of social debut. If only she could have appreciated the feel of the earth under her feet when she was a child. Instead, she took it for granted, like she would walk to her very last day and then drop into her grave. Touch was such a fragile thing, and could be lost, be taken away in a moment's notice with the swing of a hand . . . or an axe handle to the back of the neck. How foolish she had been to believe that such a simple thing as walking could never be taken from her.

The ground rose up and down before Celia, steep enough at times to leave her winded, but she kept going. Stopping meant acknowledging that she was lost, that she didn't know where she was, and could be found by creatures who meant to do her harm. More harm than had already been done.

A deep ravine dropped down before her, stairstepping down to a river that she did not know, had never seen before.

Game trails were hard to find this time of the year. The undergrowth was still thick, thriving from the bright spring sun that beamed down from the perfect blue sky. The leaves on the trees overhead were still young and tender, not fully formed. But it wouldn't be long before they bloomed completely, and caught most of the sunshine—leaving the ground covered in shadows. The weeds and flowers would struggle for sustenance then, and die slowly, withering away until the first frost turned them brown, and ground them into dust and dirt, forgotten and dead.

It was the time of mushrooms and ramps, of blooming flowers that lasted days instead of weeks. The air was filled with their fragrance. Spring was intoxicating. Unless you were lost. Lost in a woods that seemed so familiar. Woods that Celia had known since she was just a child. But different, tilted somehow, like the world had spun out of sequence.

The dream fully engaged all of her senses. Somehow she knew it was a dream. But she could smell the wildflowers, feel the soft ground under her feet, and hear the birds calling in the distance. She wanted to dance on the earth like a sprite at some earthly celebration, but she couldn't stop running.

She was drawn to the water, to the river, and to the hoarse call of a bluebird in the distance. The little bird sounded like a happy robin with a sore throat, calling after a mate.

Bluebirds were Celia's favorite birds. They always surprised her. For some reason, she never expected to see a flash of blue fly before her eyes. Red and yellow, yes, but blue was such a surprising color to see moving about in the world that it always startled her. Maybe because there was no other animal that shared the color of the sky. Maybe that was it.

Just seeing a bluebird made her happy. Celia had studied them so closely that she knew their calls, knew which was a male or female when she did see them, knew when they were happy or alarmed. The one she heard now was afraid. Something was wrong.

Celia pushed through the sticky nettle, ignoring it as she ran toward the calling bird, down the trail, toward the river.

The flow of the river, the wash of rushing water careening over rocks, heading away, pushed ahead of the cry of the bluebird, adding to a low rumble; a sense of impending doom and death.

Tears began to well up in Celia's eyes, and her heart began to race. The trail opened up before her, and gravity pushed her to the bottom of the ravine. She had to stop, catch her breath, and wipe away the sweat from her forehead. Her body felt like she had just rolled in a bed of poison ivy. There wasn't an inch of skin that didn't beg to be scratched. Celia laughed out loud then, and heard her own voice for the first time in ages. It sounded weak and distant, too, just like the call of the bluebird.

She took a deep breath, and listened for the bird to call again to get her bearings.

She was standing on flat ground. The rise of the ravine was behind her. The river stood before her, swollen from the spring rains, in a hurry to journey south. Logs and tree limbs bounced along at a quick pace, floating like little ships, some spinning out of control, caught in swirling eddies. Others bore a more direct path, and carried passengers: squirrels, possums, and a pair of baby raccoons on an extra-large sycamore tree that had fallen into the river at a most inappropriate time for the critters. Their mother was nowhere to be seen. They were lost, too.

The land was flat on the other side of the angry river. A plain, eroded by years of floods reached up to a distinct line of trees. Another thick woods, filled with its own shadows and trails, stood in wait. The flat land edged up into hills that quickly grew into mountains, the tops of which disappeared into swirling thunderclouds.

It was then that Celia saw him. Not the bird, but a man, on the other side of the river, stooped over, looking at the ground like he had stumbled upon something interesting. When he stood up, Celia nearly lost her breath.

He was a big man, with arms made of rippled muscles that looked like they had been carved by some ancient artist. His skin shone bronze in the declining light—the gray clouds in the distance were racing toward her—and at first, she thought that he might be a runaway slave. But there was no such thing anymore.

Celia could hear her heart beating, and see birds fluttering behind the man in a thicket of raspberries, perfectly red and plump. But the birds, a pair of bluebirds, weren't interested in the feast before them. They were angry at the man. He had one of their babies in his big hand.

There was no mistaking the tiny blue fledgling, or the fact that the man sought to help it, do it no harm. His back was turned to Celia. He didn't know she was there. Very gently, he reached up to a hollow tree that stood on the border of the shadowy woods, and placed the baby bird back inside, where he must have known there to be a nest.

The parents landed on a nearby limb, huddled together, and watched. They had surrendered, certain that there was nothing more they could do.

Not satisfied that the little bluebird was where it was supposed to be, the man peeked inside, reached back in, made an adjustment, then stood back.

A raindrop fell from the sky, and a clap of thunder exploded overhead, startling Celia. She gasped out loud, drawing the man's attention.

He turned around, looked her in the eye, and smiled, smiled so bright it was like a light coming on inside her head.

"Zeke," she whispered, then reached out for him.

But it was too late. The storm swirled around her, and lightning danced down from the maddening grayness, hitting the ground at her feet.

"Zeke!" she yelled, reaching for him, but he was fading, disappearing in the storm. He couldn't hear her, she was sure of it.

With all the might she had left, she screamed out again, but it was too late. Zeke was gone. Taken from her by the bright light that caused her to flicker her eyes.

She was awake. The dream was gone, fading away so quickly she could not hang on to it no matter how hard she tried.

The face of the tiny Celestial girl hovered over Celia's face. A brightly lit hurricane lamp blazed behind her, and shadows flickered on the wall of her tent, reflecting a huge amount of motion. There was a storm gathering in the waking world, too. Only it was not weather. It was people moving about in a hurry. There was tension in the air that tasted like the last storm of summer had arrived without giving notice.

"Wakey up, Missy Celia. We have to go now. Bad men

come to take you away," Little Ling said. "You no be afraid. I make sure you safe, okay? I make sure you be safe. I promise, no matter what."

"*Zeke*," Celia whispered. But Little Ling didn't hear her. No one did. *Come back, please come back.*

TWENTY

LUCAS WASTED LITTLE TIME RESTORING HIS comforts. The first thing he did once leaving the bank was catch up to Straut outside the livery. The two men then took rooms at the Planters House Hotel at the corner of Main and Shawnee Streets, not far from the bank.

The hotel was four stories tall, made of brick, and offered as much distinction and elegance as the fine hotels in St. Louis and Nashville. The furniture was the latest style, shipped from the East, as was the silverware, plates, and almost every other accoutrement adorning the hotel. The patterns and quality were hard to mistake with as much time as Lucas had spent in and around the finer things in life—even if the memory of them was dusty.

The Planters House looked to be a perfect place to seek restoration. Lucas saw no reason to be uncomfortable. He had spent enough time in a hole and was anxious to return to the life he had sought out once he'd left St. Louis. He had always liked luxury, and was reasonably surprised to find it in Leavenworth, Kansas.

Once he was settled and bathed, Lucas made his way to

a barber for a trim and a shave of his neck. He decided to leave the length in his hair, riding just over his collar, and beard, which helped cover his face from any kind of recognition. There were no Wanted posters that he knew of with his likeness, but one could be put out on him as Zeke's associate. No use in being foolhardy. He'd made enough mistakes on this trip already.

After purchasing some new clothes, he met back up with Straut several hours later in the hotel's restaurant.

Straut hadn't sought out any physical changes at all, other than a bath. He wore the same trail-worn trousers, boots, and weapons. His beard was still frayed, and his Stetson stood faded from the sun. He smelled better. That was about the extent of it.

They were stuffed in a corner of a one-hundred-and-six-foot-long dining room that stretched along the first floor of the hotel. Lucas had chosen a small table, out of sight of most of the patrons, so they could have some privacy. Not that there were a lot of eyes to be cast their way. It was late, and most folks had already indulged in their evening meal—which was a good thing. Joe Straut looked as uncomfortable as a cowboy stuffed into a banker's suit.

"You all right?" Lucas asked, spooning a bit of soup the waiter had called a consommé into his mouth after asking the question. It tasted like beef broth to him.

Straut shrugged, and stared down at his empty plate. "Never been too comfortable in fancy places like this."

"We won't be here too long. Once we find Zeke, you'll be on your way again."

"You still think this plan of yours is going to work?"

Lucas set down his spoon, and stared into Straut's eyes. He liked the man. There was no question that he was of an older order, a sergeant who was comfortable with being a sergeant and nothing more. But there was an itch about Straut that reached deep inside of Lucas's mind. Straut had been a sergeant for John Barlow. Had spent a lot of time with the man. A lot less time than had been spent with Lucas. Just months. Not years. Trust between the two of them hadn't been built up completely. It would be easy for Straut to sell out and return to Barlow's fold. He'd had to know what kind of man John Barlow was long before he'd broken ranks with him.

"I do think it'll work," Lucas said. "But we're going to need Zeke to fit it all together."

Straut, who had tucked a pure white napkin under his chin at the beginning of dinner, pulled it away and tossed it on the plate. "You might be up against something here that you didn't count on at the start of all of this."

"What are you saying?"

"Well, I been askin' around about Indians and such since neither of us has a good amount of knowledge on the subject. You sure them was Dog Soldiers that attacked you, and burned the railcar to the ground?"

"As sure as I can be." Straut had Lucas's full attention now. The cavernous room, which could seat over two hundred people, if the need arose, suddenly grew smaller.

"There ain't any reports of Cheyenne raids in that part of the country, and it seemed odd to the folks I spoke to about what happened to you. Trackers, men who've been out here for years studying the way of the redskin, scratched their chins and asked me if I was sure of what I was sayin'."

"They weren't Cheyenne then?"

"They might not've been Indians at all the way I'm thinkin' about it now."

A twinge of discomfort and anger shot up the back of Lucas's neck. He leaned forward, and spoke through clenched teeth. "What are you saying, Straut? Hobie Lawton's dead, and I've been walking around beating myself up for putting us out in Indian country unprepared. I'm responsible for that man's death."

"What I'm sayin' don't dispute that. That was a foolish thing to do, Lucas," Straut said, then glanced away quickly from Lucas's hard glare. "If you don't mind my sayin' so."

"I don't, but you need to explain your line of thinking— or what you've found out."

"Ain't found out nothin', at least not yet. Just a gut feelin'

I got. I think what you did was underestimate Mr. Grips, I mean John Barlow. I still can't quite make the switch from his made-up name to his real one, and I'd rather not speak it at all. He's a bad man, that one is. I feel the same way about Finney Deets as you do about Hobie Lawton. It be my fault that he's dead, but there ain't nothin' I can do to bring him back to life. I just have to make sure I don't do the same thing again. I figure that's your load to carry, too."

"How do you figure Barlow's involved in this?" Lucas sat back and relaxed his jaw.

"Well, you know where he's at."

"Of course, I do. He's in cell number 373B in the Tennessee State Prison. And he's going to be there for the rest of his life."

"Well, no offense, but that's your first mistake in my way of thinkin'. No cell's gonna hold that man. He'll talk his way out of there sooner or later—or just walk out with a guard's blessin'. Won't matter whether he's got no hands or a sentence, he'll figure a way out. You know what kind of man he is. You spent more time around him than me."

That was the truth. Lucas had known John Barlow since they were boys. At one time, Lucas would have followed the man through hell—and he more or less did, as his right-hand man in the war. Barlow was a lead spy for the Confederacy, the brains to a far-reaching organization that'd had tentacles beyond Lucas's knowledge.

Lucas had to agree with what Straut was saying. John Barlow had the gift of persuasion like no man he had ever met.

"What makes you think he doesn't know exactly where you're at, Lucas?" Straut asked.

Lucas sighed. "I hadn't thought about it."

"You should've."

And Straut was right again. But leaving St. Louis hadn't been a simple decision. The excursion they were on was not one for pleasure or gain. Lucas did not directly hold the intent of starting a new life, or paving west on some high-minded adventure. He was fleeing the East with grief strapped on his back. His one true love, Charlotte Brogan, had died in his arms.

"I've barely had time to rest," Lucas said.

"It didn't end once they locked Barlow in that cell. That was just the beginning. He wants his freedom as much as you want freedom for Zeke. He still wants what he was after in the first place: revenge."

"And he's got a plan for that just like I do," Lucas said, the truth of what Straut was saying, dawning on him like a bright ray of sun, had just pierced the dim dining room.

"If I was a bettin' man, and I can be at times, then I'd have to answer that question with a *hell yes*, Barlow's got a plan. A plan that was hatched the moment those chains were attached to his ankles."

Lucas nodded. "If those Indians weren't really Indians, then they were probably a crew working for Barlow in one way or another. They wanted one thing."

"Yup," Straut said. "They wanted to kill Zeke."

"And they failed."

"Yup. And then they missed him at the Tullet farm—which if you ask me, it wasn't much of a farm. I can't find nobody around that's ever heard of a farmer named Tullet, by the way."

"How about Kingsley Nash?"

"Nope."

"Son of a bitch."

"Yup."

Lucas threw his napkin on the table. "I knew there was something about those folks that felt wrong."

"Can't prove that yet," Straut said. "But Barlow's always had his fingers, so to speak, in a lot of pots all over this country. He'd know someone up this way. You can count on that."

"You think he's onto my plan?"

Straut stuck a toothpick in the corner of his mouth, and pushed his belly from the table. "Hard to say. I think it's a long-shot plan to begin with, but I agreed to come on it with you, so I'll see it out. Especially if it puts an end to Barlow and his ilk once and for all."

"A lot rides on Little Ling and Sheriff Keane," Lucas said.

"And Celia herself," Straut said.

Lucas nodded. "She's the key. If Zeke's ever going to be free, she's going to have to tell a judge what really happened to her."

"And that seems impossible."

"As far as we know," Lucas said. "But that might not be the hardest part of this whole thing."

"Really? What do you think that will be?"

"Two things," Lucas answered, pushing away from the table, matching Straut's movement to be finished with the meal. "Getting Celia to betray her father in public, and keeping her alive until that happens."

TWENTY-ONE

LANCASTER BARLOW HAD FIRM ORDERS from Sheriff Keane not to leave Nashville. He hadn't been charged in the driver's murder, a thought that the senator found absurd. He no more had the chance, or desire, to kill the schemer than the man in the moon. As it stood, he was a prisoner in his hotel room, the door locked from the inside. He was free to leave anytime he wanted, but had been advised against it.

The room was cool, and the air held a bit of moisture in it. A musty smell permeated throughout, and it annoyed Barlow. He had a great need, at the moment, for comfort, for familiar surroundings, for something, anything, to prop him up to his regular position of confidence and direction. But he was far from home, Washington, not the little house he kept in Tennessee, only as a matter of formality. Instinct demanded that he call out for Paulsen, his loyal secretary, but that request would go unheard. At best, he could order some food to the room, but that thought didn't hearten him much. He had lost his appetite.

So he paced, and began to piece together the day.

When Senator Barlow had arrived in town, there had been no communication from the people who had taken Celia. He had been contacted by the sanatorium that she was missing. That was it. There was no certainty that it was truly a kidnapping.

Upon arriving in town, he went to the prison to see his son, John, to see what he knew, which it turned out, was nothing. If John was to be believed. That was always questionable.

The senator continued to pace, stroking his chin as he regulated his breathing. He had been in more difficult spots than this before in his long life, and each time he had thought, and then talked his way out of them. Or changed them so the conclusion was satisfactory to him.

After leaving the prison, the driver had handed Barlow the note, proclaiming a man in a hood and cloak had given it to him. The note demanded that the senator leave Nashville before midnight—if he ever wanted to see Celia alive again.

Barlow stopped and looked at the clock. It was half-past ten. The night was young, but dark as a black sheet outside the window. He still had time to comply with the demand.

Except for what had happened next. The carriage had been set loose on its own, leaving the driver dead in the street, stabbed according to Sheriff Keane. It occurred to Barlow that somehow the sheriff had just happened to be in the vicinity—and he found it odd, considering the time of evening. The senator hadn't questioned the coincidence of the lawman's arrival at the time. He had been too shaken. Certain that he was going to die in a tangled wreck of horses' legs and carriage wheels—or worse, drowned in the river alone, never to be seen again, washed away like a useless piece of wood.

Barlow began to pace again. Two things had happened after the sheriff "rescued" him. One, he was informed that there had been a murder—which Barlow had not seen evidence of. The driver's body lay like a load of coal in the distance, covered by the darkness of night. There had been no personal inspection by the senator to see if what he had been told was true. He could see now that that had been a mistake. He had taken Keane's word that the driver was dead, but now, there was no proof of it at all.

"Stupid, stupid man," Barlow said aloud, chastising himself. "You know better."

From there, he considered the warning from the sheriff. "Don't leave Nashville." Which meant the senator was a suspect in the driver's murder.

"Absurd. Just absurd," Barlow bellowed as he wore a path from the door to the window, and then back again.

He was left with a conundrum. Stay in Nashville, and risk Celia's life, if the note were to be believed. Or leave Nashville and become a wanted man for a murder he didn't commit. He was between a rock and a hard place. Stuck with an undesirable outcome no matter which way he turned. It was all very confounding, but there was really no question what Senator Barlow had to do, once he thought it through.

He stopped pacing then, certain of his next move, but not, perhaps, his final destination.

Barlow grabbed up his coat and hat, then hurried over to the window, and peered behind the long, thick velvet drape, to see if there was anyone watching his room.

He saw no one, but that didn't mean the sheriff hadn't put a man on him for the purpose of surveillance. That's exactly what Barlow would have done if the opposite were his charge: posted a man to watch his every move.

At that moment, he had to consider a back way out of the Maxwell House. Surely, there was a way through the kitchen, but that was obvious, too. It would be watched, if the sheriff had put someone on him.

There was no time to back out, to reconsider his options. He had to leave Nashville. It was as simple as that. He had to find Celia.

He looked at the clock, and figured he had enough time to make it to the sanatorium before the clock struck twelve. At the very least, he wanted to make sure, for himself, that Celia was really gone.

Barlow peeked out the window again, and hoped for a fire escape. Unfortunately, there hadn't been a set of stairs attached to the building like there had been in Washington. He thought then, and decided to go up to the roof and see if he could plot his departure from there. The idea of such a covert thing did not intrigue him or excite him. Just the opposite. It made him angry. He was too old and too established to be caught up in such things. But he had no choice. If he stayed in the hotel, then he was accepting his fate as Keane's prisoner, a suspect in an unproven murder.

One thing was for certain. Lancaster Barlow hadn't achieved all of the things he had in his life by sitting and waiting for the right and proper outcome to find its way to him. No, he went after the things he wanted, the things he needed. And no matter his age or position, he was in a situation that required action, not acceptance.

Barlow hurried to the door then, certain of his path, of his plan, of what he was doing and why. But he stopped dead in his tracks just as he reached for the doorknob to exit the hotel room.

Someone was on the other side of the door. They knocked loudly, with confidence and unquestioned power. The echo of the knock was deafening. It thundered through the room, bounced off the high ceiling, and deposited fear directly in the senator's heart. Startled, Lancaster Barlow nearly jumped out of his skin.

He froze, waited, knew there was nowhere to go, to escape.

There was no way the sheriff could have known of his plan. The two men didn't know each other, so there was no offer of familiarity or clue to what the senator might or might not do.

The knock came again, followed by a muffled voice. "Open the door. We know you're in there." It was familiar, distant. But the demand only added to the senator's fear.

Perhaps he needed to reconsider the sheriff's find, that the carriage driver had truly been killed, that there was a plan afoot to kill him, too. Assassination plots were not uncommon against senators, especially in the days after

Lincoln's death. Barlow had to take the idea seriously that whoever it was on the other side of the door was there to do him harm. He couldn't help but regret ever coming to Nashville at that moment.

"We're not leaving," the voice on the other side of the door said.

The senator let his coat and hat fall to the floor. *Face it*, he told himself. *Being afraid is not your way.* He took a deep breath, squared his shoulders as confidently as he could, and pulled the door open.

The two people he saw standing before him shocked and startled him even more than the knock had.

"Hello, Father," John Barlow said with a wide smile. "You remember my assistant, Fetch, don't you?"

TWENTY-TWO

NIGHT HAD FALLEN OVER LEAVENWORTH.
Lucas stood outside the hotel, staring up at the sky, trying
to divine Zeke's location. Truth be told, he didn't even know
if the Negro was still alive, and there was no way that he
couldn't feel the weight of the possibility. If Zeke Henry
was dead, too, just like Hobie Lawton, then the trip West,
and all of the planning in the world, had been for naught.
Zeke would never be free, and neither would Celia Barlow.

Joe Straut walked up beside Lucas, stopped, and lit a
perfectly hand-rolled cigarette. "Tobacco, Lucas?"

Lucas shook his head. "Not a vice I ever picked up."

"Whiskey, then?"

"On occasion. I like to avoid things that turn a spark into
a fire."

Straut nodded, and took a thoughtful draw off the cigarette. It burned slow and even. There were years of experience in the fingers that had rolled the cigarette. "Makes
sense, I suppose, to avoid the things that set you off," he
said. "But a man needs a vice, or he might as well live in
the madness of certain death."

"I couldn't agree more," Lucas answered. "I've only had the pleasure of killing roaches for the past several years."

"My apologies," Straut said.

"No offense taken. Just facts," Lucas answered, his voice dry and truthful. A tinkling piano caught his ear. The dinner conversation had been enough to consider, and a distraction from the depths of their situation would be a welcome relief. Even that of a saloon. Perhaps, he thought, it was time to rejoin the living and rekindle his desires—and revisit one of his old vices.

Lucas pushed off the boardwalk without saying a word to Straut. The man needed no invitation to join him. He could come along if he wanted to. They were partners, so to speak, but they weren't joined at the hip.

Straut did follow along after a second of consideration, matching Lucas's step.

They walked silently down the middle of the street, shoulder to shoulder, their destination agreed on. As silently as possible, considering they were both armed, wearing their holsters openly, and fully complemented with belts full of cartridges. Only Straut wore spurs. He was the kind of man who always looked like he was on the move even when he was sitting still.

Regardless of the ordinance banning guns from inside a bank in Leavenworth, Lucas was unaware, and did not care, what other laws were imposed on the locals. He wasn't going to spend his time reading every article and restraint that governed the behaviors of its citizens. He wasn't going to be in Leavenworth that long.

As it was, there were other men out and about wearing their gear and weapons openly, and no one had accosted Lucas since the bank teller had. That woman had obviously gotten up on the wrong side of the bed about fifty years before, and decided to stay there.

There was enough light from the moon, stars, and occasional lantern, to navigate around any horseshit in the street. Surprisingly, though, the road was clean. A sign of a well-oiled local government that was concerned with the sights and smells of its growing town—which was not a surprise.

Lucas was amazed at the speed of progress that surrounded him, first brought on by the construction of the railroad, then by the desire of men, women, and children from all over the country to change their lives, to start over, begin anew, all at a great risk. Most of them would never see the East again. Their origins wiped clean like they never existed in the first place. Lucas hoped it would be the same for him.

The piano music was coming from a brightly lit saloon half a block ahead of the pair. Lucas dodged a leftover pile that the street cleaner had missed, or had been deposited after dark, which was possible, but there had been no horse traffic to be seen.

"A beer might be the perfect answer to that meal," Straut said.

Lucas slowed his gait. "We need to lay low. Tullet and Nash, or whatever their names are, are most likely looking for us."

"Looking for you and Zeke, you mean?"

"Maybe. But like you said before, if we know where Barlow is, then he knows where we are. You betrayed him. You think he's going to forget that?" Lucas asked.

Straut didn't flinch. "I've thought about that. I knew what I'd done to my future when I joined up with you back in Tennessee." He hesitated, then stopped, grabbed Lucas by the shoulder gently so he stood still, and looked him in the eye. "You still don't trust me, do you?"

"As much as I do any man, I'd guess."

"If you'd said anything else, I'd've called you a liar. Barlow's a wicked man, but I don't have to tell you that. I saw a lot of things in the war, and beforehand, if I was to tell the truth of things. That ain't no excuse for turnin' a blind eye to what Barlow was doin' as we went along after the war was over. Sometimes, I don't think it was really me standin' inside my skin. You know what I mean? It was like I was still in Chickamauga, or Shiloh, barkin' orders some other man had given me. One day, word comes along that it's time to set down the arms, but the way of blood and killin' had been goin' on for so long, a man like me begins to think it's normal. There's always a war to fight, even if the government says there ain't."

Lucas stiffened, tried to digest what Straut was saying while staying aware of everything that was going on around them. A few men filtered in and out of the saloon, and seemed not to pay them any mind, even though they were standing in the middle of the street.

"Seems to me the Indians would disagree," Lucas said. "The war's with them now. You're right, there's always a war being fought, Straut. Some men know how to profit from conflict, so they help create it. John Barlow is one of those men. It doesn't matter to him what the cost is. Hell, he had his own hands cut off to send me to prison. That's not sane, that's diabolical, but it's not a surprise. He needed more money to achieve his goals, and I had it."

Straut sighed. "There ain't no excuse for things I've done. Not after the war ended. That's one of the reasons I agreed to help you. I thought maybe I could set some things straight. Change my path. I encouraged Finney Deets to do that, but he wouldn't quit followin' me. Got him killed is what that did. I was next if somethin' didn't get my attention."

"We want the same thing."

"I think so."

Straut let his hand fall off Lucas's shoulder. "I hope you'll come to trust me completely someday, Fume. I really do."

"If it was you who'd gone missing, me and Zeke would've come looking for you, just like we're looking for him. I don't know that that's trust, but it's something. Just keep in mind that Barlow wants your hide as much as he wants mine and Zeke's."

"I've always been a marked man in one way or another."

"Me, too," Lucas said. "Me, too."

The inside of the saloon was no different than any Lucas had seen before. High ceilings covered with hand-tapped tin tiles, dotted with whirling fans to help distribute the smoke and stench of men fresh off the trail. The hand-carved bar stretched along the back wall with a mirror attached to it, making the huge room look cavernous. There were two barkeeps, both with their hair slicked back, enough pomade to grease a pig, dashing about, pouring whiskey like there was an unlimited supply.

Every chair in the place was occupied, and every spot at the faro tables was taken. If Lucas had wanted to say anything to Straut, at this point, it would have taken a deep yell. So he chose not to say anything. He just navigated toward the bar, pushing and easing by every man as delicately as possible, not wanting to offend anyone. He wasn't there for a fight.

From what Lucas could see, there seemed to be one woman for every twenty or so men. Not odds that he found favorable. The women, too, were what he'd expected upon walking inside the saloon. Working girls of all shapes and sizes, dressed in fancy, bright-colored velvet garbs that slipped off easier than they went back on. This was not a place for discriminating tastes, even though there were undoubtedly such places in Leavenworth. But seeking out high-priced girls was not in Lucas's plans. No reason to draw any more attention to himself than necessary. A regular-priced girl would suit him just as much as a high-priced one would.

But first, before he sought out such a distraction, one he was certain to have to compete for, Lucas wanted to make sure the room was vacant of any of the men who had put him in a hole, and left him there to rot.

Straut pushed by Lucas, motioning that he was heading toward the bar. Lucas nodded knowingly, glanced up to the mirror, and began to scan the room.

He didn't expect to see any sign of Zeke. That's not what they had come to the saloon for, either. There wasn't a black man to be seen, and there most likely wouldn't be. A man like Zeke would stand out anywhere he went, especially in a packed Saturday night saloon in Leavenworth, Kansas.

Lucas also didn't expect to see anyone he recognized, but he did. He did a double take in the mirror, focused closer on the face, to make sure. Recognition came quickly. There was no mistaking the girl, her perfectly sculpted face, and hard-cut eyes. Only this time she wasn't wearing a simple blue gingham dress.

No, Victoria Tullet was stuffed in a tight floor-length dress made of shimmering red velvet. The dress was cut low at the chest, exposing an ample bosom set up high to attract as much attention, and as many patrons, as possible.

She was surrounded by hungry men, the center of attention, the object of a silent auction, smiling at the one she thought was going to be the highest bidder—a well-dressed dude who looked to be enjoying the girl's fawning eyes.

Lucas smiled, looked away from Victoria Tullet, and found what he was looking for in his periphery: the madam of the house.

He slowly made his way to the older woman, dressed to the nines, with a hard-set chin and calculating eyes that suggested she didn't suffer fools gladly. She was just the kind of woman Lucas liked to do business with.

TWENTY-THREE

LUCAS STOOD OPPOSITE THE DOOR, HIS BACK solidly against the wall, the Colt in his hand, with his finger wrapped around the trigger. He had taken his jacket off, and laid it on the bed—a simple brass setup that had probably never contributed to a good amount of sleep for anyone.

The room was functional for short visits, ready for a business transaction, even though it smelled soiled and closed up. There were no wardrobes or chest of drawers for storage. Just the bed, a chair, and a dry sink, with a pitcher and bowl on top of it, butted up against the opposite wall. The pitcher was chipped at the lip, and sweated from the cold water that had recently been put in it. There was hardly room to squeeze between the bed and the dry sink.

A single narrow window looked out over the main street. It was locked, and the moth-riddled drapes pulled as tight as possible. Only a small lamp offered any light in the room, and it was dim, the wick set low, situated so it didn't give away Lucas's position with a shadow.

It didn't take long for a soft knock to come at the door. The madam, Fiona Dane, if the name was to be believed, was more than happy to accept the gold Double Eagle that Lucas had offered as a bid for Victoria's time. The coin was far more than she'd expected to get for the girl for the whole night, so it was a boon, a surprise, and perhaps a little too much to offer, but Lucas wanted to make sure he won the girl's time.

Fiona had smiled once the deal had been struck, exposing an ugly set of teeth that betrayed her age; she suddenly looked haggard and wrinkled, used up like an old barkeep's rag, tossed in the corner. "Take an extra fifteen minutes," she'd said, adjusting her hair, licking her lips, like she was about to offer herself as an added bonus. Lucas had walked away as fast as he could, and found the room.

The knock came again. Lucas eased the door open so he wasn't visible. He stepped back against the wall, the gun hidden from view, tucked behind him at the small of his back.

"Hello," Victoria Tullet said, standing at the threshold, not venturing inside the seemingly empty room.

Light cut inside the den like a knife slicing away at a dark side of beef. The jumble of sound from the saloon below quickly followed, even though it was never far away to begin with. The floor of the room vibrated with laughter, music, and demands for more beer.

Victoria's shadow loomed large into the room, frozen like a statue, a silhouette pasted to the floor as an artful rendition. For a second, Lucas thought he had been betrayed, that Fiona Dane had pulled a switch and followed up with her unspoken suggestion of desire. But when he looked again, the shadow was too thin to be Fiona, and the hair too tall.

Sweat beaded on Lucas's lip. He was certain the girl, if it was Victoria Tullet, was carrying her derringer. "Come on in." He disguised his voice, dropped it low.

The shadow waited a second, like she sensed something, then shrugged and walked inside.

It was Victoria. A relief.

She stopped just beyond the door, allowing enough room for Lucas to close it. Which he did, as gently as possible. It was tempting to slam it for effect, but he didn't want any visitors to the room any time soon.

Victoria turned to face him, offering a crafted smile until she was struck with the same recognition that Lucas had experienced in the saloon below.

He exposed the Colt to her, then dropped it to his side. There was no need to point it at her—just yet. "You make one peep, sister, stamp one toe on the floor, draw any undue attention to this room, and I will not hesitate to shoot you. Do you understand?"

Victoria Tullet, in all of her finery, looked madder than a hen left out in the rain. Her jaw drew in so sharp it could have cut steel, and her eyes raged with anger. But she said nothing. Her lips were pulled together as tight as possible.

They were standing inches apart. Close enough for Lucas to smell the sweet toilet water the girl had recently doused herself in. She had engaged in a complete metamorphosis from the first time he had seen her, from simple farm girl to a by-the-half-hour call girl. Only her face looked similar, and Lucas was more than surprised, seeing her up close, that he had recognized her at all.

"Okay. Have it your way. Nod your head so I'm sure that you understand me," he said.

The girl's glare and statue stance continued.

Tension started to grow in the tips of Lucas's fingers. He hadn't expected her to cooperate. Just the opposite. She had showed a stony attitude at the farm, a penchant for being obstinate, so he wasn't surprised by her reaction. "Really? Am I going to have to point the gun at you like you were fond of doing to me?"

"I should have shot you."

"Why didn't you?"

"You were worth more alive than dead."

"Ah, now we're getting somewhere. Why don't you move across the room, away from the door."

Victoria Tullet stood fast, never breaking eye contact with Lucas. Hate had replaced the rage that first exploded in her eyes. It looked comfortable there, like it was a regular member of her emotional family.

Lucas sighed. "You're going to make this difficult, aren't you?"

"I'm not going to make it anything."

Lucas allowed the tension he was feeling to manifest into a sly smile. "Madam Fiona will be greatly disappointed when I ask for my Double Eagle back. How will she like it when I tell her you refused me service?"

"So that's how you did it?"

Lucas shrugged. "I'll get what I want, or need, in one way or another. I don't take to being put in a hole lightly."

"You didn't bring me up for what most men want. I haven't refused you anything."

"You seem sure that I'm not here for pleasure."

"I am."

"Well," Lucas said, raising the Colt so it was aimed directly at Victoria Tullet's chest, "you might be wrong about that." He flipped the end of the barrel. "Go on, go to the other side of the room and take off your clothes."

TWENTY-FOUR

CELIA WAS AFRAID. LITTLE LING HAD DISAP-
peared, and there had been no one inside her tent for what
seemed like ages, though it could have only been minutes.
Ever since the Celestial girl had suggested that there was
trouble coming, that they had to move, Celia had been
racked with fear. Nothing that Little Ling could say could
calm her down.

Now she was left with only noises and her imagination
to surmise what was happening beyond the walls of her tent,
out of her view and abilities to react. It was a difficult situation to navigate.

She felt safe when Little Ling was near, cared for, even
though the girl did not stay with her every hour of every day.
But Little Ling had been present enough to tell Celia a little
bit of what was happening in the outside world.

She was in a place called Libertyville. It wasn't a real
place at all, but a moving community of ex-slaves and those
who sought true freedom, denying themselves the time,
ability, or desire to set down roots. They all lived in tents

and wagons, and found safe places to live their lives without drawing any undue attention to themselves. They could move any time their way of life was threatened.

It sounded like one of the Utopian communities that Celia had heard about, like New Harmony up in Indiana. She had been tempted to flee to such a place once in her life, but that hope, that chance had been lost when she had been injured, sentenced to the silent prison that she was trapped in. There would be no Utopia for her, no escape, no ability to flee danger without any help. Celia thanked her lucky stars every day for the arrival of Little Ling in her life.

Her sister, Mary Catherine, had had the same desire to flee, to find freedom and happiness away from the confines of home, out from under the gaze and control of their father. Mary Catherine had given her life over to the Lord, become a nun, and ventured to the far reaches of China—which was how Little Ling had come to her. Life had a way of making circles on its own without any interference from anyone, it seemed. The help sent to her by her dead, older sister, in the form of Little Ling was nothing short of a miracle . . . a miracle now under threat.

Wind whipped the walls of the tent, then slipped in underneath, between the ground and thin canvas, with a heavy push. The roof lurched up and down, and Celia felt like she was trapped inside a giant lung. The smell of rain hung in the air, and distant thunder rumbled far off in the distance, to the west. At first, Celia wasn't sure if the drumbeat was a troop of soldiers riding toward Libertyville, or just the promise of another spring storm.

The true sound of horses and mules was nearer, just outside the tent, along with shouts and orders, and the scuffle of hurried feet. There was worry and threat in the air, along with the uncertainty of the coming weather.

Celia was more afraid than she had been earlier, more afraid since she had found some comfort in Little Ling's presence and assurance.

A gunshot reinforced her uncertainty, the fear she felt.

She wanted to scream, to cry out, to run away, or join in with the others, and do what was needed, but, of course, she could do nothing but lie where she was, unable to speak, unable to move.

More than anything, Celia wanted Little Ling to come back. She didn't know what she'd do if something had happened to the Celestial girl. It would break her heart, kill her. She would give up. Pray to Mary Catherine's Lord for death to come and take her quickly.

As if by the magic of some silent summoning, Little Ling rushed inside the tent. "There you are, missy," Little Ling said. "Don't be afraid."

Celia blinked once. *Yes.*

Little Ling hovered over her, her moon face hard and concerned. "I know, I know."

A shadow crossed behind the girl, and Celia heard another, unfamiliar, pair of footsteps enter the tent.

"They are here to help," Little Ling said. "But I have to cover you up. I cut holes in blankets so you can breathe easy, okay? We no have to worry about you moving. Oh, sorry, that sounded mean. I no mean to be mean. Just the truth. We have to put you in the bottom of a wagon and hide you with the potatoes. Okay, missy?"

I have no choice, Celia said. *But, I will go wherever you want me to. Just don't leave me again.* She blinked once. *Yes.*

As frustrating as it was to only be able to communicate two words, yes and no, it was a relief, too, to be able to do at least that.

"It might be a rough ride," a man said. He had a soft voice, his face out of view. Celia found comfort in his words right away.

"This is Sulley, Sulley Joe Johnson. He know how you talk," Little Ling said. "Everybody here do. You not alone no more, okay, missy? You tell them what you want and they get it for you, just like me. You don't need just me, okay?" Little Ling pulled away, and Sulley Johnson came into view.

He had a soft face, and gentle brown eyes. His skin was soft, and young, not as black as she'd seen before, but bronze, like it would glint golden in the sun, if there were any.

Sulley smiled at Celia, and she felt his intentions were simple and pure, just like Little Ling's. She liked Sulley Joe Johnson right away, but deep down, secretly she had wished it was Zeke who had entered the tent to see her to safety.

"I won't let nothin' happen to you, Miss Celia. Oh, no, you don't need to worry about gettin' wet or bein' too uncomfortable. We got places to go. Far Jackson always knows where we is goin' next, you know. Libertyville don't set roots, 'specially not now, since we got you under roof."

Another gunshot cracked in the distance. There was no mistaking it with thunder.

Sulley glanced over to Little Ling with an unmistakable worried look, and the Celestial girl nodded.

"I'm gonna cover you up now, missy. It'll get dark, but we'll be right here. You no worry, okay?"

Celia sighed, and knew she had no choice. She didn't want to leave the tent. She was afraid of what was to come next. But she had to trust Little Ling and Sulley Joe Johnson. *Yes*, she blinked.

Little Ling nodded then, leaned over, and picked up a dark green blanket. "Once I cover you up, Sulley's gonna pick you up and carry you out of here, okay, missy? Then he put you in the wagon, and we go away quick. Fast, fast, so no bad men can find us again. I promise."

Make it quick. Let's go. I don't like this.

The blanket fell gently over Celia's face, and all of the light disappeared. For a minute, it got hot, and she couldn't breathe. Fear swept over her and she screamed out for Little Ling. But, of course, no one heard her.

The world started to spin, and Celia knew that she was being moved, that she was in Sulley's arms, cradled as gently as possible. She wished she could feel his strong arms, the bounce of his walk, but she couldn't. All she could do was regulate her own breathing, and give herself over to the man and the Celestial girl.

Maybe, she thought, *this is nothing but a nightmare, and I'll wake up, and walk out of my room, and then I'll run, run as fast as I can to New Harmony.*

TWENTY-FIVE

JOHN BARLOW STOOD AT THE HOTEL ROOM door expectantly, like he should be afforded the respect of an invitation to enter it.

"What are you doing here?" Lancaster Barlow said, peering around his son, and the dirty scoundrel that stood next to him, to make sure they were unseen by any of the hotel's boarders.

John Barlow pushed by his father without an offer of concern. Fetch followed on his heels. "Oh, Father, you look pale. Come, close the door, have a drink. Surely you have some fine bourbon to share?"

"You're supposed to be in prison." The senator looked down the hall again, then closed the door as softly as he could, and locked it.

"What makes you think that I am not still in prison?" John Barlow asked.

Fetch, dressed in rags just like he had been the last time the senator had seen him, stood off to John Barlow's right, in his shadow, unmoving, watching everything with an unnerving focus.

Lancaster Barlow moved across the room, led with his chin, and walked straight up to his son. "You need to explain to me what the hell you're doing here, and you need to do it now."

"Calm down, Father."

"Calm down? How am I supposed to calm down with an escaped convict in my room? I am a United States senator. Do you know how this would . . ."

John Barlow raised his gloved hand and put up a fake, nonexistent index finger to his father's mouth, and stopped him midsentence. "I know what you are, Father. Make no mistake about that. Relax," he said, taking his glove away, dropping it to his side, so that he looked nearly normal. "I have not escaped. As far as anyone of importance knows, Fetch and I are sound asleep in our bunks, just like we are every night, and will be again, when the bright light of day cracks through the murky windows of my home, sweet, home, the Tennessee State Prison. Isn't that right, Fetch?"

"Yes, oh, yes, sir. We'll be all tucked in come mornin', just like every ol' day," Fetch said.

The senator nearly gagged when the smell of the rot hit his nose. He looked away in disgust, then quickly regained himself, and eyed his son as directly as he could. "So, you just come and go as you please?"

"Something like that," John Barlow said.

Silence followed as the senator waited for an explanation. None came right away, and it was obvious from the smug look on his son's face that what was expected wasn't going to be forthcoming any time soon. "So, you can assure me that my reputation is not at risk by your presence here?" he finally asked.

"I can't assure you of anything, Father, especially when it concerns your reputation. That was put at risk the moment you stepped on the train and left the comforts of Washington."

"Are you suggesting that I shouldn't be here?" Lancaster poured two fingers of bourbon into a crystal glass and offered it to John.

He shook his head. "I've sworn off the stuff, for now. Perhaps once I regain my true freedom, I will allow myself to indulge in some of my favorite vices. Until then, I will remain dry and clear-headed. Just like you should do."

"I had no choice but to come. Celia . . ."

"Yes," John interrupted again, "you had no choice, and because of your knee-jerk, poorly thought-out reaction, you have done exactly what *he* wants you to do."

"*He*? You know who is responsible for this? Tell me, now. Tell me, goddamn it." The senator's face flushed red, and he felt his heartbeat quicken to a dangerous level.

"Calm down, Father. If you think about it, you'll figure out for yourself who has swept in and absconded with our poor dear defenseless Celia. You know who. You just don't want to admit it."

"Fume," Lancaster Barlow seethed. "Lucas Fume." He threw the glass of whiskey at the wall.

The explosion of shattering glass caused Fetch to startle and jump. He eased up behind John Barlow so he was out of direct sight of the senator. The ragman hunkered in the man's shadow, like a frightened child.

"Ah, that's the father I know and love," John Barlow said.

"How can this be? How can he just ride in and take the one thing that can't defend herself? That is unacceptable. Plainly unacceptable. What the hell is his intent?"

"To get you here," John said, almost matter-of-factly. There was a thick smile burgeoning on his lower lip.

"To get me here? That doesn't make any sense."

"Father, you have lost your wits. The time in Washington has made you soft and blind. Lucas Fume wants revenge, can't you see it?"

"Revenge? That's silly. He has everything a man can want. More money than he will ever be able to spend in his life, and you, locked away in prison for the rest of your life. At least, that's what he thinks." Lancaster looked at his son from head to toe, still unable to fully comprehend what he was truly seeing.

John Barlow scowled. "He has his freedom."

"Yes, he does. What else does he need?"

"His friend's."

The room went silent again, and this time the senator nearly buckled at the knees. "Zeke Henry. Free."

John Barlow nodded. "There's only one way for that Negro to be free, his face not on every Wanted poster west of the Mississippi, and you know it, Father. It's for you to be held accountable."

"I didn't . . ."

Barlow stepped forward so he was an inch from his father, so they looked evenly, eye to eye. "You don't have to lie to me. I don't care what you did, or didn't do. The fact is that Lucas Fume is on to you, and he has a plan, and that plan involves Celia. Can she talk, Father? Can she tell anyone what you did to her in your moment of rage?"

"No." It was a gush, a half-finished answer.

"You say that like you don't believe it."

Senator Lancaster Barlow stiffened. "I don't know. I don't think so. No," he whispered.

"You better hope not."

"What do you want, John?"

"I only want to help you."

"I don't believe that."

"Believe what you want. Come on, Fetch, let's go. Our time grows short. The guards will be making their rounds soon, checking the beds. We mustn't come up missing. That would be an awful event for us all. Imagine the punishment, the time spent in solitary, in the hole, unable to communicate with anyone. If we are discovered, Fetch, we won't be able to help anyone. Father would be left all alone with the sheriff sniffing about, trying to hang a murder on him that he didn't commit. The irony of it all is too awful to think about, isn't it?"

Fetch peered around Barlow, and smiled at the senator again. "That would be bad, sir, we wouldn't be able to delight in no midnight walks no more. I like talkin' to the boy. Don't mind bein' in his hands at all. I ain't no Bojack Wu, but he likes me."

"Don't mention that name," John Barlow snarled, glaring at Fetch.

The man cowered. "I'm sorry. Don't hit me. I won't do it again."

"Make sure you don't. No, we wouldn't be able to walk at night again, Fetch, and that would be a tragedy." Barlow squared himself then, smiled at his father, and walked toward the door.

"Stop," Lancaster bellowed. "What do you really want?"

"So, you see it my way. I'm the only one who can help you?"

"Yes. What do you want?"

John Barlow stopped at the door, stood to the side of it, and motioned for Fetch to open it. "I want my freedom. Weren't you listening? I want it now. You don't have time to waste. Fume's plan is swirling all about you, threatening to pull you under, to expose to the world what kind of temper you really have, and exactly what you did to my weak little sister. An appeal will take years, Father, and to be honest, you don't have that kind of time. Lucas Fume is a very smart, and persistent man."

"I know all about Lucas Fume and his talents. Just like I know yours." The senator picked up the decanter and took a long swig of the bourbon straight out of it. "There's only one way that I can help you."

"Yes," John Barlow said. "There is only one way. A pardon."

Lancaster Barlow nodded. "A pardon. A pardon from no one but the president himself."

John Barlow smiled then. "Make it happen, Father. Call in all of your chips. The president surely owes you a favor or two. If not, shame on you. And, if you don't, or are unable to arrange a pardon as quickly as possible, then you will be sharing a cell next to mine, or dangling, toes first, from the end of a rope. Either way, I'm sure it's not what you have in mind for your future. The clock's ticking, Father. We have to go. But have no fear. I'll be in touch." With that, he walked out the door, quickly followed by the little weasel of a man, Fetch, who closed the door behind him as loudly as he could. The thud thundered across the empty room like a drum had been banged for the final time.

The whiskey burned the back of Lancaster Barlow's throat as he crumbled into the nearest chair.

He was suddenly alone, afraid, uncertain of what to do next, paralyzed by the prospects his son had just presented him. If Lucas Fume was truly on to him, then there was only one thing left for the senator to do: He must use every resource he had available to him to return the favor. Go after Lucas Fume with all the fervor and power he could muster.

With that thought, Senator Lancaster Barlow grabbed up the decanter, and took another long drink. This one didn't burn nearly as bad as the first.

TWENTY-SIX

LUCAS AIMED THE COLT DIRECTLY AT VIC-toria Tullet's head. "I'm serious. Take off all of your clothes."

"You'll regret this," she said with a sneer.

Lucas chuckled. "I can't think of a time in my life when I've regretted seeing a whore take off her clothes."

Victoria flinched at the word, and narrowed her eyes at Lucas. Other than that, she didn't imply any movement or compliance to his command.

Lucas replied with the same silence, and let the thin smile on his face fall away into a sternness that wasn't faked.

The room they stood in was hardly quiet. The floor vibrated from the saloon below; fast piano music, laughter, and the joys and disappointments of the faro tables all shook the building with a vitality that suggested it was a living, breathing entity all its own. Besides the floor, all of the other rooms were occupied with patrons and their chosen girls, engaged in the pursuit of physical pleasure, and a good time. The smell of tobacco smoke, beefsteaks cooking in the kitchen, and an overabundance of toilet water all mixed together and formed a unique and recognizable smell to any man that spent time in a saloon, or the upper floors of one.

Lucas found no pleasure holding a gun on a woman, but he knew she was armed. That had been his experience with her previously, and he had no indication to suspect otherwise.

"What's your real name?" Lucas asked.

"Victoria Tullet. You know that."

"Nobody around here has ever heard of any Tullets. Why do you suppose that is?"

"Maybe you ain't talked to the right people."

In that moment, Victoria Tullet's face changed from highfalutin call girl, to a young, scared country girl. Lucas almost felt sorry for her, but the change of expression didn't compel him to lower the Colt. He flipped the tip of the barrel again. "Go on, then, whatever your name is, take off your clothes. You can start by handing over the gun you've got hidden inside that dress."

"Why, mister, what makes you think I have a weapon hidden about my pearls?" She flicked her eyelashes, taking pleasure in mocking him.

"Because I have had the pleasure of having it pulled on me more than once, and it's not going to happen again."

"And now you want the pleasure of seeing my body."

"For starters."

A roar of laughter erupted underneath them, a different kind of thunder, one that didn't promise a storm, but gave them notice that life was going on unguarded in the saloon, and no one was concerned about their pairing.

"You're serious, aren't you?" she asked.

"I am," Lucas said. "The gun first, and then we'll go from there. No funny stuff. Ease your hand under your dress, pull the gun out, and toss it to the center of the bed. If you make one false move, I will kill you."

"You've done that before? Killed a woman?"

"I've done what I had to. Now, go on, don't make me prove it. Just do as you're told," Lucas said.

Victoria lowered her head, sighed with defeat, and

slipped her hand inside a secret slit in the velvet dress. She pulled out the familiar derringer, and did as she was told—tossed it gently on the bed. She obviously believed that Lucas was serious that he would kill her if he had to. And she was right. He would have pulled the trigger of the new Colt in an instant if he thought he had cause.

"Now, is there anything else? Another gun? A knife sheathed to your thigh?" Lucas asked.

"You must have an interesting history with women, Mr. Fume. You don't seem to trust easily."

"We're not here to talk about history. We're not here to talk at all."

"That's sad. That's all most men want really. Most of them are quick with their business, and then they use the rest of their time whimpering about their lives and lost loves like beaten pups."

"I'm not most men."

"I never said you were." She slowly moved her hand up to her neck and started to unbutton the dress. Every move had intention with an added sway of the hips meant to arouse. There was no mistaking the move Victoria was making, slipping into business mode, but Lucas was not interested in what she had to offer physically, at least at the moment.

"What's your real name?" he asked again. The gun was still trained on her, as was all of his focus.

"You're not going to give that up, are you?"

"No."

She slipped the dress to her waist and let it rest, exposing an expensive whale-bone corset and a pert figure that didn't require much tightening. She was amply endowed with solid breasts, unscathed by child-bearing, or the destruction of age.

"Do you like what you see?" Victoria glanced to the buttons on his trousers, and seemed disappointed not to see any sign of excitement. "Too bad. Maybe I don't have what you like."

"That has nothing to do with it," Lucas said. He was willing himself not to be tempted by the sight of her flesh. It was difficult. He enjoyed spending time with a woman as much as he enjoyed a fine meal. The last time he had lain with a woman was in Libertyville, and just the thought of Avadine, of the girl who had nursed him back to health, and the sight of Victoria Tullet in the midst of disrobing was nearly enough to cause him to lose control of himself. "This is business. Your people left me in a hole to die."

"Hardly, I told you, you're worth more alive than dead. They was coming back for you."

"Roy and Kingsley Nash? If that's their names, which I'm convinced they're not since no one has heard of them, either."

Victoria shrugged and let the dress fall the rest of the way to the floor. Her legs were as shapely as the rest of her. More so. She was perfect in every way, a prime choice, an obvious moneymaker for the house madam, Fiona Dane, except Victoria could be bought, and couldn't be trusted. "Should I continue?"

There was no evidence of any other weapons. The empty derringer holster was the only evidence of her attempt at self-protection.

"I expect to get my money's worth," Lucas said.

Victoria smiled, said nothing, reached around behind her and unclasped the corset. She let it tumble to the floor without any attempt to catch the contraption.

Lucas did his best not to react to the suddenness of the girl's nakedness. He had expected it, demanded it, and did his best not to be excited by it—but some things were out of his control. He felt a stir below his waist, and wasn't sure that he had the strength, or desire, to fight it off.

Victoria Tullet smiled knowingly, and stepped forward, away from the pile of clothes, toward Lucas.

Lucas stiffened his arm, reaffirming his aim with the Colt. "Stop right there."

"Oh, Mr. Fume, you are no fun at all. Wouldn't you like to get your money's worth?" Victoria did as she was told and stopped, employing a pout across her lips that continued her mocking and overacting.

It was like all of the air had been sucked out of the room. Even the noise below sounded dim and distant. Lucas could feel his heart beating inside his chest, blood coursing through his veins, and the demand of desire building up to a point that would eventually need to be released, or at the very least, expressed. He wanted to touch Victoria Tullet, pull her to him, take her and sate his growing hunger. But that would be a mistake. A fatal mistake.

"I would, and I will get my money's worth." Lucas walked to her then, met her in the middle of the room, leading with the barrel of his gun. It was difficult to ignore Victoria. She was a beautiful, willing, attractive woman. The likes of which he had not seen, or experienced, in a long, long time.

The smell of her hit his nose, and the toilet water, obviously meant to smell like a spring flower, didn't disappoint. She would make a fine meal.

"Who are you?" Lucas demanded.

"I'm just a girl, tryin' to make a living and have a good time. Who are you?"

"I'm just a boy trying to figure out what the hell is going on, who you are, and who hired you to come after me and Zeke," Lucas said. He raised the Colt and pressed the barrel against Victoria's temple. "Who hired you? Who do you really work for?"

A look of fear passed across Victoria's eyes, but disappeared as fast as it came, and was quickly replaced by hate. Her pupils vanished into a deep black pool that promised to be endless. Without any warning at all, she grabbed his crotch. Not in a provocative way, but she squeezed hard, with the intention of inflicting pain, of controlling Lucas, of bringing him to the floor.

It was a brave and risky move. All it would have taken was a squeeze of the trigger, intentionally or not, and her grasp, along with everything else would have come to a quick end. Instead, Lucas pulled the gun back, grimaced, and jumped backward, pulling himself out of her grip as quickly as he could.

She had not expected him to pull backward. It was an unusual reaction, and the assured confidence in her face vanished.

"Don't move," he demanded.

The well in Victoria Tullet's eyes lost their hate and bubbled with amusement. "I just wanted to see how much of a man you really were, Lucas Fume. Can't blame a girl for that, can you?"

It was a quick recovery. Lucas admired her confidence and intelligence, but there was something in her voice that he recognized. Each word was slow, enunciated, prolonged, just like her moves. She wasn't trying to entice him. She was killing time. Somehow, she had sent a distress signal, and was waiting to be rescued.

Unfortunately, the recognition of Victoria's ploy came a minute or two too late.

The door to the room burst open, and Roy Tullet, or the man who had claimed to be Roy Tullet, rushed into the room with a rifle aimed directly at Lucas's head.

Lucas didn't panic. At his recognition seconds before, he had taken a deep breath, realized where he was standing, and knew what was about to happen seconds before it did. He had been in that circumstance before, in the war, as a spy, but he was rusty now, and not immune to the allure of a beautiful woman like he had been when he was fully engaged in a hired plot.

So he stepped back, making himself the tip of a triangle, and kept his gun trained on Victoria.

They both had expected Lucas to react, to spin and point his gun at Roy, giving Victoria the chance to get out of harm's way, so Roy could pull the rifle's trigger and finish off Lucas. One false move and he would have been dead as a doornail—but now was not the time to reflect on that.

"You make one more move, Roy, or whoever you are, and I will kill this girl as sure as there are stars in the sky," Lucas said.

Roy Tullet, slim, and still dressed like the farmer he had

posed to be, flop hat and all, stopped like he'd been smacked in the face with a skillet. "You won't do it." The rifle barrel didn't waver. It was still aimed at Lucas's head.

Lucas said nothing, didn't react at all. He pulled the trigger without offering even a blink of regret.

TWENTY-SEVEN

THE SHOT EXPLODED IN THE SMALL ROOM, temporarily deafening Lucas and, most likely, the surprised and stunned Roy Tullet, too. Gun smoke hung in the air like a storm cloud that had instantly appeared out of nowhere.

There was no time to check for damage. There would be none. Lucas knew where he had aimed—just a hair to the left of Victoria's head. At the most, she would suffer a powder burn and a bad headache; maybe a scratch from the shave of the bullet tip as it edged along her cheek, but a blink told him there was no sign of blood on her nearly perfect porcelain face.

Victoria stood where she had been, upright, on two feet, bewildered and afraid.

Lucas knew he only had seconds to take advantage of his act—and like Victoria's intentions, his own plot had been set into motion the moment he had walked up the stairs to meet her. Entertainment for them both, if they survived, would come later.

The next part of Lucas's plan came fast. He kicked as hard as he could into Roy Tullet's groin. To hell with the gentleman's rules of fist fighting. The Celestials had the right idea: When it came to a life or death situation, use every limb you have to defeat your opponent. Nothing's off the table. The price of defeat was too high to play by any rules.

Still shocked by Lucas's pull of the trigger, and his concern for Victoria, Roy was an easy target. The heel of Lucas's boot connected directly with the man's balls, causing him to inhale deeply, groan loudly, and fly back into the wall butt first as he doubled over in pain. Roy's rifle, a Winchester '73 that looked fresh out of the crate, fell to the ground, and spun out of reach.

Confident that his kick would disarm Roy Tullet, Lucas never lost sight of Victoria, or the realization that the discharge of his weapon would sound an alarm and send a platoon of men, employed by Fiona Dane, as well as others who worked for the same man as Roy Tullet, running toward the room.

It only took Victoria Tullet, naked as a newborn, a few seconds to realize that Lucas's aim was off, that she wasn't wounded. Her eyes darted toward the direction of the rifle on the floor, then to the derringer on the bed. It was closer, but still out of reach. Her eyes calculated the movement, and tried to sum up the future, determining whether or not Lucas would really shoot to kill.

The rising tide of the guffaws and laughter in the saloon below them dimmed, distracted and alerted by the gunshot. The moment of silence was unsettling.

Time was ticking.

If one thing was out of place, then the next move Lucas had planned on taking was going to hurt like hell.

But he had no choice.

He took a deep breath as he brought his boot solidly back to the floor from the kick, then bolted forward with all of his might.

He pushed past Victoria, nearly brushing her hip, aware enough of her naked skin that he didn't want to touch her at all. Seconds before, he could have allowed his drive and desire to overcome his logic and ravage her, or at least try to, right then and there.

By the time a look of recognition crossed Victoria's face, Lucas was well past her, halfway across the room, breaking into a full run with only one place to go.

He didn't hesitate. There was no time for that, or to reconsider his mission, which had failed miserably. He still didn't know who had hired the Tullets, who they were, or what the score truly was. Too late to turn back now. He tucked his head, and leapt into the air feetfirst, leading with his boot.

The thin panes of the window shattered and exploded outward as he flew through the air into the darkness of night. He immediately searched the ground for his target. He hoped like hell that Joe Straut was where he was supposed to be, sitting underneath the window in a wagon loaded with straw, recently purchased from the local livery, like the slew of information that had led them to the saloon.

The fall, or jump, would have gone better if Lucas'd had wings, but he was no bird, and had never held any desire to fly, to be Icarus. That story hadn't turned out too well. But as it was, Joe Straut was exactly where he was supposed to be.

As much as a relief as that was, there was something odd that caught Lucas's attention, even in the tumble and quickness of his flight.

He fell two stories into a soft bed, that allowed for an uneventful crash, but Lucas could see the shadow of a man just off to the right of the wagon, just on the edge of his periphery, running toward them.

Lucas gripped his gun tightly, certain to hold onto it. He wasn't sure whether Straut was aware of the threat or not.

He tumbled into the wagon just like he'd planned. The straw softened the blow of the fall, and Lucas had twisted in the air so that he fell prone—he knew better than to try to imitate a cat and attempt a landing on his feet. The last thing he needed was a broken leg.

The sudden stop knocked the wind out of his lungs, and he gasped loudly, just like Roy Tullet had when he took the surprise kick to the balls.

Lucas jumped up as quickly as he could, orienting himself, and the aim of the Colt, in the direction of the shadow.

By that time, Straut had turned around, with the reins of the two-horse team firmly in his hands, to check on Lucas's condition.

But that didn't matter to Lucas. He knew they had very little time to deal with the man running toward them. There'd be guns coming after them from above and from inside the saloon in a matter of seconds.

Lucas aimed his Colt toward the figure, his finger fully pressed on the trigger, ready to fire. He had five cartridges left, plenty to end this situation, if need be.

But he restrained himself, pulled back as he realized the shadow running toward the wagon was familiar. It was a big shadow.

"Hang on, we gotta get the hell out of here," Joe Straut yelled as he flipped the reins. "Giddy up! Go! Go!"

The wagon instantly lurched forward throwing Lucas off balance. He stepped backward, then forward, then back again, wavering around in the bed of straw like a child's top tumbling on its last spin. He dropped to his knees, and focused on the shadow, who was now close enough to identify. It was Zeke.

Lucas made his way to the back of the wagon, scooting on his knees, knowing two things. Zeke was a big target, and he'd need to cover him if the Negro was going to make it safely aboard the wagon.

Straut pushed the team of horses as hard as he could, looking over his shoulder at every chance. He had to know it was Zeke who was running behind the wagon trying to catch up, but Lucas didn't expect Straut to slow or stop as that would be certain death for them all.

The first gunshot cracked in the air.

"Run!" Lucas yelled out to Zeke, motioning him to go off to the side, into the shadows of an alley.

The gunshot had come from the broken window, from Roy Tullet most likely. It was too dark to tell, and it didn't matter who the shooter was, only that it was a rifle that had been shot. It had the range to hit them; they hadn't gone that far.

The bullet bit into the hard, dry street just behind Zeke,

close enough for Lucas to see a puff of dust explode at his friend's heels.

Zeke ran hard, was closing in, didn't give up his attempt at reaching the wagon.

Lucas could see the whites of Zeke's eyes, the sweat on his forehead, and the heave of his lungs, as he pumped forward with all of his might. He was five feet away, reaching out with his long arm.

Another gunshot and a quick glance up to the window told Lucas that it was more than one man now. The drapes had been ripped down when he had jumped through the glass. Bright light emitted outward from the room. There were at least three men taking up aim.

"Faster, Straut," Lucas yelled over his shoulder.

"We need more horses for that," Straut answered back as loud as he could.

Lucas refocused, and stretched out his hand to meet Zeke's. They were inches apart.

Two shots rang out at the same time, and Zeke stumbled, slowed, then quickly fell out of sight, into the darkness of the street.

"Go back, go back," Lucas yelled to Straut.

But the ex-sergeant acted like he didn't hear a word. He just kept driving straight away, as fast as he could.

TWENTY-EIGHT

IT DIDN'T TAKE SULLEY LONG TO GET CELIA settled in. She could breathe easily enough through the slits that had been cut in the blanket, but it was dark, her eyes covered. She could hear and she could smell—at least there was that.

There was no question that she was in the back of a wagon, just like Little Ling had told her she would be.

Celia could hear the horses hitched up, anxious to move, snorting, concerned about what was going on around them. The air was buzzing with energy, nervousness, frantic movement, yelling, more wagons moving out like a bad storm was coming. It was like Libertyville was on fire, and it sounded much bigger, and far more populated than Celia had imagined it was. She had hoped to see it all, look into the eyes of those she shared the town, or whatever it was, with. But that was not to be. Not now. The beasts tied to her wagon had reason to be anxious if what Celia had been told was true—that there were men coming after them because of her presence in Libertyville.

"You be fine, Miss Celia," Sulley whispered close to her ear. "I be right up on the seat not a foot away from ya. But I can't acts like you here, you understand?" He waited a second. "Of course, you does. Now you jus' relax. Sulley Joe Johnson ain't gonna let nuthin' bad happen to ya. I promised Ling, and I keeps my promises, you jus' ask anybody that know me. I'm the one to be counted on. Far Jackson say so himself. Miss Lainie, too, and she don't put up with no guff from no peoples 'round here."

Where's Little Ling? Celia panicked, started blinking rapidly, her own personal SOS. *Help, help, help, where's my Little Ling?*

"They be lookin' for Ling, too, just like they is you," Sulley whispered again, like he could read the words in her mind. "You don't need to worry about that little girl. She be hidden safe, just like you. But they find her, they know you here, so's we had to split you up. Understand?" He waited a second again, then said, "Of course you does. You a smart one. Ling say so, and that be good enough for me. Now, be comfortable in your spot, we gonna go, and we gonna go fast. Far Jackson done got us another place to hide in, but it be a hard ride, and they's badness about. I got a gun. Don't you worry none. I won't let 'em find you. I promise, ya hear?"

Okay. Breathe, Celia, breathe deep, it'll be okay. Thank you, Sulley Joe. I wish I could say that out loud. Is that too much to ask? Thank you.

She heard movement, heard Sulley pull away, and Celia had to accept that she was alone. But the sweet man wasn't far. She wasn't so tense now, though she was still afraid. Still packed in among the bags of potatoes like the lug of useless flesh that she was, but that was all right, too. She liked how the potatoes smelled. The back of the wagon had an earthy aroma, hopeful, with an offer of sustenance. Celia wasn't hungry, she hadn't been since Little Ling took over her care in Libertyville. But it was the potatoes, the consistency and comfort of them, that calmed her, made her feel safe, like she couldn't be found now that she had trust in

Sulley Joe's presence, and was stuffed in the midst of the burlap bags full of them. She could smell the burlap, too. Most times, it made her itch, but not now. If it did, she couldn't feel it.

The potatoes reminded her of home, of the past, when things were right, normal, and life was easy and peaceful.

Was it all just a dream? Celia wondered. *Was my life before just an imaginary existence? I can hardly remember what the bottom of my feet felt like, let alone running, or dancing. Oh, how I loved to dance. I think I miss that the most. Yes, that and just lying half asleep in my feather bed dozing in and out, Tippity Tom, the big old black cat of the house, at my feet.*

She closed her eyes then with the hope of drifting off, of recreating the feeling of home, of her bed, but the wagon lurched forward, startling her back into the reality she existed in.

Celia heard the crack of a whip, the distant scream of a girl, and a rolling thunder that did not cease. It sounded like a troop of a thousand horses had descended on the camp.

They had waited too long to leave. Celia was certain that it was her fault that they'd been caught. Fear returned to every fiber of her being as the wagon bounced away at a high speed.

"Run, run, run!" Sulley shouted. "Run as fast as you can!"

There was nothing Celia could do but lie there, stuffed underneath the pile of potatoes, hoping with all of her might that she wouldn't be found.

There was no way to know what would happen to her if that occurred. But she wasn't so worried about herself. She was worried about Sulley and Little Ling, and all those in Libertyville who knew about her and had tried to help her.

It would've been easier if she had died, if her father had just killed her instead of leaving her like this, unable to speak, unable to run when she needed to, and most of all, unable to help those who needed help the most. She was useless. Even a potato had more value, more to offer the world than she did.

At that moment, Celia let all of the hate that she had struggled to keep buried rise up into her throat. When it escaped, it was the first groan that had come out of her mouth since she'd been beaten into her current state.

The sound of her own voice nearly scared her half to death, then made her happy, and not so afraid.

A tear slid over her cheek, but she could not wipe it away.

TWENTY-NINE

LANCASTER BARLOW STOOD AT THE FLOOR-
to-ceiling window, gazing out at Nashville as the sun
broached the horizon.

The growing city looked foreign to him, unfamiliar.
Buildings had come and gone in a flurry of progress at the
end of Reconstruction. Change had come in waves, then
became a constant presence in most Southern cities of any
size. It had been more than ten years since the war had
ended, and the scars, at least the physical scars, had finally
started to heal—at least, outwardly.

Even in the quiet of morning, it felt like there was a great
heave underneath the foundation of the earth, pressure
building after taking a long, deep breath, pushing forth into
something unseen, something unknown, that would come
next. There was no grand war on the horizon, other than with
the savages out West, but the senator was confident that war
would be won, and the redskins put to the earth in the way
of the buffalo—near extinction. The savages would be
placed on reservations with their enemies, so they would
kill each other. Regardless, that war would be won. No, what

was boiling, what was coming into being for the United States, was a destiny beyond most imaginations—but it was visible everywhere. Even before him, in Nashville. A smart man in the halls of power could be even more powerful, more wealthy than any senator who had come before him—and Lancaster Barlow fully expected to become that man.

Barlow exhaled and reined in his thoughts, focusing again on what lay before him.

The presence of the river, and the prescient vision of the city's forefathers in plotting the location of Nashville, had almost guaranteed a continued and prosperous future.

There was a time when Barlow knew all of the nooks and crannies of the city: pockets of population, full of crime, overflowing with ne'er-do-wells and scoundrels ready to do his bidding, or tell a needed lie all for the asking and payment of a penny or two. But along with his influence and practice in this city, that network had withered and died when his aspirations had taken him to Washington. Left unattended, the crooks had all found another way to fill their pockets, as had Barlow by investing his own future in another city, a larger canvas where more seemed to be at stake, and more could be gained.

There was no question that his son had taken his place, to a degree, since most of John's efforts and aspirations had been focused on the advancement of the country's boundaries to the west of the Mississippi. While the senator had funneled all of his fortune and passion into the machinations of Washington, his son had bet everything he had managed to build on the growing appetite of the civilized population to start over and begin anew. The railroad, and the money made there, with Congressional help, of course, was proof that John had been right in his thinking. Unfortunately, the senator's son had allowed his business brilliance to be overcome with a personal grudge, with petty vendettas, wrapped around the cause of love and jealousy. The downfall of many a man, no matter how smart or driven. *Such a pity*, Barlow thought.

"Or maybe it was more than that," the senator said aloud, not breaking his gaze from the roofline of the city.

It was impossible not to consider the visit the night before, from his son, as a cavalier and dangerous act. There
was nothing unusual in that. John had always been the type
of boy to exceed one's expectation when it came to getting
into trouble, and then just as quickly, finding his way out,
even if it meant taking unconventional or devious methods
to achieve his freedom. But walking in and out of prison at
will, and presenting a face that suggested he enjoyed such
a thing, almost led Lancaster Barlow to believe that John
Barlow had managed to get himself incarcerated in the
prison on purpose, like it was a necessary part of a plan that
needed to finish playing itself out.

"But why?" the senator said aloud, again to no one.

The room was empty, but Barlow was accustomed to
talking to himself, or presenting his theories and thoughts
to Paulsen without filters or consideration. The secretary
had always been a fine sounding board, and he was beginning to regret leaving the man behind in Washington. But
there had to be someone in the capital city who he trusted
to attend to his day-to-day business, and Paulsen had proven
adept at that over the years. If there was any man Barlow
trusted in this world, it was Paulsen. Even more than his son.

Soft pink light began to rise up along the horizon, just
over the river. Among all of the new buildings that had
sprouted up recently, a furniture factory had been built there,
capitalizing on the vast hardwood forests that edged the city.
The owners—men Barlow did not know yet, but would make
a point to gain an introduction—were in the process of
scouring all of Europe for the finest talents, woodworkers
who had practiced their craft for generations. The search
had been started in Switzerland, a distant place of unimaginable beauty, and one Barlow knew he would never visit. But
he admired the sense of commerce, the effort to make the
city, and ultimately, the country, a center of wealth, even if
it was in skills and not brains. *Perhaps*, he thought, *I've
missed more than I considered by leaving.* But gain, at least
financial gain, was not what he was after at the moment.
There would be a certain breed of man to be found in that

factory. Or maybe the smaller ones that surrounded it. Men desperate to feed their growing families. German men, skilled men, who needed money. Perhaps it would be a place to look, if all else failed . . .

Regret was most often an unvisited island for Lancaster Barlow, but his current situation was cause for a different kind of reflection. This visit to Nashville had seemed doomed from the start when word came of Celia's disappearance. And now, the shroud of murder hung over him. The murder of an unknown and unnamed carriage driver: It was preposterous to him.

"If I were going to kill someone," the senator said aloud, "it would be for the advancement of a cause, not for the pleasure of it." He pulled away from the window then, no longer interested in considering the hope that a new day brought to him, or to what once was the city he considered to be his home—a safe haven for his dreams.

Lancaster Barlow squared his shoulders, strode to the wardrobe, and pulled out his best suit. He was going to get ahead of this madness, set things straight with the sheriff, and get on with his primary mission—which was to locate Celia and return her safe and sound to the sanatorium. It was that simple.

If Lucas Fume was trying to set him up for a fall, then he was in for a grand disappointment.

Just the thought of Lucas Fume made the senator seethe with anger, anger that could have very easily boiled over into a full rage.

Wealth had come easy to the thickheaded Scot by way of his father. The boy had once claimed to be a friend of John's, but that was highly questionable. Fume knew nothing of scrapping for every dollar, for every ounce of respect. He'd been born with a silver spoon in his mouth to a family already teeming with more land holdings than they could make use of. Just to think of the trouble Lucas Fume had brought on his family was unthinkable.

"If you harm my Celia, I swear to you, Lucas Fume, wherever you are, you will suffer in ways you cannot imagine . . ." Barlow swore through gritted teeth.

He tore out a suit, shirt, and fresh collar from the tall wardrobe, and dressed as quickly as possible. Every second counted now that the sun was up, and he knew that there was a plot against him. Best to get ahead of it, cut the head off the snake as quick as possible.

If there was one thing to be thankful for, it was that his son had the means and wherewithal to alert him of Fume's presence and intention.

Lancaster Barlow smiled then, planning his next move. First thing he had to do was go into the village of shanties by the riverside and see if he could find an old friend or two, ones that remembered him and how well he had rewarded them for doing his bidding. If none were to be found, he would make his way to the factory employment lines. Then, he would send a message to Paulsen and set the gears in motion to get a pardon for John in front of the president. If there was one thing that the senator needed more than anything, it was his son's freedom, so they could find Celia together, and put an end to Lucas Fume and his games once and for all.

THIRTY

ZEKE POPPED UP OUT OF THE DARKNESS like a determined bull. He had stumbled, quickly regained his footing, and pushed toward the speeding wagon with all of his might, reaching out, trying his level best to grab ahold, and not get left behind. That would be certain death.

Lucas leaned out as far as he could, grabbed Zeke's hand, and pulled him forward with all of his might into the wagon. It was like wrestling a three-hundred-pound catfish, only this one—Zeke—was willing to be caught and landed.

It was a relief, and somewhat of a surprise to see the Negro. Zeke was the last person Lucas had expected to see as he dove out of the second-floor window.

Gunshots crackled in the air behind them, and it reminded Lucas of the battlefields that he had fought in during the war. He had avoided fighting as much as possible, choosing instead to spend his wartime in the cities, undercover, gathering intelligence, and transporting messages from one place to the next. Spying had come easier to him than shooting did. He had wanted to get as far away from the gunshots as he could then, and even more so, now.

Zeke tumbled into the bed of the wagon, nodded at Lucas, then scurried into the corner, cowering, covering himself with straw, making himself as small and invisible as possible.

Lucas followed suit, took the other corner, but didn't bury himself. He grabbed up the Winchester that Straut had ensured would be there, and returned fire, emptying the rifle of its ammunition as fast as he could. He tossed it off to the side, then grabbed another rifle, and did the same thing.

A cloud of gun smoke followed the speeding wagon away from the saloon. Straut was headed out of town, away from Victoria Tullet and her protectors as fast as possible.

"Can you go any faster?" Lucas hollered.

"These horses are at their limit," Straut answered.

"We needed a bigger team."

"Too late for second guessin' now."

Lucas peered back toward the saloon, down the street into the darkness. "We got a chase coming on. Three riders, maybe four. We're going to be outnumbered in a hurry."

Straut glanced over his shoulder. "There's five Winchesters back there, and a crate full of cartridges. Hold 'em back, if you can. That's the best I can do, unless you want me to stop so we can put three men on their five."

"Keep going. We'll do our best."

"I figured you'd say that."

Lucas nodded. "You all right, Zeke? I need you, man. Come on out of there, and grab up a weapon."

Zeke rustled out of the corner tepidly, his black face barely visible in the dark of night. His eyes were wide with fear and hesitation, white as a sheet. "Ain't gonna shoot no mens, Mistuh Lucas, if I don't have to. Them fellas aim to hang me. I heard 'em say so. I ain't in no hurry to see the end of no rope. I thought maybe I was, but I was wrong. I sure was. Them bad ones scared the life right back into me."

"Shoot into the air then," Lucas barked, unable to contain his anger. "If you don't, none of us are going to see tomorrow."

Zeke didn't have time to answer. A shot ripped into the side of the wagon, shattering the wood of the rail into splinters, sending it flying like shrapnel from an exploding bomb.

It felt like a swarm of bees had landed on Lucas's arm. Biting, stinging pain exploded upward, and he realized that he'd been glanced by a scattergun as well as the splintered wood.

The projectiles were weak, at the end of their range, causing them to tumble off his arm instead of digging in, but they still hurt. He gasped out loud. "Damn it!"

"You all right?" Straut yelled over his shoulder.

"Buckshot scratched me," Lucas said. "I'm all right. Go. Faster! There's more coming, and their aims are going to get better the closer they get. I'm in no mood to die in Leavenworth, Kansas."

Zeke hadn't taken his eyes off Lucas. He grabbed up one of the Winchesters, and joined in as Lucas shot back at the encroaching riders.

The ruckus had drawn attention from more than just the men chasing them. Curious folks stepped out of brightly lit saloons to see what was going on. Most stood back against the exterior walls, not showing any intention of getting involved. There was not a surprised look on any face to be found. It appeared this type of chase happened all of the time.

Lucas could see two riders closing in, well within range of his rifle, but before he could get a solid aim, Zeke fired off as many rounds as he could.

The Negro's cartridges hit both riders square on, which didn't surprise Lucas at all; he'd kept a keen eye on Zeke when he was target shooting out on the plains. The big Negro had more skills than he was willing to let on.

The riders flew off their horses onto the dirt street with familiar thuds that could be heard all around. Other horses coming from behind stopped, and the riders dismounted to offer aid, allowing for the wagon to gain distance from them, and finally race out of town.

The fire was low and shielded so it couldn't be spied easily. Joe Straut stood over it with a stick in his hand, turning a day-old rabbit slowly, like it was on a spit.

The cooking meat was a comfortable smell, and both

Lucas and Zeke seemed at ease, sitting just off to the right of Straut, watching out over the flat land continuously, waiting for the riders to come at them in a full-on assault—but so far, there'd been no sign of anyone. It had been quiet, but it was deep into the night, and Straut had driven the wagon as far as he could, only stopping when he thought he would endanger the horses.

"Where were you?" Lucas asked Zeke.

"Not too far. I tore out once them riders showed themselves at that farm."

"Wasn't much of a farm."

"Figured that to be true."

"I have a hunch that those two were waiting for us."

"I'm sorry," Zeke said.

"Sorry for what?"

"For not comin' for you. I was scared them men was still around waitin' for me to come rescue you."

"You're probably right in that. It's best you went on," Lucas said. "Straut showed up. It worked out."

"Who knows we out this way, Mistuh Lucas?"

"Can only be one person that I know of that wants to do us any harm."

"That Barlow boy?"

"That's right. I think he's set out after us just as much as I set out after him."

Zeke looked at Lucas curiously. "I done thought you left all that behind, that we was startin' a new life out here? But somethin' don't add up, since Mistuh Straut be along for the ride. I knowed you was up to somethin' when I saw him."

"I was waiting on Straut out on the plains," Lucas said. "He has some information for me, then he was going to see you back to Tennessee."

"Tennessee? I thought you done said we weren't never goin' back there?"

"No, Zeke, I said I wasn't going back. But I think you have to if you're ever going to be a free man. Those Tullets had a Wanted poster with your likeness on it. That crime's going to follow you wherever you go. You have to know that's true."

"I ain't gonna be free, I knows that. You should, too."

"I've put some things in motion, Zeke, and for them all to come together, well, you have to go back home, or you're going to be looking over your shoulder for the rest of your life. Me, too, as far as that goes. You can ride with me as long as you want. I owe you my life."

Zeke leaned in to Lucas with a strange, unusual look on his face. He looked annoyed. "What'd you go and do, Mistuh Lucas?"

"I took Celia, Zeke. I stole her away from the terrible place she was in, and I'm going to give her a better life. You, too, if you'll let me."

THIRTY-ONE

LUCAS HAD THE LAST WATCH. NIGHT TILTED
toward dawn, but it was still dark and quiet. There were no
whip-poor-wills calling out to remind him that he was not
alone in the world. He didn't even know if such a thing as
a whip-poor-will existed in Kansas. For all he knew, the only
place the unseen night bird called out was Tennessee, and
points east. The uncertainty that came from being a thousand miles from home was never far from his mind.

There were no owls about, either, and as odd as it might
have seemed, Lucas would have gladly shared the darkness
with one of the wise-looking birds, or the distant yip of a
coyote. But there was nothing, nothing but the soft push of
a breeze that couldn't even rightly be called a wind.

From what Lucas could tell, the land was flat for as far
as the eye could see. Not even a hill cast a shadow. Trees
were thin and sparse, and there was no hint of a creek or
river that would affect the lay of the land. Only knee-high
grass covered the hard ground; grass that seemed to go on
forever—and might have for all Lucas knew. Whatever lay

west was a mystery to him, regardless of what the maps and other men said was out there.

The overhead sky was cloudless, black as the back of an eyelid, but dotted with pulsing stars, points of silver light too far away to offer a glow to navigate by. The air was cool, but moist. Lucas was comfortable, accustomed to the middle summer weather, with just a shirt and no need for a coat of any kind.

The camp they'd struck, and low fire, were behind him about twenty-five yards. Dim orange coals glowed on the surface of the ground so close that Lucas had to squint to see it.

He couldn't see Zeke or Straut; they were nothing more than invisible and unmoving boulders. Straut was happy to come off of watch hours before, and Lucas assumed both men were fast asleep, glad to be away from the dangers of Leavenworth. It was a less comfortable setup than the fine hotel in town offered, but backtracking for the sake of comfort was out of the question.

Leavenworth was behind them a good ways, but they were hardly out of the reach of danger. A good scout would have no trouble finding them. Plans would be made in the daylight among all three of them, but the ultimate goal was to get Zeke back East as quick as they could. They'd have to find a train for that, and dodge the bounty seekers that would most likely be on the hunt for them.

That's what the Tullets had to be, Lucas concluded. Bounty hunters financed by the Barlows.

Lucas pushed the immediate thought of Victoria away as fast as he could. He did not even care for her, found her to be a threat, not the kind of woman he would ever find compatible; attractive, yes, highly attractive. But she troubled him like a splinter under his fingernail. No matter how hard he dug to remove it, it pushed farther back out of reach, deeper under his skin, irritating him, threatening infection.

He stood up from the spot he had perched in, and began walking the perimeter of the camp again, doing anything to get the naked female out of his mind. A woman, especially that woman, was the last thing he needed to be preoccupied with.

He was fully armed, carrying one of the Winchesters along with a belt full of cartridges thrown over his shoulder. He still had the Colt on his hip, and he'd tucked a derringer over his bare shoulder, hidden out of sight by his shirt—though in the bright light of day it could have been easily seen. He also had a long knife sheathed on the opposite hip of the six-shooter.

The variety of weapons seemed plenty, and there was no doubt that Zeke and Straut would come running at the first sound of trouble—if they were able.

Lucas thought about whistling as he walked, but decided against it. Pushing through the endless grass, albeit slowly and with intention, made enough noise the way it was. His skin itched at the touch, and he wondered if he would ever get used to the grass. He hoped to put Kansas behind him soon.

About twenty yards away from the spot where he had rested for a while, he stopped again, certain he heard an out-of-place sound. It was a brief, but alarming sound. It was like a horse had come to a stop, and cleared its nostrils. The sound was muffled, and came directly from the north, to the left of him.

The team that had pulled the wagon was resting directly ahead of him, which was due east, in a stretch of grass that held a few cottonwoods and nothing more. The trees offered what little cover could be found, and that was minimal since they were tall, full of leaves at the top, and thin trunked with only a few branches that jutted out about ten feet up.

After a few seconds of intent listening, Lucas could only hear the steady breeze, and the constant rhythm of his own heartbeat.

He gripped the Winchester tighter. The distant sound of the horse, if that's what it was, reinvigorated his vigilance. There were men on their trail; men who would shoot first even if Victoria Tullet had said that the three of them were worth more alive than dead.

It had been a good while since Lucas had circuited by the camp, so he decided to check on the sleeping pair, check on Straut and Zeke, just to relieve his worry.

The sound could have been a bird coming awake, or any sort of creature stumbling upon another. Coming or going at this time of night wasn't out of the question. The horizon was showing signs of diffused light, like a thin gray fog was slowly rising up from the other side of the earth. Dawn was breaking slowly, taking its own time, like always.

Lucas would be glad to see daylight, have a mug of fresh coffee, and get on the trail. Stopping put them at risk, but there had been no choice. They had gone as far as they could in the deep darkness.

The coals of the fire were barely breathing by the time Lucas reached the camp. They offered little heat, less light, and threatened to die soon if no wood was thrown on them. But Lucas's eyes were well adjusted to the darkness, and it only took him a second to realize that Zeke and Straut were gone, nowhere to be seen.

A twig snapped behind Lucas. His training was distant in the past, and there was no question that he was rusty from the time spent in prison, but as he spun around, he brought the Winchester up to his shoulder, and easily found the trigger.

"Drop the rifle, Fume. You're surrounded," a familiar voice said.

A bright light erupted, a snap of a Lucifer followed the quick crackle of fire eating something dry, like a broom—or a torch.

Lucas felt the heat, and had to shield his eyes from the unexpected brightness. In a blink or two, he saw five figures standing beyond the light, a torch held by the closest man.

Lucas didn't drop the Winchester. He held his aim directly at the fire.

"If you want to live another second, you'll do as I told you," the man said, stepping forward so Lucas could see him clearly. It was Roy Tullet.

"Not going to happen, Tullet, or whatever your name is," Lucas said, keeping the rifle level at him.

"There's no difference between stubborn and stupid the way I see it," Tullet said. "Now, if you don't go about lowering that weapon, I'll just have my men here take care of your two friends and then there won't be anythin' to argue over, will there?"

Lucas focused his attention past Tullet, who was covered head to toe in trail dust and anger. He could see that both Straut and Zeke had their hands bound behind them with heavy rope. The two other men, one of them being Kingsley Nash, stood next to each man with their pistols drawn.

Beyond the men, another figure, still in the shadows of dawn and hard to discern, sat on a horse with a rifle aimed in Lucas's direction. There was no question that he was outmanned, outgunned, and at a huge disadvantage.

"All right," Lucas said. "I know when I'm beat. I'm going to ease the rifle to the ground." He began to lower it to the ground.

"I'm serious, Fume, no funny stuff. You do anything stupid, that Negro'll be the first to get a bullet in the head. We done saw how fond of him you are."

Lucas let the Winchester slip from his hand to the ground.

"Now, kick it to me," Roy Tullet said.

Lucas stood up slowly and did what he was told. He tried to make eye contact with Straut, but his head was to the ground. So was Zeke's. It was like they had been ordered ahead of time not to communicate with Lucas in any way.

"All right," Tullet said, "now do the same with the Colt and the knife. No funny business."

Lucas exhaled deeply, did as he was told, then stood up. "Why not just kill us here and now? Put us out of our misery."

"You ain't no hurt dog," Tullet said.

"I doubt you'd be so generous."

"Don't matter what you think now, does it?"

"I suppose not."

"Ben," Tullet said over his shoulder, "bind his hands like the other two."

The man, or more to the truth, boy, since he looked to be about fifteen, smooth-faced and big-eyed, nodded, and hurried away from Straut.

The man who had said his name was Kingsley Nash

stood stoic next to Zeke, the long barrel of his Walker Colt pressed against the Negro's temple. There had been an indication of money, of gentry and high breeding upon their first meeting, but that had been when Lucas believed what Tullet had told him. It was an elaborate tale that seemed well thought out, a signature of John Barlow's, but Lucas hadn't been looking for a trap when they all had first met; now he trusted nothing when it came to this trio, nothing but the truth of their intention.

Ben smelled like he hadn't had a bath in a month. Lucas assumed the position, and put his hands behind him, but not too tight, so it would pull his shirt tight.

"You done act like you've done this before, mister," Ben said. His breath smelled foul, too, and Lucas was glad the boy had spoken to him from behind.

It was tempting to surprise Ben with an elbow jab, but there was too much at stake. Instead, Lucas stood there, focusing on the horse and rider with the rifle on them. Up until that moment, it had been hard to see beyond the flare of the torch, but daylight was coming on quickly. It wasn't a man. It was a woman. Victoria.

Almost as if she knew she had been identified, she nickered the horse, who protested with a recognizable snort. She rode forward, still carrying the rifle. She came to a stop next to a tall cottonwood.

The move got Nash's and Tullet's attention, but they stayed focused on their prey. So did Ben. He pulled the binding tight on Lucas's wrists. There was no way he was going to escape. At least right away.

Victoria Tullet glared at Lucas with an eyeful of hate. She stuffed the rifle, a Winchester like he carried, into a scabbard, then grabbed up a coil of rope, and tossed it upward so it flipped over the lowest hanging branch. "Let's get this hangin' over with as soon as we can," she said with authority, like she was the one in charge.

THIRTY-TWO

LANCASTER BARLOW OPENED THE HOTEL room door to leave, and came face to face with Sheriff Keane.

"Going somewhere, Senator?" the sheriff asked. He was standing to the right of the door, allowing room for exit, but the hallway was blocked behind him. Two serious-looking deputies, one burly and one skinny, stood with their shooting hands resting on the grips of their side arms, ready to use them if the need arose.

The sight of the three men took the air out of Barlow's lungs, and the propulsion out of his feet; he wasn't expecting to see anyone, hadn't heard them. Barlow stopped dead in his tracks. "I have business to attend to, Sheriff Keane. If you don't mind."

The middle-aged sheriff wrinkled his brow, then stepped directly in front of the senator. "I do mind, since you asked."

Barlow wrinkled his nose. The man still smelled of stale tobacco smoke. And of a skunk, too. He was a traitor, a lawman on the take if John was correct. The star on his chest was owned by Lucas Fume, not the loyal citizens of Nashville.

"Is there a problem, Senator?" Keane said.

The deputies stood as still as statues, but there was no mistaking them for idiots. Barlow was sure they had their orders to shoot first and ask questions later—which there was no worry about. He was no troublemaker, and less a marksman than most men his age. Words and documents were his weapons of choice.

"No, no, Sheriff Keane, of course not. What do I owe the pleasure of your visit?"

"I have some bad news," the sheriff said.

"About Celia?" Barlow put his hand over his chest to steady himself. "She's been found?"

"I'm afraid there's no word of her location . . . yet."

"What then is your mission? News of the murder for which you put me falsely under suspicion?"

Keane shrugged. "Well, as a matter of fact, that matter has been cleared up. There was no murder at all."

"As if that is a great surprise. I shall speak to those who oversee your position about your fictitious claim of murder. Accusing me of such a horrendous act was way out of line, sir. I told you last night that it was a fool's errand. An unjust accusation that could do a great amount of damage to my reputation and standing in the community. I shall have your job if it's the last thing I do."

"You wouldn't want it," the sheriff said, offering a twist of his lip in defiance. "The pay is poor, and the clientele is of a lower standard than you are accustomed to dealing with."

"Well, then," Barlow bellowed, "if you are not here to arrest me for this murder that did not happen, and you have no news of Celia, then what is so important that I cannot pass and get on with my business? I have important matters to attend to, or did you not hear what I had to say?"

"I have come to arrest you, Senator Barlow," Sheriff Keane said. His voice was deadpan, and his eyes void of any emotion at all.

"Have you lost all of your senses, sir? Or are you just mad? Whatever preposterous game you are playing will come to a bad end. You and Lucas Fume will rue the day when you set your fool plot in motion. Don't think I am unaware of your connections to that man, or who your benefactor really is."

Sheriff Keane exhaled deeply and looked upon the Senator sadly, like he was speaking to someone who did not understand the language he was talking. Lancaster Barlow was offended, and outraged. Highly outraged.

Keane said nothing right away, just stood there staring at the senator.

Finally, Barlow could no longer take the silence. "Am I supposed to ask what the charge is this time?"

Keane shrugged. He looked like he was enjoying himself. "Yes, of course, it is your right to know what you've been accused of, I suppose, but it won't change a thing." He looked over his shoulder, and nodded. The move set the two deputies in motion, and they each took a step toward Barlow, who instinctively stepped back inside the hotel room. "It doesn't matter, sir, you have no place to run to or hide. Not now," Keane said.

The senator's face was boiling red from his neck to his forehead. He felt funny inside his head, suddenly tipsy like he had been drinking, but of course, he had not. His anger was having an effect on his body. He could feel his heart racing inside his chest. But he girded himself, squared his shoulders, then stamped his feet, rooting himself in place. "I must remind you that I am also a lawyer in this state as well as a respected United States senator," he said.

"I am well aware of that," Keane answered. "You'll need to come with us now, sir, or we will have to bind your hands and consider you to be hostile. It is your choice how this goes."

The two deputies stood directly behind the sheriff, blocking the way out. The only exit was to dive through the window, and there was no way the senator was going to do that. He hadn't planned for an escape, and he would never survive the fall anyway.

"What is the goddamned charge?" Lancaster Barlow yelled.

"You are under arrest for the aggravated assault and beating of your daughter, Celia Barlow, sir. A beating so severe that it has left her in a state worse than death. That is only one charge. Would you like to hear the rest?"

"You have no witnesses," Barlow hissed.

Keane shrugged again, exhaled heavily, and said over his shoulder, "Get him, boys. He's hostile, and I've wasted enough of my time with this scum."

The wagon stopped, and Celia finally relaxed. There had been shooting, screaming, and the bounce of the rough ride, all making enough noise to make her tense and unsure of what was happening. Coupled with the sudden recognition that she could utter a sound, even if it was an unintelligible groan, her world felt like it was turned upside down. She was anxious, excited, afraid.

Thankfully, breathing was easy enough through the blanket holes, and she had grown accustomed to the warmth underneath it, so she was not physically uncomfortable.

The battle, or whatever it was, was over. She had not heard a gunshot for a long time—long minutes that could even have been a half hour, or more. She had never been a good judge of time, especially in the dark.

Her hearing seemed more focused, and Sulley rustled on the driver's seat, turned his body to the bed of the wagon, and stepped down into it after the team of horses settled down.

Celia was relieved. She wanted more than anything to see Little Ling, to find herself inside a tent, and return to the normal she had quickly grown accustomed to after arriving in Libertyville. She was sure, *positive*, that Little Ling would be thrilled to find out that the muscles in Celia's throat could pulse from the inside out. Though, obviously only on occasions of extreme fear. Celia had tried to recreate the groan, but it had not happened again. But she wasn't discouraged. Something felt different. She could feel movement inside her throat no matter how tiny. That was progress. Something to share, something to celebrate.

Even though she could not see him, she could hear Sulley

come closer, pulling away the burlap sacks full of potatoes, oddly from the front, like he was looking for something.

Maybe he lost something in the hard ride. If only I could help.

She could hear the sacks of potatoes thumping on the ground as Sulley threw them over the side, unloaded them; thunder and rocks raining from the sky.

And then came the voice, a voice she did not know. "Come out, come out, wherever you are."

Panic rose up inside of Celia once again. It wasn't Sulley moving around in the bed of the wagon. *Where is Sulley?*

The blanket was suddenly yanked back, exposing her eyes to bright sunlight. She couldn't see, couldn't breathe, couldn't bring herself to scream. It was like everything was paralyzed inside of her all over again.

"Well, looka here at what I found." A man Celia didn't know, stringy long hair, beady black eyes to match, and flaky skin that looked and smelled like it hadn't seen a bath in years, stared down, and smiled toothlessly at her. "I think I done found me enough bounty money to eat dinner for a month a Sundays. Yes, sir, I surely do. You that senator's daughter everybody's lookin' for, ain't you?"

The man had a hooked nose, and was dressed in an over-sized black frock coat and tattered black trousers. He looked like a vulture flapping his wings as he reached in to pick her up.

Celia screamed, but it did not deter him because he couldn't hear her.

PART III

Escape from Hangtown

I do not ask for any crown,
But that which all may win,
Nor seek to conquer any world
Except the one within.

—LOUISA MAY ALCOTT
FROM "MY KINGDOM"

THIRTY-THREE

ZEKE HENRY SAT ON THE BACK OF THE HORSE with a rope around his neck. The big Negro offered no protest, nor uttered any desire for last words. He had his head lowered, resigned to his fate, to losing his life at any moment, and with his hands tied behind his back. From what Lucas could tell, it almost looked like Zeke was relieved, glad for the end to be at hand.

The sun had pushed up over the horizon bringing light to the flat grassland; the wind reignited. The force of the unrelenting gusts nearly pushed Lucas's hat off his head. He flinched, a natural reaction to catch it before the felt Stetson tumbled away—but it was out of reach. If things progressed as they were, a lost hat would be the least of his worries.

"You move again, and I might let my finger catch an itch on this trigger," Ben said, standing behind him. "Nobody'd mind."

Lucas rolled his eyes, and was thankful that the wind was hitting him straight on instead of from behind so he wouldn't have to smell the boy. But he doubted what Ben said to be the truth. Victoria Tullet had told him more than once that he was worth more alive than dead, which gave Lucas hope for time and opportunity to show itself. But she had said nothing of the kind about Zeke.

Lucas didn't say anything to Ben. No use egging the boy on. There might be something to prove; for all Lucas knew, the boy was trying to make a place for himself in the small band, and killing a man might just prove something. At least in his little rat-sized brain.

Lucas knew he was being watched, not only by Ben, but by Roy Tullet, Kingsley Nash, and Victoria, who had remained on her horse. Her eyes were hard and her shoulders were straight as a board. She looked like an overseer, a general ready to bark orders. It was an odd sight for Lucas. One minute Victoria Tullet was a farm girl; the next, a naked working girl; and now she commanded respect from a position that was more often, if not always, held by a man. The three men jumped at her orders like they feared her more than anything on earth. She would have made a great spy during the war with those talents, but the way Lucas's luck was turning, she would have been on the wrong side of him, not next to him.

If the circumstances were different, he would have been wholly intrigued by Victoria. As it was, he needed to consider a route of escape. One that would free Zeke, and not put Joe Straut in any immediate danger. Bad thing was that Victoria Tullet had proven unpredictable, and she sat directly in the way of the most obvious path of escape. On top of that, he was out of time. There was no plan, no window to jump out of into a waiting wagon. There was only the moment at hand, and it looked like he was going to be forced to watch Zeke Henry die.

Payback. Perfect payback from John Barlow. No one had mentioned the scoundrel's name, had not implied that he was pulling the strings in any way, but it sure felt like he was involved. Even if it was distantly, orchestrating the campaign to capture Zeke with the Wanted posters.

There was no question that Barlow, or his father, the

corrupt and self-serving Lancaster Barlow, had cause to see Zeke dead. He was their fall guy. Zeke had been accused of raping Celia Barlow, John's sister, and Lancaster's daughter, then beating her senseless—stopped at the last minute from killing her by the only witness, the honorable senator. Zeke had been sentenced to life in prison, but had escaped from prison with Lucas, only to have to continue running. If Zeke was dead, and Celia couldn't speak, there would be no way anyone could prove that the story was false, that it had been Lancaster Barlow who had beat Celia . . . not Zeke.

The Negro needed to be dead. And now, beyond the Mississippi, the reach of the Barlows was about to grasp their one long-held desire.

Lucas lowered his head. They had stopped too soon. Hadn't run far enough away from St. Louis. He hadn't put his plan to vindicate Zeke and free him in action soon enough. Regrets would be many. Add on to the regret he held with the death of Hobie Lawton, and Lucas hoped that they would kill him, too, and end his suffering. But he doubted that was the plan. John Barlow loved to prolong pain, not take the risk of ending it.

Victoria Tullet raised her rifle so the barrel pointed straight up into the air, and pulled the trigger. As the report of the gun cracked across the ground, Roy Tullet slapped the rump of the horse Zeke was sitting on with all of his might.

The slap was not near as loud as the gunshot, but it caused Lucas to jump inside his skin.

To everyone's dismay, the horse hesitated to bolt. The beast was a swayback mare the way it was, with some age on it, so any spirit was questionable on a good day. Add in Zeke's size and weight, and the burden of running looked like it might have been a little much for the old horse to take.

The mare lurched forward, but stopped, leaving Zeke pulled back at an angle.

"Christ, Roy, can't you do anything right?" Kingsley Nash asked.

If there was ever a chance, this was it. Lucas drew in a deep breath, and caught sight of Ben, who had stepped

forward with a smile on his face, taking his attention off of
Lucas, anticipating the sight and sound of a snapping neck.

Lucas's hands were bound tight, but not as tight as they
could have been. When Ben had cinched the knot, Lucas had
positioned his wrists so they were side by side, pressed out as
far as they could go. He had spent a lot of time practicing escape techniques in the Confederate camps. Capture was always a risk. Especially when he put on a Yankee uniform and
walked right into Union headquarters. He could move his
wrists back and forth now that Ben had taken his eyes off him.

Hang on, Zeke.

"Shut the hell up, Nash, we ain't in no hurry. Look at the
boy sweat. He done gave up," Roy said. He smacked the
horse again, and it just stood there, refusing to budge.

"Don't look like no mule to me," Ben said. And then he
laughed, guffawed, and imitated the heehaw of a mule.

Both men cast Ben an angry look.

Lucas glanced up to see Straut doing the same thing he
was doing: calculating a move. To get his hand out of the
rope there needed to be more time, more of a distraction;
he couldn't pop his shoulder out of its socket quickly, un-
noticed, like he'd been able to do when he was younger.

Like she could read what was happening, or see the silent
planning going on between Straut and Lucas, Victoria Tullet
leveled the rifle, aimed it, and pulled the trigger without any
warning.

The shot was perfectly placed. It caught the horse right
behind the ear.

Thunder clapped, and echoed from the rifle. Time
stopped. The horse looked stunned for a second, then tipped
over, like it had been pushed. No sound came from the
horse's mouth, or if it did, it was muddled up in the rest of
the commotion. Blood rained down to the ground, following
the horse in a splatter.

As the horse fell over, Zeke went with it, until the rope
caught hold and yanked him back. He dangled for a second,
strangling, his toes just inches off the ground.

It was not a straight drop like it should have been, and

none of the gang had compensated for Zeke's weight and size—or bothered to check the capacity of the limb to do the job it had been assigned. In a matter of seconds, the limb snapped, and Zeke tumbled to the ground, bouncing off the horse and rolling into the thick grass. His neck did not snap, but his hands were still bound. All that was free were Zeke's big feet. But he was smart enough to know if he stood up and ran, he would present himself as a target.

Gun smoke hung in the air, along with the shock and reverberation of the broken limb.

The commotion gave Lucas just the time he needed to free his hands.

THIRTY-FOUR

THE CELL WAS EIGHT FEET BY EIGHT FEET. A wood frame bed with a thin, yellowed mattress was the only furniture that could fit inside the small room—beyond that there was barely room to move. There was no window, no vent to offer fresh air, and no toilet for private matters, just a bowl and pitcher left to sit with the human consequences for days on end. The door was made of iron bars, just far enough apart to put a finger through, much less a hand. It faced a brick wall that was halfway above ground, and half below. The bottom bricks sweated with moisture, and smelled bitter, pungent, acidic, of urine and tobacco spit.

Lancaster Barlow had not seen anyone since he had been tossed in the cell and left, it seemed, to rot.

There was no way to tell if it was day or night. All matters of time, and value—like his watch—had been stripped from him. The light outside of the cell was dim, like a distant torch burned low, even though it had been the beginning of the day when he'd arrived at the jail.

Shadows flickered on occasion, reflecting silhouettes of

large rodents on the wall as they scurried to and fro, searching for something to eat. Barlow feared going to sleep. He
was certain he was going to wake up without an ear. He'd
heard of such things, rats attacking humans, but he'd never
expected to experience the horror for himself.

Outrage only began to describe how he felt. He had protested violently with words, objections, of course, at the very
thought of being locked away, but Sheriff Keane and the
two deputies had looked upon him with deaf ears, like he
did not exist. There was no way out. No escape. All the
senator could do was wait for the ways of the law, jurispru-
dence, to take control, dictate the chain of events that were
certain to come. There were rules, laws that had to be followed. As it was, Barlow was stuffed away in the basement
of some county building with no representation, under false
charges; charges so outrageous that no one in their right
mind would ever believe that he was capable of such acts.

The senator sat on the edge of the bed, trying to ignore
the growing ache in his back, and the dryness in his throat.
He'd had no breakfast, no lunch, and there was no water in
the pitcher to quench his thirst. He thought of yelling out
again, but from past experience, he knew it would do no
good. No one would come to his beck and call. So, he eased
back into the corner, put his back against the cold, hard wall,
and settled in for the wait, defying any feelings of sleepiness.
But they came quickly once he lowered his head to his knees.

Someone scraped the iron bars of the door with a tin
cup, rousing the senator from a deep slumber. He startled
awake without any memory of where he was, expecting to
see Paulsen. "What now?" he bellowed, jumping to his feet,
nearly smacking his face on the interior wall of the cell.

"Water for the man?" It was the skinny deputy that had
helped bring him in.

Barlow shook his head, trying to wake fully. He stared
at the man, who on second glance, and up close, looked
weak, mousy. "Just water?"

"Beggars can't be choosy," the deputy said. The *can't*

sounded like it rhymed with paint, and the rest of the deputy's words were tinged with the familiar twang of the not-so-far-away hills. He wasn't a city boy. "You want this or not?"

Barlow stared at the man, trying to size him up completely. *Could he be bought?* "Of course, I'm parched."

"Parched?"

"Thirsty. Yes, I'm thirsty."

The deputy nodded his head, stood back, and searched a brass key ring for the key that would open the door. "Stand back, and don't try nothin' funny. They's a guard at the end of the hall ready to shoot if'n they's any kind of ruckus down here. You understand?"

Barlow nodded. "I'm not the escaping kind."

The deputy twisted the key, opened the door slightly, and offered the senator the cup. "Go on, now. Don't take all day. We only got so many cups."

"I can't keep it?" Barlow took the cup and the deputy closed the door, then locked it back up just as quickly as he'd unlocked it.

"No, sir, there ain't nothin' to have in that cell but you and your own."

The deputy cinched his lips, and his cheeks inflated, like he was licking an empty hole in his gum. Or perhaps it was a nervous tick. The little man looked over his shoulder every other second, like he was waiting on someone, or preparing to do something he wasn't supposed to.

Barlow looked into the cup. The water was brown, or deep red with rust from the pump; it was hard to tell in the dim light. He wrinkled his nose at the smell of rotten eggs. "This is the best you got?"

The deputy stepped in so that he was nearly touching the bars of the cell door with his nose. "Looka here, mister, I brought you the best I could. They be more later, once time for supper comes on. And then, they may not. Depends on my duty and who it is that I serve." He'd lowered his voice considerably.

Barlow noticed, saw it as an opportunity. He held his

breath and took a quick swig from the tin cup. It tasted like it looked and smelled. He almost spit out the water, but swallowed it quickly. As bad as it was, the drink offered some relief.

"Come closer," the deputy whispered.

The senator looked at the deputy curiously, then did as he was asked. "If you help me, I will reward you greatly."

"Ain't me that'll be any help, other than this: Your son says you will have the same power that he has."

"What power is that?"

The deputy shrugged his shoulders. "I don't understand the messages. I just deliver them."

"When did you hear from my son?"

"Lower your voice. They's gonna hear you and wonder what the hell is goin' on in here." The deputy paused, looked over his shoulder again. "I can't say no more. Now, give me the cup." He unlocked the door and reached in.

"What if I say no?"

"Then I won't be back for a long time." The deputy flexed his fingers. *Give it to me.* It was an unspoken command, but completely understood.

Barlow looked at the cup, and downed the remaining contents in one deep gulp. He nearly gagged, then offered the deputy the cup.

Nervous, the deputy checked the hall again quickly, then reached in for the cup—but Barlow grabbed his wrist and squeezed it as hard as he could, threatening to the pull the little man into the cell. "You tell my son to get me out of here. I can't do anything for him in here. You hear? Tell him no pardon from the president." Barlow paused and narrowed his eyes. "If you don't, then when I'm a free man, you can count every penny you have that I'll come after you. It will happen sooner rather than later. It might not be me, but someone will, and when they find you, you'll wish they hadn't. You understand?"

The deputy nodded his head as furiously as he could. "I'll tell 'im, I swear, but you have to let me go."

Lancaster Barlow stared into the man's eyes as hard as he could, then released his grip, and stood back.

The deputy slammed the cell door so hard that it echoed like a thunder boom. The entire building seemed to rattle. "I'm serious, little man. You tell him. Get me out of here. Get me out of here now. This instant."

The deputy didn't answer. He hurried off. Leaving Barlow alone with a fast-beating heart, and a rotten taste in his mouth.

THIRTY-FIVE

LUCAS PULLED HIS SHOULDER IN WITH A twist, then popped it out of the socket. He yanked his gun hand up as fast as he could out of the rope, bracing for the pain as he went, and reached for the derringer that was hidden in the holster inside his shirt. He knew the pain, the suddenness of it, would only subside once he put his shoulder back in place. Adrenaline and desperation made the pain tolerable, then nearly undetectable.

The sound and movement drew Ben's attention, but the boy was slow in reacting to what he was seeing. Lucas had counted on that, hoped for an extra second or two. It was what he needed to get his finger to the trigger.

Any concern about Zeke, Straut, or what the others were doing, or saw, was the least of Lucas's concerns. If he stopped and thought about everything that was swirling around him—all the possibilities and capabilities of Nash and the Tullets—he wouldn't have to worry any longer. He'd be dead. He might be at any second, anyway. So be it, he wasn't going down without a fight.

Lucas yanked the derringer out of his shirt as hard and

forcefully as he could, but that wasn't his only move. He jammed Ben directly in the jaw with a hard jab.

The force of the blow stunned the boy. Rotted yellow teeth and blood immediately spewed outward as Ben tilted to the side. He nearly toppled over from the surprise, from the impact, but stayed on his feet.

The rope that had bound Lucas's hands fell to the ground, and he jumped behind Ben, catching him with one hand so he didn't fall. He rammed the derringer to his temple with the other hand.

Ben was a shield, a sudden hostage. There was no time to offer a threat, to warn the boy from moving or saying anything out loud. If the message wasn't loud and clear, then his death would be quick. It was that simple. Lucas had no problem with pulling the trigger.

There was no sign of Zeke, but Straut stood with Nash at his side, his Walker Colt jammed into him. Roy Tullet wore a look of shock on his face, like he wanted to say something, but the words were caught in his throat. The earth had practically stopped moving. Every breath was a step closer to death.

The only one to react swiftly was Victoria Tullet. Her lip quivered, then twisted into an angry sneer as she saw the ploy unfold before her. She blinked, tensed up, raised the rifle tighter against her shoulder, and pulled the trigger with a forcefulness that released all of her confidence and rage in one swift action.

The shot echoed away from the thin clump of cotton-woods, and rolled along the grassland with nothing to stop it except the scream that came out of Lucas's mouth at the same time. The two sounds met in the middle, clashed, but nothing could be done to deter the impact of the lead flying through the air. It caught Joe Straut behind the ear. Victoria had aimed at him just like she had at the horse. He was no more than a pack animal to her, a beast to be dropped with no regret, consideration of morality, or chance of redemption.

There was no time for any last words, any offer of trade,

or even a look of surprise. Blood, bone, and cartilage exploded outward from Straut's face as the shot exited underneath his nose. The force of the blow propelled him forward, down onto his knees. It was not a kill shot. It was not meant to be. That would have only taken a rise of a hair of the barrel, into the brain, or lower into the heart; she knew the difference.

A shot to the head would have been a moment of pain for Straut, and then certain blackness; a painless merciful death. Victoria Tullet wanted Straut to suffer, to linger like a pig with half its throat cut. She knew it would give her an edge over Lucas, an extra second or two that meant life or death, possible salvation for her and her crew, as he reacted emotionally instead of strategically.

Straut was a smaller target on his knees, but one in need of relief of his suffering.

Every ounce of moisture dried up in Lucas's throat. His joints felt hot, like they were caught against one another, instantly rusted closed, unusable. The derringer was a Colt .41 caliber, a single shot with little range. He could waste it on Ben, try to shoot Victoria off the horse with a hope and a prayer, or come up with something else.

Half a second was like an eternity. Gun smoke hung in the air like clouds set on staying around for a while. But in truth, there was little time to make a move.

The only advantage Lucas had was the shield he had made of Ben, and there was no guarantee of its effectiveness, that Victoria wouldn't shoot the boy with the hope that the lead would pass through his body and take out Lucas. It was a possibility to consider.

As if she could read his mind, Victoria nickered her horse, gave it a hard press with her legs, and drove the beast forward, right toward Straut. She stuffed the reins in her teeth, and kept the rifle aimed at the crumbling Straut.

His hands were on the ground, and blood dripped from his face in a grand waterfall: runny, pure red, not like molasses. His eyes were wide open, and he snorted through half of his nose, what was left of it, trying to right himself, trying to find the strength to rise and continue the fight, shoot instead of being shot. His wrists were trembling, and his skin was white as a newborn lamb being led to slaughter. He didn't take his eyes off of Victoria Tullet, off of death riding straight toward him. He was determined to look her in the eye.

There was no way Lucas could rescue Straut. It was too late for that, and he couldn't stop Victoria.

There was only one thing to do.

He pushed Ben toward Roy Tullet, who had turned to see what his daughter was doing. The rustle and noise the groaning boy made drew Tullet's attention, and he started to raise his gun in defense. But it was too late.

Lucas was ten feet away. Ben struggled as Lucas pushed him square in the back, and held the derringer to his head. The boy was sweating, mumbling unintelligibly. Even though the words were unidentifiable, Lucas knew the boy was pleading for his life, that he was scared he was going to die. And he had reason to be afraid. It had been a bad choice to hook up with Roy and Victoria Tullet. The decision showed his character, or the lack of it, and made him no better than they were as far as Lucas was concerned. The boy was an outlaw, a killer like them, like her, even if he hadn't killed yet himself. He would soon enough.

Lucas didn't hesitate any longer. He pulled the trigger.

Ben gasped, and swung his arm up like he was trying to bat away the hornet who stung him, then started to collapse—but Lucas kept him from falling, at least straightaway.

Like the shot to Straut's head, this one emitted blood, but to a lesser degree. The lead didn't exit the boy's head. It just bounced around inside his brain until it ran out of steam. New pathways were cut into the useless gray glob, disconnecting every command and connection from head to toe. Ben immediately shit his pants.

The shot to the boy's head drew Victoria's attention, and she tore the reins from her mouth, and brought her horse to a stop. She answered back with a shot of her own.

This one caught Straut in the back of the neck, severing

his spinal cord, finalizing the deal she had dealt out. He was dead, out of his misery.

Lucas dropped the derringer, and let go of Ben.

As the boy fell, Lucas grabbed the gun out of Ben's opposite holster. The gun was an 1860 model Colt that had been converted for metallic cartridges. It was fully loaded, and it only took him a solid second to raise it and fire.

In all of the confusion and action, Kingsley had paled with fear, and had decided to tuck tail and make a run for his own horse. Lucas let him go, figuring that he would take him sooner or later. His target was Roy Tullet. There was no choice. Tullet had to die. It was the only way to stop Victoria in her tracks.

Lucas pulled the trigger and the cartridge caught the elder Tullet at the base of the throat, just under the Adam's apple. The report of the shot echoed away and was replaced with deafening silence. Any birds or other creatures had long since hightailed it away from the thin grove of cottonwoods.

Tullet didn't have time to lurch backward. Lucas fired again, stepping over Ben, hitting him in nearly the same spot. He pulled the trigger again, ensuring the outcome of his intention. He didn't want Tullet to suffer any more than he wanted Ben to suffer. He wanted them both dead.

"Nash!" Victoria screamed out. "Get back here, you coward."

But Nash was gone, and Victoria was running low on ammunition. Terror struck her face at the realization of what Lucas had just done. Like he had hoped, she was stung, frozen in the realization that Roy Tullet was dead.

Tullet collapsed to the ground in a bloody thud—and Lucas kept walking straight toward Victoria. It was like he was unafraid, wearing protective armor, but he was neither. He had lost any sense of life or death. He wanted revenge.

Lucas raised Ben's 1860 Colt, and brought Victoria's forehead into view. He repositioned his finger on the trigger, felt the warm metal against his skin, smelled the gunpowder and blood in the air, took a breath, blinked, then stopped.

Victoria stared down at Roy Tullet, her eyes off of Lucas

and Straut for a long second—long enough for Zeke to jump up out of the grass and throw himself onto the horse. The impact was sudden and unexpected. The first thing to go was the rifle. It flipped into the air out of her grasp. Then Victoria fell off, careening to the ground with no weapon, no one to save her from Zeke and Lucas as they rushed to subdue her.

THIRTY-SIX

IT DIDN'T TAKE MUCH EFFORT FOR ZEKE AND Lucas to capture Victoria Tullet, to keep her from going anywhere fast.

Zeke scooped her into his arms, and she fought him like a wildcat. She scratched, bit, and clawed, but her efforts were lost to the tree trunk–sized muscles locked around her; a bear hug instead of chains.

After she was bound up, Lucas stood back, staying a safe distance from her flailing feet; he gathered his senses.

"Don't you touch me, boy. I know what you did to that girl." Victoria hissed, then spit in Zeke's face.

He didn't react to the mention of Celia. Zeke just stared at Victoria Tullet with a bemused sadness.

She tried to kick backward, tried to free herself any way she could, but it was wasted energy. Zeke wasn't letting her go for love or money. "Might as well stop the strugglin', miss," Zeke said. "I can't let you free. Not till Mistuh Lucas say so anyways, and I don't think that's gonna happen anytime soon. You done made him sad."

Lucas heard every word spoken, but he chose to not react.

He scanned the horizons around him, turning slowly in a complete circle, looking for anything unusual, anything that posed a threat.

"You listen to me, slave," Victoria threatened in a low tone, "you let me go now. That's an order. If you don't, you'll come to regret it, I promise you that. You'll have another charge on you for touchin' a white woman in a way you shouldn't't."

Zeke flinched then. "I gots my regrets, miss, but lettin' you go ain't gonna be one of them." He glanced up and made eye contact with Lucas, who had stopped his rotation, and focused on the Negro. There was a question on Zeke's sweaty black face, like he wanted to make sure what he was saying was right.

Lucas shrugged, and wandered back to the spot of the deadly melee, about ten feet away from Zeke and Victoria. He stopped in the center of the triangle of death: Straut, Roy Tullet, and Ben, lying dead at measurable geometric points. It was like their deaths had been planned that way, like a play at an opera house, or in a child's backyard, but it hadn't. Luck or fate had let them fall where they did.

There was no point of rescue for any of the three men, no point in putting forth the effort to attempt to revive them. Death had been swift, unquestionable. Their eyes were wide open, staring at hell, heaven, or a void of nothing. Lucas had no idea what Straut believed in when it came to an afterlife, and he didn't much care when it came to the other two. If there was such a thing as hell, he hoped they were getting their taste of what an eternal toasting was all about.

"Your days of bossing anyone around are over, Victoria," Lucas said as he turned back to the living pair. He looked past her, to the empty horizon. "Nash is gone. Ran off at the first sign of trouble to leave you and your father on your own like the yellowbelly coward he is."

"He went after more men, you wait and see." She struggled against Zeke's arms, but he just pulled her tighter. "He'll be back, and I'll take pleasure in watching you die slowly. You ever hear about how the Cheyenne kill a man? Peel off his skin a bit at a time, cut off his manhood and cook it in a stew for their dogs? That's your fate, Lucas Fume, you wait and see."

"Didn't have the look of a man after reinforcements if you ask me. He's gone. Looks like if there's any fate to worry about, it's your own. It's been left to us," Lucas said.

Zeke eyed Lucas closely. There was no worry on the Negro's face, nor did he look any worse for the wear from almost being hanged.

It had been a foolhardy attempt, and the truth was, they were both lucky to be alive, standing there as the captors, and not the captives—alive instead of dead like the trio Lucas stood in the center of.

It had only taken Lucas a second to pop his shoulder back into its socket. There was a sharp ache, but it would grow distant with time and movement. Being able to do such a thing was more a skill than a talent, and he was glad for the time in the past to have perfected it. Without it, he would have had no plan, no way out. Rewards from the past had been rare recently.

Lucas stepped over Ben. The boy had died with a surprised look plastered on his face. "We'll tie her to that tree, Zeke." He nodded toward the one Zeke had been strung up in. "While we bury Straut."

"What about Roy?" Victoria demanded.

"Roy?" Lucas asked. "I thought he was your Pa."

"You're an idiot," Victoria seethed. "He was my husband."

The announcement stopped Lucas in his tracks. The Colt he'd snatched from the dead Ben dangled in his hand, and he almost let it fall away from the surprise of what she had said. "You need to tell me what the hell is going on."

"I'm not telling you anything."

"Suit yourself. We'll leave him on the ground, and you can watch the critters come in and feed on him for all I care."

"You can't leave me here."

"You were going to kill me, us. You killed Joe Straut, and he had no quarrel with you at all. He was just here because of us, me."

"That's on your shoulders. Or his. He should've picked better friends."

"I beg your pardon? Straut's dead because of me?"

Victoria tried to shrug but Zeke's grip was too tight. "You can't leave me here." She struggled anyway, still doing her best to break free.

Lucas shrugged back, and walked past her and Zeke. He didn't stop until he found the hanging rope that Zeke had freed himself from. "Then maybe we can make a deal. You tell me exactly what was what here, and I'll take you into Leavenworth and deposit you on the sheriff's doorstep."

"The sheriff? Why would you do that?"

Lucas picked up the rope, stiffened, and looked Victoria Tullet straight in the eye. "Because you're a cold-blooded killer, that's why. You murdered Joe Straut, and I'll see to it that you pay for that crime if it's the last thing that I do."

"They'll hang me," Victoria protested.

"Unlikely," Lucas said.

"Why, because I'm a woman? You've forgotten about Mary Surratt."

Lucas sighed. "I suppose you're trying to tell me that we fought on the same side in the war? I know full well who Mary Surratt was. A boardinghouse owner convicted for being involved in the conspiracy to assassinate Lincoln."

"We have that in common, we do," Victoria said. Her voice had changed, softened. Lucas didn't trust her, or believe her right away.

"You're not old enough for it to have mattered," Lucas said.

"My family, Roy's family, they all fought for the cause. Our blood runs gray, I swear."

Lucas knew desperation when he heard it. He looked past Victoria to Zeke, and said, "We need to get her bound up so we can get on with what we need to do. The flies have already found Straut." He looked up to the clear sky and searched for vultures, but didn't see any. "If there's a bargain to be made, Victoria, it's not going to be found in our commonalities, but in the divulgence of information. But one thing is for sure. I will see you to jail for the killing of Joe Straut. What I tell the sheriff depends on what you tell me. Think on that awhile."

Victoria lowered her head, defeated. "Please, don't tie me up. Please. I can do things to you that no other woman ever has." It was a last attempt, and Lucas was unmoved.

"I wouldn't count on that." He aimed the 1860 Colt at her. "Now, Zeke's going to let go of you. One wrong move, and I'll pull the trigger and dig one more grave than I was counting on. If you don't believe me—then try me, because right now, as I look at my dead friend over there, well, justice needs to be served, and there isn't a judge close enough to dish it out as fast as it needs to be dished. My angry heart could explode, and then I'll ride in and tell the sheriff my side of the story, and tell him where to find the graves, yours included. So, you decide."

"I know when I'm beat," Victoria said, giving up the struggle, wilting in Zeke's grip.

Lucas nodded a silent, unmistakable command.

Zeke unlocked his arms and released his bear hug on Victoria. To both of their surprise, Victoria reacted submissively as she was walked to the tree to be tied up. It was like watching a snake charmer at a carnival, and there was no question that Lucas was ready at any second for the snake to stop dancing, and turn to bite him.

THIRTY-SEVEN

THE GROUND WAS HARD, BOUND WITH TAN-
gled roots that ran deep, making it difficult to dig a grave.
Luckily, there was a small pick and shovel attached to the
side of the wagon that Straut had purchased in Leavenworth.
Zeke's strength was also a great boon to the task, but that
didn't make the digging much easier, or quicker. Even with
the tools, the ground was stubborn, offering resistance, like
it didn't want to be disturbed, or share space with anything,
or anyone.

Neither Zeke nor Lucas spoke much as they went about
the business of making a place for Joe Straut's eternal rest.
The wind offered the only voice—a constant whisper pushing through the grasses, lost and uninterested in finding its
way home. It circled about aimlessly, but reverently, never
rising in volume to the scream it could have. The sky was
cloudless, and vultures soared overhead, floating without
flapping their wings, riding the wind and heat rising from
the earth. They were silent birds, scavengers, not great hunters. Voices were not needed. Songbirds were distant, if no-
ticeable at all. Even Victoria Tullet had given up her struggle.

She watched, tied to the tree, her head drooping at the neck like a flower in need of water. Tearstains cut through the dry dirt on her face. She had cried until she couldn't cry anymore, threatened until there were no more threats, and screamed until she realized that no one was listening, or would come to her rescue. She had given in, given up, for the moment.

It was obvious that Lucas and Zeke both had plenty of practical experience at digging graves. They went about their business methodically. One on one end of the plot, and the other on the opposite end, digging in rhythm, even though they weren't trying to. Zeke had started humming at first, an old slave song Lucas recognized right away, one Lucas had heard in his childhood.

Hoe Emma hoe, you turn around dig a hole in the ground, hoe Emma hoe.

He glared at Zeke and compelled him to stop humming without asking outright. The last thing he needed reminding of was his childhood, or slave days.

But there was no escaping it. When he was older, and joined the war, Lucas had had to dig more than one grave. He was certain that Zeke had, too. There was always a sadness that came along with the digging, and the realization of the shortness of life, of the fragility of it, that the next grave dug could be your very own. It was an old line of thought, one Lucas had pondered many times before. He needed no reminders that death was always nearby on this day, or any other, as far as that went.

His adult life had not been one of leisure, even though it should have been considering his position of birth, born to a man of financial and land wealth. But as Lucas had learned the hard way, money sometimes made for more troubles, not less, and in no way did it ever fend off death, sickness, or suffering.

Zeke stood waist-high in the grave, and glanced up to the sky. "Laws have mercy, this ain't what I wished to be doin' on a beautiful day like this one turned out to be." He had tossed off the maroon velvet jacket long ago, and his shirt, torn and tattered from all the recent trials he had been through. He was soaked with sweat.

Lucas stopped digging, too, and stared at Zeke. It was easy to see the slave that the big man once was. Now they were friends a thousand miles away from home, burying another friend. "This is never easy work," Lucas said. He wiped the sweat from his own brow.

Zeke looked to the bottom of the grave. "What you gonna do with her?" he asked in a low voice.

Lucas glanced over to Victoria. Her head was still bowed in resignation, and her eyes were closed. If her chest wasn't moving with each breath, it would be easy to mistake her for dead. He felt bad for tying her up, treating her like some kind of animal, but there was no way he could trust her. She'd either run off, or find a way to try to kill them if she wasn't caged somehow. It didn't seem right to do that to a woman, but it didn't seem right that she should kill Joe Straut, either. She'd offered him no chance. Just shot him behind the ear just like she had the old tramp horse.

"Exactly what I said. Turn her over to the sheriff," Lucas said.

"Then what?"

Lucas sighed, then looked to the sky as if he were searching for an answer. "I need to get you back to Tennessee safe and sound."

Zeke put the last shovelful of dirt on the grave and stood back. He looked over to Lucas, and said, "You wanna say a prayer?"

For a second Lucas looked stumped, like he had been asked to calculate a math problem he didn't know the formula for. "Thank you," he finally said.

"That it? Ain't no prayer, Mistuh Lucas, if you don't mind my sayin' so."

"Why isn't it?"

"You didn't ask the Lord nothin'. This man might not get safe passage to heaven without our pleads and prayers."

"I know your father was a preacher man, spread the gospel of Jesus to those who would listen."

Zeke nodded, and interjected, cut Lucas off from speaking, which was rare. "He done built that church you hid in in Libertyville."

"I know," Lucas said. "It's not the day to argue with you about such things, or prove why I believe what I do. Thank you from me has to be enough.

"I'm grateful that I met Joe Straut, that we became fast friends, and that he believed in my plan enough to give his life for it. He knew the rest, Zeke, we talked about it. But he wanted to put a final end to the Barlows.

"Straut could have had an easy life on a little farm, but the truth of it was that that kind of life bored him to tears. He'd been a sergeant most all of his life. He didn't know how to do anything else other than join up with a group of men and fight for a cause of some kind. I'm grateful he took up our cause, your cause. I doubt it was easy for him to carry a flag of sorts to free a Negro. He fought in a war to keep Negroes as slaves. He believed in the Confederacy, in the way of the South. He wanted to persevere, and like now, he was ready to give his life for that cause. But he survived, and he came to know you, saw you as a full human being, and put his life on the line for you. I don't know, Zeke, you can pray to the sky all you want, but me? I'm more comfortable looking at the ground and saying thank you. It's all I know to say."

Zeke's eyes were instantly bloodshot, and even though he'd set his jaw hard, a tear escaped out of the corner of his eye. "I never told him thank you. Never thought this would happen, Mistuh Lucas. You think he'll be forgivin' me in heaven?"

"Sure, Zeke, I'm sure he will. Now let's get ready to go. We got a little bit of a ride into Leavenworth."

"You really gonna leave those other two to the critters?"

"That's what I said."

"I'd like to say a few things here, for the Lord," Zeke said.

"Suit yourself." Lucas grabbed up the shovel and walked away, stepping over Roy Tullet as he went.

"You can't do that," Victoria yelled out. The fight and struggle in her had returned. At least she had been decent enough to give them some peace while they buried Straut.

Lucas stopped, then walked up to her, standing ready to dodge any spit that came his way. "Are you ready to make a deal?"

"A deal? With you?"

"It's simple. You tell me exactly what I want to know, and I'll bury Roy."

"How about I tell you everything I know, and you let me go free. I'll bury Roy my own self."

"Not going to happen, and you know it."

"There's no way I can convince you?"

"No."

"I can . . ."

"I don't care what you think you can do. I'm not going to bed a grieving widow under any circumstances."

"You were going to buy a whore."

"I was deceived." Lucas paused. "It's my deal. The truth for a grave, or nothing."

"What about the boy?"

Zeke finished up his mumbling, and walked away from the grave, back to the camp, and started gathering up what had been left there.

"How's that your concern?" Lucas asked.

"He rode with us."

"Depends on what you tell me. First thing is that I'm going to have to believe you."

Victoria exhaled, then looked past Lucas, out to the horizon, scanning it, it seemed, in search of anything living—or moving. After a long second, she looked Lucas in the eyes. "They always said I was the weak one on the account of bein' a female, that I'd break if something like this happened. If I got took. Nash said I'd squawk like a chicken at the first sign of trouble."

"That's his real name?"

Victoria nodded. "Kingsley Nash, as far as I know. But he ain't no big landowner like we told you when you stumbled upon us. He's a bounty hunter through and through. Him and his momma was taken by the Injuns, and he was taught their ways of huntin' and trackin', and other ways, too, I 'spect."

"He still keep word with those Indians?"

Victoria nodded again. "Yes."

"They the ones that attacked the train?"

"They was supposed to kill that one then." She nodded at Straut's grave. "But leave you two to us."

Lucas flinched, flexed his free hand, and gripped the shovel tighter. "How'd they know we were there? Where we were going?"

"There's magic is those telegraph lines, Mister Fume, and there's more eyes lookin' for you and that slave than you might have figured."

"Really? Tell me more. This is a big country. I could have gone anywhere, hidden anywhere."

"But you didn't," Victoria said. "You took a familiar railcar. A man operated out of that same railcar for a long time, built up a favorable network of friends and thieves who owed him a favor. You wasn't that hard to track. Especially for a man like Lanford Grips."

The wind picked up into a scream, and drove straight at them. The sudden gust surprised Lucas, and it nearly knocked his hat off his head. He reached for it, catching it just in time. "Barlow."

"That fella betrayed him. Turned on him. There was a debt to repay."

"And you get to collect the reward? Over my dead body."

"Gladly," Victoria said, a slow smile growing on her face. "Let me guess. Roy was Nash's righthand man, and the reward for me and Zeke is even greater than it was for Straut. But you and Roy wanted it all for yourselves. You had a plan to knock out Nash and Ben and take it all for yourselves. Why else would a man offer his wife up as a whore?"

Victoria sneered, and acted like she was going to spit at Lucas, just like he thought she would. But a sharp, distant crack of thunder erupted from behind Lucas, and the spit never had time to form.

Victoria gasped and her head thumped back against the tree. A red dot appeared on her forehead, and it grew in size, running down her face like a sap bucket had been untapped.

Lucas dropped to the ground as the next shot came in, catching her in nearly the same place.

The shot echoed across the wide-open land, betraying the shooter's position. Lucas crawled to the other side of the tree, rising up with Ben's 1860 Colt ready to fire, but the distance was too far, and the range of the gun too short to get a good shot off.

Kingsley Nash turned his horse, kneed it hard, and rode off as fast as he could in the opposite direction of Leavenworth, leaving Lucas and Zeke with another grave to dig, and another reason to look over their shoulders while they did.

THIRTY-EIGHT

ALL CELIA COULD SEE WAS THE MAN'S hooked nose and beady black eyes as he picked her up out of the wagon. He turned his head away, allowing her to see the gray sky beyond his head, roiled with clouds that looked like dirty cotton still on the boll.

He smelled of perspiration and hate, and for the millionth time since Celia had taken to being an invalid, she wished more than anything to just be able to turn her head away from a disgusting stench of one kind or another.

There was fighting going on close by, out of her line of sight. The man who was stealing her began to get nervous, as he tried to keep his balance as he made his way over the sacks of potatoes, and out of the wagon. She was certain he wasn't her savior, a friend. She knew that feeling, had found it in Little Ling and Sulley.

The air was thick with gunpowder and the crackle and pop of gunfire, some close, some distant.

Somehow, Celia had been transported to the middle of a battle. It all reminded her of the war, even though those sounds and fears were distant. She spent most of that time in New York City, miles away from the desecration that occurred on the land of her birth, her childhood, and dreams.

Even now, in her current state, all she longed for was to return home to a normal life. But that was impossible, would never happen no matter how hard she wished it.

"You light as a feather there, miss. What is you, skin and bones under that rag?" the man said. "Ain't they been feedin' you since they took you away?"

He looked at Celia in an uncomfortable way, and she became more afraid than she already was. She didn't know where Sulley or Little Ling were, what happened to them, or if they were still alive. She didn't know where on earth she was as far as that went. But most of all, she had no idea what this man's intention with her was. Celia wasn't sure she could endure much more—she wanted to scream for help, but knew it would do no good, even if the unintelligible grunt that she was newly capable of slipped from her lips. No one would know it was her, understand what they heard.

The man had Celia cradled in his arms, and he spun around as soon as he stepped down from the wagon. A horse snorted close by, behind them. The spinning movement made Celia dizzy, faint. The thin-as-a-wicket man had thrown her over his shoulder, and had started to trot, running away from the wagon where she had been hidden.

Everything inside of Celia bounced, and she felt a stream of bile starting to bubble up her throat. There was no way to control it, to stop it, and even if she could, she probably wouldn't have. What remained of her last meal spewed outward, onto the man's back, just above the waistline. He stopped running almost immediately.

"What the hell?" he yelled over his shoulder. He squeezed her harder, like it was some kind of punishment. Inside her skin, she flinched, but one of the benefits of her physical restrictions was that there was no reaction to man's meanness. He would think she was stubborn, or immune to pain, which in the end, could be a bad thing.

Celia's face was buried in the small of his back, forced into the moistness of her vomit. She couldn't have answered him if she wanted to. Her eyes were closed, preparing for what came next.

Could this be it? Will he kill me? Put me out of my misery like a lame horse? Or use what's left of me for some vile purpose?

But what she expected to happen next didn't happen at all. A sudden loud slap exploded in the air, like wood meeting flesh, and then the man groaned, quivered, and collapsed to the ground, taking Celia with him.

"You moves another inch, mister, I swears, I will stick the barrel of this here gun in your mouth, and pull the trigger without nary a concern for who you is, or what is the right thing to do. You unnerstand me, mister? I'll kills you if you moves a hair." It was Sulley's voice.

Celia had secretly feared that he was dead. She had never been so happy to hear a familiar voice in her life. She had fallen on top of the hooked-nose man. Instead of her face being pushed into his back, it was sideways on the ground. She could see off into the distance. Rolling green hills littered with bodies, the smoke of battle, and an angry sky overhead. The storm was not over. Lightning danced down from the black clouds seeking a place to punch the ground with its fiery fingers. Thunder boomed like a thousand drummers were marching toward them, out of the west. Sheets of hard rain advanced, but had yet to reach them.

There was no way to know what had just happened, but she had a bad feeling that a lot of men had just died so she could live.

The man flinched, then relaxed, like he'd changed his mind about fighting back. "You ain't gonna get out of here alive, Negro," the man sneered.

Celia couldn't see Sulley, but she heard him take a deep breath, then heard another smack of wood against skin. This one was harder than the last.

"You's lucky I didn't kill you," Sulley said. He stepped over the man, and settled his boot in front of Celia's face. "I'm gonna picks you up now, Miss Celia, then we gotta run hard and fast. They's a horse just over the ridge. We gots to go. There still be mens with guns that aim to do us harm. Not sure where they all come from, but I knows *who* they come from. You, too, if you thinks about it long enough. I gotta gets you safe."

Sulley picked her up as gently as he could, but with the urgency he suggested. His grip was tight, just below the sting of the pinch left by the straggly-haired man. Celia wanted to scream out, but she didn't want to alarm Sulley with her guttural plea. He might stop at the shock of it, and put them both at risk. She could endure the pain. She had imagined something much worse than this.

Her first glance at Sulley's sweet face nearly took her breath away. His left eye was almost swollen shut. It was a black bulbous mess of inflamed tissue and dried blood. His other eye was barely a slit, and looked almost the same, like he had been struck across the face with a board, or a double set of fists. It was a wonder he could see. His nose was broken, too, a mess of shattered bone and cartilage. He smelled sour, sweaty, so pungent that the smell of him nearly brought tears to her eyes. A quick glance to the sky sought out a pair of soaring buzzards. She feared they might try to make a meal of Sulley even though he still had the ability to stand on two feet.

What happened, Sulley? What was this all about? But she really didn't want to know—her gut told her the truth along with her eyes.

Sulley did exactly what he said he was going to do: He ran as fast as he could—which wasn't fast at all, more like a man running a potato sack race after church on Sundays— away from the man, in a direction of safety, she hoped.

The battle continued, but the shots grew distant, like a faint heartbeat: *pop, pop, pop.* The earth jiggled and bounced, green grasses, wet and sticky with moisture. At least Celia was upright, not looking at the world upside down.

Before they disappeared over the ridge, Celia caught one last glance of the ugly, smelly, hook-nosed man. He was a crumble of black material lying on the ground, starting to stir, starting to struggle to his feet. Celia was glad he didn't have wings to come after them with. He looked like an injured buzzard trying to fly again. And then he was gone, lost from her vision. Celia started to breathe easier, relax the tension she felt in her neck and belly.

The horse that was waiting for them was pure white. "I'm gonna lay you up over the sides now, Miss Celia," Sulley said in between deep painful pants of breath.

She blinked once. *Yes. Be careful.*

He eased her up on the saddle, faced Celia forward, then leaned her down gently. It took a great amount of effort and struggle, but Sulley climbed up behind her, got himself situated, feet in the stirrups, butt as centered in the saddle as he could, then pulled her to him, and wrapped one arm around her waist, holding her as tight as he could.

"You hang on now. We got a long ride to Nashville. Little Ling be waitin' for us there," Sulley said. "And she sure be glad to see you, I promise."

THIRTY-NINE

SHERIFF KEANE STOOD AT THE CELL DOOR.
"Wake up, Barlow. I've got news for you."

The fear of sleeping had not been able to keep Lancaster Barlow awake. When he blinked his eyes open, he wasn't sure if the visit from the deputy had been a dream, a nightmare, or if it had really happened.

There was still no clue of the time of day, whether it was morning or night, dinnertime or breakfast. "What do you want, Keane? I'm in no mood for more of your lies."

"I don't bring you lies." There was a tray in Keane's hands. It held a glass of fresh water, a piece of freshly toasted bread, and a steaming bowl of broth of some kind. It smelled of chicken, of days long past when the senator was a student struggling through law school on long nights and little sleep. He had eaten well in Washington.

"I can see that." Barlow sat up slowly, giving leeway to the creak in his joints, flinching only slightly at the pain of old age.

"You're in luck, Senator Barlow," Keane said. "The circuit court judge will be here in three days. Your case has been expedited to the top of his docket. I'm certain he wants to put the hubbub of it behind him as quick as he can."

Barlow stood straight up ignoring any further pain. "Hub-bub? What is that about?"

A slight foxlike smile crossed the sheriff's thin lips. "The papers are having a field day with your arrest, Senator."

The senator made his way to the bars of the cell door, and pressed his face against the cold iron. "You did this. You and that good-for-nothing liar that you work for. You set out to ruin me. Well, you and Lucas Fume won't succeed, I can guarantee you that. You won't succeed." He was tempted to spit at the man, but he restrained himself. His hunger over-rode all of the actions that posed a threat to his survival—except the words that came out of his mouth. He pulled back when he realized that he was enraged, threatening.

"I have told you more than once, Senator Barlow, that I am a servant of the people. I do not take my orders from one man. I take orders from the written law, documents that govern all behavior. To suggest otherwise is a huge mistake on your part."

"You do not deny that you and Fume are acquaintances, have been in communication?"

"My friends and acquaintances are my personal business, sir. Who I communicate with and why is hardly your concern."

"You have charged me with crimes that are, were, my family business. Private matters. They are none of your business, either."

"Your crime involved the life of more than your daughter."

"A Negro," the senator sneered.

"A man, with full rights. Even the right to vote. In 1870. The Fifteenth Amendment, if I remember correctly. Were you in Washington then, Senator?"

"You know I was." Barlow stared at the bowl of broth. He had never felt so helpless in his life. "I have rights."

"You do. Which is why I have brought you your food."

"I can't say that I'm grateful."

"I wouldn't expect you to be. Stand back against the wall. You make one wrong move, and I'll be happy to save them the trouble of hearing your case." Keane set the tray down at his feet, pulled up a ring of keys with his left hand, and pulled out a .45-caliber single action Army Colt with his right hand. "You want this grub, do what I told you, and do it now. The rights of hostile prisoners are different from those that cooperate."

"I know the rule." Barlow put his hands up and edged back to the far end of the cell. "There, are you satisfied?"

"No funny business, Senator. I'm serious."

"I can see that."

Keane clicked the lock with the appropriate key, and pushed open the cell door. He stood there for a second facing Barlow like they were standing off for a duel in the street, then he nudged the tray inside the cell with the toe of his boot. Half the broth sloshed out of the bowl. He offered no apology for the spill, and locked the door.

Barlow grimaced at the puddle on the floor, but didn't protest. "I expect to see an attorney before this so-called trial is set to begin."

"As soon as one is available."

"I'd like to see a newspaper, too. I would like to know the damage that has been done to my reputation, and start planning on how to repair it. Who is this judge? I would like to know that, too."

"The Honorable Jacob Freely. Does the name ring a bell, Senator?"

Barlow felt a bolt of rage career through his entire body. Of course the name rang a bell. It was the man he defeated not once, but twice in previous elections. Freely was an angry, ambitious, puny little man who would like nothing more than to even the playing field and make way for a victory, however it came, that would take him straight to Washington.

"You and Fume arranged this. You know Freely and I are mortal enemies."

"Perhaps he will recuse himself, Senator. I'm sure there will be a glare of light on this proceeding, errors will be spotted straightaway, broadcast from here to Washington and throughout the territories. Do you really think Judge Freely will make any mistakes at all? I'm sure he knows what's at stake."

"Scoundrels and thieves. That's what you are."

Keane shrugged. "Senator, it's really not my place to remind you that you are here because of your own actions, but it seems as if you are determined to force me to."

"You just did."

"Not entirely. It is claimed that you beat your own daughter to the point of being an invalid, that she cannot speak for herself any longer. And, you orchestrated the arrest of an innocent man, put him in prison to keep him quiet, out of sight."

"A Negro."

"You are persistent with the idea that Zeke Henry is not entirely a man, but again, I will remind you that he has the same rights as you do."

"That is not true. He does not have the right to violate a white woman with his eyes, his touch, or have the ability to marry."

"You do not have the right to violate another human being, either, Senator. You have disgraced yourself, and lied to the public you serve, sir. You have misled them into thinking that you are a kind, generous man, who has their best interests at heart, and that is simply not true. You are the scoundrel and thief, sir, and much, much more. You are a very dangerous man, a threat to society. But that is for the judge to decide. Not me. Judgment is not mine, though I wish it were."

"You have no proof."

"You are here, under lock and key, and that is not a charade, or a mistake. The law has been followed, every incident documented so that it will stand up in court. Don't think for a second anything has been left to chance."

"I would like to see my attorney now!"

Keane cocked his head, and narrowed his eyes. "Anything else you'd like me to bring you, Senator? A bath, a whore, a bottle of fine champagne?"

"Don't mock me. Don't you dare mock me."

The sheriff shook his head, then turned and walked away, whistling "Dixie" as he went.

FORTY

LUCAS STOOD ON THE PLATFORM OUTSIDE the train station, staring down the empty tracks. The sky was gloomy and angry. Even though it was midmorning, the day looked like it was about to end, not start; darkness threatened to stay for the entire day.

A hard wind blew out of the west, pushing a tall bank of clouds so black that it was hard to believe that a sun existed anywhere at all, like the glowing red orb had been consumed, never to be seen again. The weather perfectly reflected the condition of Lucas's heart and mood. He was stiff with tension. It wouldn't take much at all to rile him, to force the snap that was building inside him. His Scottish blood was boiling, and a fight, any fight, would have been welcome. As it was, he stood alone, by choice, trying to keep his wits about him. He knew he didn't need to draw any more attention to himself than he already had in Kansas. *Get out while you can*, he told himself. *Get out while the getting is good.*

Rain had yet to fall, but the smell of it was in the air. There was no hint of relief, as if the rain would wash the ills of the world, resolve a drought, or bring sustenance to a hungry crop. It threatened to be a cold and hard rain, frozen and painful if it hit you in the face, the kind of rain that could ruin a sod house farmer, squash his dreams in one fell second.

The train was late, and Lucas was starting to get nervous. He felt vulnerable, anxious to get out of Leavenworth even though he held no enthusiasm for his destination.

"Saw a sky like this turn green once," an unknown voice said, drawing Lucas's attention away from the barren tracks. No matter how hard he tried, he couldn't will the train into existence.

"Really? What happened when it did that?" Lucas glanced over, sized up the man and decided right away that he posed little or no threat.

The porter had eased up next to him undetected. He was a little taller than a burro at the ears, and about ten shades darker than Zeke. Dressed in the expected black uniform, the little man was almost invisible in the darkness of the rising storm, save the whites of his eyes, his fresh collar, and puffs of curling white-as-cotton hair protruding out from under his billed hat.

"Fear come down without the inclination or decency of thunder. Hail and lightnin' announced the End Times for three dozen folk that was in the path of a spiral of madness that no man had ever seen b'fore. I believe it was the hand of God himself, doling out punishment to the wicked." The porter's voice was steady, even though he had to put his hand to his hat to keep it from blowing away. "One minute the town was there, and the next it was nothin' but splinters scattered about for miles. Tore one man's head straight off his neck. The sheriff he was. A man who drank up power likes some men drink up whiskey. He was hateful and angry. Then he was no more."

"This is that kind of sky?" Lucas asked.

"It is."

"Train late for a reason?"

The porter shook his head. "Not that I knows of. But I ain't got no reason to know that. Train'll show up, or it won't. Bandits rob the treasuries, or the Injuns take the hair as a prize. Trains be ducks in the water with nowheres to go but the way the rails says they can, east or west, can't break off and run from troubles. Some days that be a good thing, some days, it be bad. Everybody need a place to hide from time to time."

Lucas eyed the porter a little more closely. The little man's tales were hitting a little too close to home. "Maybe this God of yours picked up the train and took it away. Could be a load of wicked people heading your way."

"Redemption would be swift." A gust of wind pushed up against the little man, and he took a step back to steady himself. He shook his head, looked to the sky, then stepped up next to Lucas again and looked at his watch. "Well, loads of folk come and go these days. More comin' than goin', I suppose. Those that deserve a blessin' will surely find it. All is not lost."

"If you say so."

"I do."

Lucas sighed and looked down the track again. This time he saw the train pushing toward the station, slowing for the stop, adding black smoke to the black sky, so close in color that he couldn't tell where one ended, and the other began.

"Any trunks, sir?" the porter asked, seeing what Lucas saw.

Lucas shook his head, and offered no further explanation. He looked over his shoulder, just in time to see Zeke walking up the boardwalk, freshly shaved, bathed, and fitted into the finest clothes available—in the time and size available. He still wore his old boots, because they didn't have time for a new pair to be made. But it wasn't what Zeke was wearing that interested Lucas. It was what was walking beside him, or more to the point, who. Fiona Dane. The madam from the saloon where Lucas had purchased time with Victoria Tullet. And beside her was a girl Lucas had never seen before. Supposedly, the best Madam Dane had to offer. She was going to accompany Lucas on the trip East, to St. Louis.

"Nice talkin' to you, sir. I hopes you has an easy trip home."

Lucas glared wordlessly at the porter as he eased away,

and made his way to another passenger who had pushed out of the station door in need of help with three trunks, and who, most likely, would reward the porter with a coin or two, if he was lucky.

"So, we meet again," Fiona Dane said, coming to a stop before Lucas. There was a hint of an accent on the tip of her tongue: French maybe, certainly European, maybe real, maybe not. She struggled to hold onto an open parasol, a decorative instrument not up to the task of keeping her dry from the coming storm. The wind buffeted and tried to jerk the parasol out of her grasp, but she won the fight to keep hold of it—for the moment. She offered Lucas her opposite hand to kiss, but he only stared at it, then at her. She withdrew her hand hesitantly with the turn of a lip, like she had just been insulted.

"Your last girl tried to kill us," Lucas said. He was in no mood for charades or false manners. This was a business transaction and nothing more as far as he was concerned.

"You had a history with that girl," Fiona Dane said.

"I didn't even know her name."

"Who did?"

"And I have to take your word for that?"

"Yes, you do." There was a long hiss at the end of the word. Lucas had no desire to see if her tongue was forked. "Or stand here and get blown away, soaked to the bone. You should not be so angry. You got what you paid for," Fiona Dane said.

The train crept up, rumbling the ground under their feet.

"You're right, of course," Lucas said, ignoring the train. "I was interested in what she knew, what was between her ears, not what was below her neck, or between her legs."

"You don't sugarcoat anything, do you, Mr. Fume?"

"Not on a day like this." Lucas glanced over to Zeke, who was standing on the other side of Fiona Dane's girl, looking nervously at the sky.

"And this time?" Madam Dane stepped back and opened her arms in presentation of the girl she had brought along with her. "Are you interested in her beautiful smile, her secret knowledge, or something else?"

Lucas offered no hint of emotion on his face. He looked the girl up and down quickly, glanced at her red hair, green eyes, and pale alabaster skin with approval, and said, "I try to never make the same mistake twice."

FORTY-ONE

THE RAILCAR WAS FASHIONABLE, COMFORT-able, but not as luxurious as the one that had brought Lucas and Zeke west, out of St. Louis.

Comfort and safety were Lucas's primary concerns. That, and he wanted out of Leavenworth, Kansas, as quickly as possible. With Kingsley Nash still alive, he still had an enemy close at hand, a paid man who had more at stake now to finish the deed he'd been hired to complete than ever before. Working for John Barlow was one thing, but Lucas knew the kind of man Kingsley Nash was. Most bounty hunters were persistent, fueled by the thrill of the chase, until things turned personal, like this had, then that thrill transformed into deep-rooted revenge. And there was no stopping that. Only one outcome was acceptable. One of them had to die. Lucas hoped today was not that day, that it could be avoided, put off indefinitely. Getting as far away from Kingsley Nash, and Leavenworth, was extremely important. So far, so good. There hadn't been any sign of him.

The train sat motionless on the tracks, the engine idling, sending the vibration of the wait through every car. The storm boomed overhead. Wind rocked the train sideways like it was moving at top speed, and the air was filled with energy; nervousness was in every set of eyes met.

A different porter had shown Lucas, Zeke, and the red-headed girl to their car. Not their quarters, but an entire railcar, leased for the purpose of the ride back to Nashville. Lucas had wired ahead and purchased the services of two extra railroad detectives to stand guard at each entrance so he and Zeke could get some rest, have some space that was reasonably secure and safe.

Lucas opened the door to the room next to his suite, and looked to the girl. "You can make yourself comfortable in here."

She looked at him oddly, then pushed up against him. She smelled of freshly doused toilet water: violets and lilacs, spring, the season of opportunity and hope. "I'll be waiting."

Lucas sighed and stepped back. "Make yourself comfortable. It'll be a while." He gave the girl a gentle nudge, and she walked into the small berth with a pout on her face. He offered nothing else, and locked the door behind her.

Zeke was standing in the narrow hall that led in and out of the railcar. His head nearly rubbed the ceiling, and his shoulders missed hitting the walls by a mere inch on each side. "I'll sure be glad to get a move on, Mistuh Lucas. Don't like sittin' still in no storm. Unsettles me."

Lucas remained silent. Storms made him nervous, too.

He made his way into his suite next to the girl's room just as a thunderclap boomed overhead, rattling the train from the wheels up. Zeke hurried after Lucas like a small child seeking shelter, who was afraid of storms.

"I doubt the bed in your berth will be big enough, Zeke. I didn't have time to make special arrangements for you. I was lucky to get those two guns at the doors. They came at a price I was willing to pay. There was no time to rebuild a train car to fit your measurements."

"I'll be jus' fine on the floor, Mistuh Lucas. I done slept in a whole lot of places worse than this." Zeke paused and looked at the ceiling as an even stronger rain started to fall.

It sounded like a thousand daggers falling from the sky. "You sure we gotta go back to Nashville?"

Lucas stood in the middle of the room, getting his bearings, hoping that the roof was strong enough to hold, to keep them dry. "I'm not any happier about going back than you are, Zeke. Straut was supposed to be your escort, but that's impossible now. I have to make sure you get there."

"Ain't no cause for it that I sees. A nice fella done got killed for such a thing. Gave me a debt I can't repay."

"It's my debt, Zeke. I owe Hobie, too. They both died because I employed them. You owe them no debt."

"They died 'cause of me, Mistuh Lucas. Ain't no way around that. If'n it wasn't for me, you and Straut'd be off on a pleasant adventure of one kind or 'nother. I shoulda given myself up in St. Louis."

Lucas walked up to Zeke, and stopped in front of him. He had to look up. If he stared straight ahead, he'd be dead-eyed straight with Zeke's hard-as-a-rail chest. "There's going to be a trial, Zeke. A trial for the man that set this whole thing in motion. If anybody's going to hang, or pay a debt, then it'll be him."

Zeke started to quake at the toes. He trembled mightily, and it wasn't caused by the outside storm, which continued to rage. It was so loud inside the railcar that Lucas could barely hear himself think, but there was no mistaking the fear that had struck the big Negro.

"It'll be all right, Zeke."

The frightened ex-slave shook his head. "Ain't goin' back there, Mistuh Lucas. Don't matter how much money you got or is willing to waste. That man, he has more than you. More money, more powers. He'll kill me slow and easy on the first look. I can't goes back there and face Mistuh Barlow. He be a big time senator, a man of Washington. Why, I see'd a picture of him with the president. How he gonna pay against a simple man likes me? He says what I done, well, folks, they jus' gonna believe it no matter if'n it be true or not. I never did what he said I did. Never would have thunk it, Mistuh Lucas, not in a million thousand years." A thunderclap cracked overhead, and Zeke hurried away from Lucas to the door.

"Zeke, you have to go. It's the only way you're ever going to be free."

Zeke gripped the door handle tightly, but held fast in the room. He looked like a scared dog ready to bolt at the first opportunity. "I can't, Mistuh Lucas. Not only will they kills me, they'll kill you."

"Celia will be there, Zeke. Celia will be there."

The room was dark, but Lucas's eyes were adjusted to the lack of light caused by the grayness outside, and the pulled shades on the window. There was a constancy now to the rock and sway of the train as it pushed its way east across the flat plains as fast as it could roll, trying to outrun the storm. Rain beat on the roof, but at a steady rate, a soft drumbeat, a patter. The threat of destruction seemed less and less the farther away from the station the train drove.

It was easy to see the girl, even in the dimness of the room. She was lying on her side, facing the door, naked as the day she was born. "What took you so long?"

"I told you it would be a while." Lucas stood in the middle of the berth, a few feet from her, staring at her, taking her in. He could still smell violets, the hint of spring, the promise of feminine company about to be fulfilled.

The pleasure of a woman, of a knowledgeable woman, was something Lucas had sorely missed in prison, and had had very little of since being free. He aimed to satisfy that need, that want, that desire, all the way to St. Louis.

"You just gonna stand there in your clothes, or do you expect me to come up and undress you, too?"

"You just stay right there."

"Oh, you're a talker."

"Not necessarily." Lucas struck a match on the bottom of his boot, bringing an immediate and unexpected blast of light to the berth. The girl shielded her eyes, but made no effort to cover her body, to hide under the cover from shame or embarrassment.

"You like it in the light?" she asked.

"No," Lucas said, directing the match to a small flat-wick kerosene lamp, assuring the light would stay in the room. "I want to make sure what I'm dealing with."

The girl allowed her hand to fall to the thin mattress. "You should've taken in the preview back at the saloon if I don't suit you."

"You suit me just fine. I just want to make sure you don't have any weapons about you."

"Only what you see, mister."

"I guess I have to take your word for it."

"Unless you want to search me." She smiled, licked her lips, then rolled over onto her back.

Lucas looked around the room, and saw nothing of concern. He was most likely being overly cautious. He chastised himself silently, then turned and closed the wick, shutting off the flame. The berth went dark, and Lucas, left with nothing but time on his hands, reached down, unbuckled his gun belt, eased it to the floor, then dropped his drawers, and took off the rest of his clothes. He climbed into the bed, happy to feel the welcoming softness of a beautiful woman, leaving all of his concerns about the trip back to Nashville behind as much as he could.

FORTY-TWO

NIGHTTIME HAD FULLY ENVELOPED NASH-
ville, though it was difficult for Lancaster Barlow to know
for certain what time of day it really was. He had begun to
detect a pattern of meals, of distant sounds, of guards coming and going, but to guess at the time of day or night was
just folly—and he had little patience for folly at the moment.

It was as silent as a church on Monday inside the jail, and
it had been for several hours. Even the rats were quiet, which
usually meant that it was deep into the night, their quest for
food satisfied. Roaches, it seemed, never slept, waited for
darkness to completely engulf the world so they could scurry
about doing whatever it was that roaches did. They climbed
over Barlow like he was nothing more than a hill, a bump to
traverse, nothing of concern to them. The floor was littered
with their dead brothers who thought the same thing.

A dim lamp flickered from somewhere down the hall,
out of sight, so low that the shadows almost melded into the
darkness.

The senator could barely see his hand, though it was clear
enough to detect a new tremble. Either the effect of old age

had finally settled in to stay, or his deeply held fears were boiling under his skin trying to release themselves out of every pore. He didn't know which. He was sweating even though there was a wet chill in the air.

He settled his head against the wall, about to give into sleep, when he thought he heard a slow, measured bit of breathing. A new sound barely audible over the beat of his own heart.

A cock of his ear toward the cell door told him that he wasn't hearing things, imagining the presence of a human being in the hall. It was real breathing. "Who's there?" He kept his voice low, concerned about drawing attention to himself and the visitor.

No answer came. Just the continuation of the breathing.

The tremble in Barlow's hands increased in severity, and he had to press them firmly on the thin urine-stained mattress to make them stop, or at least buffer the shake. The harder he pressed the steadier his hands became. After a long minute, he got up and made his way to the cell door, then tried to peer down the hall, but the shadows were too thick, and the light too dim. But the breathing remained, was closer, stronger. "Who are you? What do you want?" he asked.

"I want a pardon. I want to walk free without worry again."

"John." The senator buckled at the knees, slid to the floor. Both of their voices were whispers hiding just under the surface of silence. "I was hoping it was you. I'm so happy to hear your voice. I'm sorry, I did not have time to send Paulsen the request."

"You failed."

"I didn't have time. They came and got me. Locked me up. You could have contacted Paulsen. You know how to walk in and out of prison. Why couldn't you do it?"

"Because you are in here. You are no help to me now. There is nothing you can do for me. Your good name is sullied, everything that you have worked for has been destroyed. You should have never come here. The papers are having a heyday, do you know that? You're a Washington fool, a carnival, a sideshow."

"I came here for Celia." He ignored the carnival remark.

He could only imagine the fun that journalists near and far were having with his troubles.

"And I will have to finish that journey. See it to its most fitting and satisfactory conclusion. I knew I would have to do that anyway, clean up after your weak attempt to stop her."

"Stop her? What do mean, 'stop her'?"

"Please, Father, you didn't come here to rescue her. You came here to put her away again, to silence her. You came here to do away with her so there was no way she could ever damage your reputation, reveal to the world what kind of man you really are. Please, do not treat me like a fool. That has always been your downfall. You don't think anyone is smarter than you. But you are wrong. You are as clear as a glass of water to me and to the rest of the world now."

"I had to stop her, then. She couldn't be with that . . ."

"Man?"

"He's a Negro. Not a man."

"Tell them that."

"You approve?"

"Oh, Father, you are such an idiot. Of course not, but if they would have been left alone, been allowed to let whatever happen that was going to happen, then they would have paid that price. Not you. Look at you now."

"She would have been soiled."

"And that is worse than what she is now?"

"Whose side are you on?"

Silence returned to the last cell in the dark corner of the basement of the county jail. Only John Barlow's breathing gave any indication that he had not trailed off, and disappeared again.

Lancaster Barlow crouched on the floor, trembling like a frightened two-year-old. He couldn't believe what he was hearing, where his life had taken him. He never dreamed he'd end up like this, a prisoner, a criminal without the right to come and go as he pleased.

"You need to get me out of here," the senator demanded. "You can come and go as you please. Make it so for me. Please, get me out of here."

A slight chuckle erupted, then quickly muted, so it wouldn't grow into a laugh. "You're begging."

"Of course I'm begging. You know how it is in jail. It is the most horrible thing that has ever happened to me."

"I can't go back. Not now."

"What do you mean?"

John Barlow eased out of the darkness and faced the cell, looked down at his father. A distant flicker of flame glinted off the metal hooks that took the place of each of his hands. "I have escaped, Father. It is the only way to clean up your mess. The upcoming trial has created the perfect opportunity to put a final end to your inept attempts to silence Celia. I will use the chaos to accomplish just that, once and for all. She will be forever silent."

Lancaster Barlow stood up, and looked his son in the eye. "You better not hurt her."

"I promise you, Father, she won't feel a thing."

FORTY-THREE

SULLEY HELD ON TO CELIA AS TIGHT AS HE
could, but she was still afraid she was going to fall off the
galloping horse. They rode relentlessly, fleeing the melee,
the battle, whatever it was, without stopping, without hesitation of any kind. Sulley hadn't said, hadn't stopped long
enough to explain what had happened to him or why—and,
of course, she couldn't ask.

There was no question that Sulley was hurt. Celia could
smell his blood mixed with his sweat, could hear him groan
at every hard bounce, but he didn't complain, didn't waver,
just punched the horse with his legs when the beast slowed,
and kept on going. She barely knew Sulley, but she loved
him for scooping her up and taking her away from the
straggly haired man. Sulley had rescued her, saved her from
unspeakable horrors, and she was forever in his debt for that
valiant act . . . but she needed him to stop. She needed water
and some food. A weakness was growing deep inside of her,
a weakness she didn't know, one that felt different, more
powerful than anything she had ever felt, if that were possible. The feeling felt like it could pull her away, drag her

down: a riptide, invisible to see but unmistakable in its strength. She felt a strange gnawing in the pit of her stomach, and in the back of her head an ache pulsed that had never been there before. She hoped it was just dizziness, an effect of the recent events, of the hunger and thirst that she was experiencing.

Please stop, Sulley.

But he didn't hear her, couldn't hear her, not even when she tried out her newfound voice. The moan that escaped her lips was more of a smack than a plea. It couldn't be heard over Sulley's own pain, the run of the horse, and the wind that pushed into her face. The gusts of wind felt like a punch from a bully, forcing every attempt at salvation back at her, then tossing her scream away from her in a tease that felt full of intention and malice. Even the weather seemed to be her enemy. But she was safe. Safe in the arms of a man who meant her no harm. Celia was sure of that. Regardless of what was going on around her, inside of her, Sulley gave her comfort and hope. Most importantly hope.

In that moment of certainty, Celia stopped struggling, and realized that even if Sulley did stop, he couldn't feed her, probably wouldn't know how. And he wouldn't be able to ease her pain, the dizziness inside of her, the funny feeling in the back of her head. Fear only weakened her. She had learned that much since being locked inside of herself, but living with it, calming herself was hard, difficult, almost impossible in times of trouble. But there was no trouble now. So she relaxed as best she could, held up tight against Sulley, and allowed herself to slip away to sleep, into the darkness of no feeling, and perhaps, if she was lucky, into a dream where she could feel the cool grass between her toes, and see those that she missed—her lost loves, and the one with generous eyes that she dearly missed. She always hoped to see Zeke. There was nothing more that she wanted than for him to caress her face gently, softly, with those giant fingers on those giant hands—hands that wouldn't hurt a fly—unless he had to.

No dream came to Celia. Sleep wasn't deep enough to

transport her to another land. She woke in fits and starts then dozed away again, as the horse rode on. Her throat was dry, and this time when she woke it was because of the noise around her.

At first, she was startled, afraid, like she had been at the onset of being taken from the sanatorium, but that fear subsided as soon as she looked up and saw Sulley's sweet face.

His eyes were still swollen, and the blood from the battle had dried on his face in streams—dark red, almost another shade of brown, caked on his shiny brown skin. But there was a light in the slit of his eyes that she could see. A happy light, a light that held no worry, just restrained pain, which Celia fully understood. He smiled down at her.

"We here, Miss Celia. We be in Nashville. Now, yous need to be quiet so's you don't draw no undue attention. I gots you covered up like a hurt dog, and hopefully no ones will stop me. The hotel be close. We be with Little Ling b'fore long. You just settle in. She gonna get you in a hot bath, and feed you a nice hot meal. I know she will. You jus' wait an' see if Sulley is right. I knows he is. Been prayin' all the ways here. And look, here we is in Nashville jus' likes we suppose to be."

Sulley stopped the horse in front of a tall building that cast a shadow halfway down the street. A chill had come over Celia, and the lack of sun only made the shiver deeper, though unseen, like all of her physical responses. It didn't matter that she was wrapped in an old green Army blanket that smelled of saddle soap and straw. She was cold. Her dizziness had matured into a hungry weakness that had spread throughout her body—a body unable to defend itself inside or out. But she could see Sulley, then see beyond, down the street, and recognize what he said was true. She was in a place that she recognized. Nashville. Almost home, but not quite. That made the weakness bearable. Almost. Slightly. If that was possible. She could hardly remember the times when she was strong and healthy, when she could come and go as she pleased.

Sulley didn't dillydally about once he arrived at the

proposed destination. He hurried around the horse, hitched it tight, and retrieved her off the saddle. "You hold on now, Miss Celia. Don't make no noise, no noise at all," Sulley said. "You be quiet as a sick dog, and no one will be the wiser. I sure is glad you light as a feather. Lawd have mercy if you was heavy as a tar bucket."

Celia blinked once: *Yes, I won't utter a peep,* and held her tongue. Any sound that she could make was rooted firmly in the bottom of her throat. It would need water to prime it, to release any sound. *Had he heard her after all? Or had he just forgotten that she couldn't speak?*

He eased her into his arms, stumbled a bit as he went forward, regained his balance, then hurried to the door. They were at the back of the building. It was easy to see that. Crates and barrels crowded a platform, and chickens in wire crates clucked nervously next to a tub of boiling water. Even here, there was the smell of blood and death in the air. It seemed like she was never going to escape it.

Celia closed her eyes, and steadied herself. She felt like she was lying on a precipice, an outcropping of some great mountain. If she rolled one way, she would fall into a deep black abyss and never stop falling until she hit a bottom unseen by any man, present or past. If she rolled the other way, she would wake from the long dream, stand up, dust herself off, and make her way to her home, a home where Zeke would be tending the garden, and Mammy Faye would be simmering a chicken of her own on the big wood stove in the kitchen of her childhood. Neither outcome was possible, but it was how she felt. The abyss seemed to have a draw, like the darkness had the power to pull her to it. It was the weakness. She knew it was going to win her over. She just knew it.

Sulley entered a door, and stepped up on a creaky floor. The smell of cooking food hit Celia's nose, and she knew by the smell and sounds that they were in a cavernous working kitchen of some kind. *Are we in a hotel, Sulley?*

He couldn't answer her, and wouldn't have even if he could have heard her. He hurried forward, up a set of servant stairs that led to more stairs.

By the time they were on the fourth floor, Sulley was winded. Celia could feel his heart beating so fast she thought it was going to explode inside his chest. She wanted him to stop, to take care of himself; she wasn't worth the trouble. But he didn't stop. He kept on climbing. He didn't stop until they had traversed two more sets of stairs.

"We almost there, Miss Celia," Sulley said in between heavy pants. He was soaked in sweat. It had nearly washed away the dried blood on his face.

Celia could see that Sulley was weak, too, but his eyes were determined, fierce with purpose. He wasn't about to give up now. She loved him even more for that.

Something caught Sulley's attention as he pushed through the door that led onto the sixth and final floor. He looked over his shoulder, and the purpose fell away from his eyes as panic replaced it. He tightened his grip on her, pulled her as tight to him as he could. There was no time to accept an apology for the pain he was causing her. She understood. There was no need to be sorry for his efforts, for trying to save her.

Celia heard what Sulley heard. Footsteps in the stairwell, coming up behind them as fast as they could. More than one set. More like three heavy-footed men. All in a hurry.

Please, Sulley, don't let them take me away again. I don't think I can survive it.

As if he heard her, Sulley girded himself. "Hold on." Then he broke into a hard run, pushing down a hallway of hotel room doors so fast that the numbers and details were nothing but a tearing blur. It was like the blurry doors were screaming for her.

Celia didn't know where she was, who was behind the doors, or what the plan going forward was. All she wanted was to stop moving. She wanted to be safe and comfortable. Funny thing was, when she was in the sanatorium, all she wanted to do was go, move around, have an adventure, anything but the same thing every day—she had been a prisoner there, she knew that now.

Sulley ran all the way down to the end of the hall, and stopped. He pulled Celia tight with one hand, and rapped on the door three times as quickly as he could with the other one.

It only took half a breath before the door yanked opened.

A man with warm eyes and a star on his chest stood at the entrance. Little Ling was at his shoulder. Anxiety and happiness were painted on her perfect Celestial face.

"They's mens on my tail," Sulley said, panicked, hardly able to talk, to breathe.

The man with the star on his chest seemed to understand every word. He pulled the two of them inside as quickly as he could, and slammed the door closed.

The first gunshot rang out behind them just as he twisted the lock shut.

FORTY-FOUR

LUCAS LAY ON HIS SIDE, NAKED, CATCHING
his breath from the latest go around with the redheaded girl.
Her name was Molly McKay, if she was to be believed. At
the moment, she could have called herself Lilly Langtry for
all he cared. She was as skilled at her trade as he'd hoped
she would be, as he'd needed her to be.

Their time together had put some distance between the
storm and deaths that had occurred in Leavenworth. His
time there was like a bad dream, like it really hadn't
happened—but there was no denying that it had. Lucas still
felt the soreness in his muscles from the struggles, and the
loss of Joe Straut and Hobie Lawton in his heart.

The girl had been nothing more than a much-needed
distraction. She'd been the best roll in the hay he'd had since
he'd left Tennessee. The only one, in truth. His time with
Avadine, the girl who'd nursed him back to health after his
escape from prison, had been much more than a simple roll.
There'd been no money in that transaction, even though one
of them had been left broke and despondent because of their
being together—Avadine. Lucas tried his best not to think

of the Scottish girl, the regret he felt for leaving her. But riding west with him was no life for a girl like Avadine. She deserved something more settled, more consistent, a real life. Lucas wasn't ready for that, and he wasn't sure he ever would be. What had happened in Kansas had proven to Lucas that he was right in leaving Avadine behind.

Molly had her back to Lucas, the easy rise and fall of her breath gave the only clue to her resting state. The blind on the window was pulled tight, offering only varying sprays of dim light as they moved back and forth with the sway of the train. Any weather outside was undetectable as the constant roar of the engine and roll of the iron wheels against the iron rails drowned out almost every sound in the berth. Lucky for that. Molly had been quite vocal in sharing her pleasures.

The time in the girl's berth seemed perfect, allowing Lucas a long stretch of time to relax, to regain himself, and prepare for a return trip home he'd hoped to never have to make.

Molly McKay's alabaster skin glowed in the dark. It had felt like satin against Lucas's skin. Sweat from the exertion she had expended beaded in the small of her back. Other than that, there was not an imperfection to be seen on her. It was almost like she had been created fresh, just for him. But Lucas knew better than that. It was a fantasy to think such a thing—but a necessary one so he wouldn't consider all of the other men she must have been with in the past.

Lucas liked being with Molly McKay. The pleasure he felt was most welcome, and he was glad that he had thought to bring her along for the ride as a traveling companion. As much as he liked her, it would also be easy to leave her. Once their transaction was concluded, he would see her off in St. Louis, put her on a return train to Leavenworth, and get on with the business at hand: seeing Zeke free of the false and erroneous charges held against him.

He needed to be relaxed, to have all of his senses about him to pull off his plan with any certainty of success. Facing down the Barlows would be Herculean, if not impossible.

Lucas knew that he was risking his own life—his own freedom—again by helping Zeke. But he owed the Negro as much. Zeke had risked his own life for Lucas over and over again. Whatever the risk, it was worth taking. No question. Zeke Henry deserved to walk the earth as a free man, and Lancaster Barlow deserved to rot in jail, right along with his son, for what the senator had done to Celia—and Zeke.

Lucas was tempted to touch Molly again, trail his finger up and down the bumps and ridges of her backbone in an attempt to arouse her passions once again—it wouldn't take much for him to have another go with her.

Molly was thin, but not sickly, round and comfortable in all the right places. There was little to complain about when it came to her beauty. Lucas had always wondered what drove a girl to the line of business she was in, especially a girl at the beck and call of a madam, or worse, an angry man who sought only profit from his stable. Women in such circumstances were no different than cattle, bought and sold without thought to their welfare. Lucas hoped that Fiona Dane was a fair and just madam. Molly didn't seem angry, or hold a complaint against the woman. That would have been easily detected. As it was, she seemed to enjoy her "work." Her story was none of his business. Not on this trip. Not on any trip if he had any sense about him. Knowing more than he did would make it hard to leave her—and if he was honest, that's what he had paid her for: companionship, and the opportunity to be free of her emotionally—unlike he had been with Avadine. He still held feelings for that girl, even though they weren't strong enough to hold her to him.

Lucas didn't touch Molly. Instead he restrained himself, pulled back, and stared at the ceiling, at the light dancing on it, trying to get in and invade the darkness. He was done. With that realization, Lucas sat up on the side of the bed, and stared to the floor, looking for his pants, for his gun belt. Thankfully, everything was where he left it.

He took a deep breath, glanced over his shoulder for a second, and considered a change of mind one last time, but Molly hadn't moved. She seemed as spent as he was.

Satisfied that he was ready to get a move on, that he'd gotten his money's worth, Lucas put his hands on each side of himself, and prepared to propel himself off to the next part of the trip, but something stopped him. Something sharp. The point of cold hard steel poked on the right side of his back, just at the kidney.

"You move toward that gun, and I'll stab you straight through," Molly McKay said. "Won't give you no time to jump. By the time you scream out, I'll stab you again. That Negro comes in, I'll be to your gun before he opens the door, and I'll kill him, blast him through and through. Be an end to you both."

"Let me guess," Lucas said as he froze, tried not to move a muscle. "You get paid for delivering us to whoever hired you."

"Do you want to live or die?"

"Makes no difference, does it?"

The point of the knife jabbed a little deeper in an attempt to convince Lucas that she was serious. It didn't break the skin, but it was close to it; wouldn't take much strength or push from Molly's hand at all to draw blood, to do some serious damage.

"I want you to stand up slowly, you hear? Slowly. I'm gonna stand up with you. You make a wrong move, and I'll kill you. I swear I will. Don't matter whether you're dead or alive, I get my money," Molly said.

Lucas doubted that, but he wasn't going to argue with Molly McKay, or try to convince her otherwise. She was a pawn in an old chess game, and the truth of the matter was, she probably didn't know what a pawn was. She wasn't going to get paid, no matter how this turned out.

He did as he was told, and stood up slowly, offering no resistance or hint of a false move. Lucas didn't want to provoke her if she really *was* capable of killing him. But he doubted it, doubted that she had ever killed a man before. If that were the case, she would've already done so. She'd had plenty of opportunities to stab him in the back while he was on top of her. There were worse ways to die, but today hadn't been his lucky day—he'd die from a stab in the back if she had such a thing in her to do it.

Molly stood up behind him, keeping the point of the knife pushed into his back. It was probably a small knife, most likely a folding utility knife, easily stowed away and hidden—but big enough to do the job if it was used right.

"I want you to move the gun away from your clothes with your foot. Then I want you to get dressed. Slowly. I'll have the gun on you then," she said.

Lucas was tempted to ask her why she wanted him dressed, but he didn't say anything. He moved toward the gun, toward the pile of clothes slowly. He could feel the seriousness of her hot breath on the back of his neck. But there was also a slight tremble in her hand. It was the sign that he'd been looking for, hoping for.

There was no question that there were women in the same trade as Molly who had the capability to kill a man. Some of them hated men, would be glad for revenge for what had been done to them, take it out on any man; it didn't matter whether they were culpable or not. And then there were trained women killers. Lucas had known a few in the war. They had skills and a cold heart to rival any man. Molly was neither of these types of women. She was a fool sent on a fool's errand.

About three feet from the gun, Lucas dove forward, grabbed up the Colt, rolled, and came up standing with a draw on Molly. His finger was securely on the trigger.

It was the first time he could ever remember holding a gun on a naked woman while he was naked himself. "Drop the knife, Molly. You flinch, and you're dead. If you doubt that I will pull the trigger, just keep in mind there's a couple of fresh graves outside of Leavenworth. I didn't bother to dig out the bullets on any of those that I killed."

Molly's face grew pale, making her already white skin grow whiter; she could have faded away right then and there. She didn't hesitate. She dropped the knife to the floor.

"Now, kick it to me," Lucas said.

She did. "What are you going to do to me?"

"What I said I was going to do. Send you back to Leavenworth, from where you came, with a message for whoever sent you to kill me—that you failed. And, when I get done doing what I set out to do, I'm coming after them. I'm going to return the favor, and kill them. They've made an enemy they're going to regret making."

"He ain't far behind."

Lucas nodded. "Nash is on this train isn't he?"

Molly shrugged. "Don't know exactly where he is, but come St. Louis, he would've been comin' for you. I know that much to be true, and you best believe, and don't believe nothin' else."

"Good to know. Good to know. I'm not surprised."

"He'll kill me if he finds out I didn't kill you."

"I doubt that."

"You don't know Nash."

"I know men like him. He's got bigger game to hunt. He might do something to you, but he won't kill you. Not here anyway. I'm sure of that."

"What are you going to do to me?"

"I'm going to get dressed, and so are you. Then I'm going to tie you up and make arrangements to get you back to Fiona Dane, unless there's a reason not to. Is she in on this?"

Molly shook her head.

"All right, then." Lucas proceeded to do as he said he would. To his relief, Molly McKay offered no resistance to the plan. He dressed, and held the gun on her as she did, then tied her to a chair with one of the sheets on the bed. "Don't worry," he said. "I'll make sure you get some food and water." Then he slipped a handkerchief across her mouth, and gagged her.

A knock came at the door, causing Lucas to keep the Colt out of the holster. "Who is it?"

"It's me, Mistuh Lucas, just a checkin' on you. Thought I heared some extra loud goings-on in there."

Lucas smiled, tucked the Colt into the holster, and walked to the door. He opened it just enough to see Zeke, and allow Zeke to see in.

"Just making sure it's just you," Lucas said.

"Ain't no ones here but me. What happened?"

"She tried to kill me."

Zeke glanced at Molly, shook his head, then said, "You sure does has a way with the womens, Mistuh Lucas. Ain't never seen anythin' like it in my life. What's you gonna do?"

"Get me something to eat. I'm starved. How about you?"

FORTY-FIVE

THE HOURS PASSED BY QUIETLY AND WITH-
out event on the train. As they slowed for the station in St. Louis,
Lucas made no effort to prepare to exit the railcar.

He had made arrangements with the railroad detectives
to have Molly McKay deposited on the first train back to
Leavenworth, and felt as sure as he could that the task would
be completed satisfactorily—in other words, he had no
reason to mistrust the detectives.

The only concern Lucas held deeply was the fact that
Kingsley Nash was on his trail, and could very well be on
the same train as he, waiting for the right opportunity to
strike. He had known that the trip back to Tennessee came
with a new set of perils—the Barlows surely had traps set
along the way—but Lucas had hoped for an easy ride. Advice from an old spymaster, Friedrich Helms, warned him
against the comfort of quietness, of letting down one's
guard. That's when the wolves strike. But that advice was
old, buried deep in Lucas's memory. He hadn't thought about
Helms in years. The man was most likely dead by now.
Lucas didn't know for sure; he had disappeared at the end

of the war like so many men. Helms could have gone back to being a farmer, or his misdeeds and tricks could have caught up with him at the end of a gun barrel. The man had made plenty of enemies during the war. They all had.

Zeke sat by the window staring out at the shacks that announced the city was drawing closer. "They gonna kill that girl, Mistuh Lucas, if'n you send her back. You knows that, don't you?"

A shimmer of some kind of emotion ran up Lucas's spine. A flash of the girl's bare breasts flickered in his mind, and somewhere—it might have been the train slowing down—he heard a slight groan of pleasure. A real groan. For a second, Lucas thought they had both touched a place that wasn't bought. "You don't think I should put her on the train back to Leavenworth?"

"You does, you gonna have to live with another death on your shoulders, that's all I think. She be a dead girl walkin'. A purty one at that."

"What makes you say that . . . that she'll be dead?"

"She can be bought. They gonna be a feared that she'll talk too loud. Tell somebody important what she was hired to do. Then what? They got somebody onto them 'cause of her, and theys only one way to make that go away, and that's to put her in a ditch somewheres."

"Or under a train trestle like Straut and Deets did, trying to hide those folks that Barlow had killed."

"Don't know nothin' about that. But it sound right. People throws people away when they's done with them. Don't fear the Lord and his wrath, the fires of hell, nothin', they jus' go on doin' the evil that they knows how to do. I don't like all this killin'."

"Kingsley Nash is on this train. Or close by. Not too far, no matter what. It won't matter much to him here. Chances are he isn't going to go back to Kansas if he finds me and does the deed that he's been hired to do. So, she might not be in as much peril as you think," Lucas said.

"That woman, she gonna care."

"Fiona Dane?"

Zeke nodded his head.

Lucas stood up and walked over to Zeke, glanced out the window, then turned his attention straight on the Negro. "What makes you say that?"

" 'Cause I heard her says so, that's how. Didn't knows what I was hearin' when I heared it, but I does now."

"What'd she say, Zeke?"

"She says, 'Ain't no use comin' back here, you don't do to him what you's supposed to.' "

"Why didn't you tell me?"

" 'Cause I didn't think nothin' of it. A woman tellin' her whore to do what she supposed to do to a man. I heard that kind of talk more'n once in my life. I was thinkin' she was talkin' about pleasurin' you, not killin' you."

"Damn it." Lucas walked away from Zeke, and started to pace. "You're right. If I send her back to Fiona Dane, then I'm sending her to her death. But if I keep her here, then she's at risk from Nash as much as I am."

"And," Zeke said, turning away from the window, "if you lets her out of them ropes, she gonna try to kill you at every chance she gets. You gots a big problem layin' there in fronts of you, Mistuh Lucas, you sure does. What you gonna do?"

The train came to a stop, releasing steam as it did, to slow itself down. The belches sounded like a giant exhale—a relief from the quick ride from Leavenworth to St. Louis.

"I don't know," Lucas said. "But I need to figure something out before we get moving again."

Molly McKay sat in front of Lucas, dressed in a simple shift, her hands tied behind her. A desk separated them, and Zeke stood behind Lucas, dangling a Walker Colt in his big right hand. Just his presence, and the gun, offered a threat, but there was understanding and softness in his eyes. He looked uncomfortable in the role of enforcer.

There was no mistaking the scowl that had settled on Molly's face.

In the light of day, Lucas could see a peppering of freckles on her cheeks. They stood out like little scars, more pronounced against her blazing red hair, and skin so white that it looked like she had bathed in straight lye for years on end instead of just using soap. But the thing that bothered Lucas the most was that she looked younger, like a pugnacious child, sitting before him, her ears closed to the scolding she must have thought she was about to receive. In the night he had thought she was well into her twenties, especially considering her talents, but now, vulnerable and angry, she looked like she was in her late teens at the most.

"Do you like tying girls up, Mr. Fume?" Molly asked. Her Irish accent was as prominent on her tongue as the freckles on her cheeks.

"Only when they try to kill me."

"Must happen a lot then," she said.

Lucas shrugged. "More lately."

"Are you gonna kill me?"

"No." Lucas paused and narrowed his eyes, trying to ignore the defiance he heard in her voice. "Unless I have to. Who hired you?"

"Now, what makes you go and think such a thing?" Molly asked, her tone changing, mocking him.

"It doesn't really matter. I know who hired who to start with even though it ended with you. I doubt you know the truth of that, or care for that matter. Have you ever killed a man, Molly?"

She shook her head. "You was to be my first. I'd liked to have cut one or two's balls off them, and watched 'em bleed like they did me. But I ain't had the chance at a reward for such a thing till now."

"How much?" Lucas asked, not showing any interest in the anger at her past.

"To kill you?"

"Yes."

"Ten gold eagles."

"Did you see them? Were you given an advance, one or two eagles, up front, so you could trust the man to pay up once the deed was done?"

"Ain't none of your business. Besides, why would you think it was a he that paid me?"

"I didn't think that at all, just seeing if Fiona Dane was the go-between or not. You pretty much just told me she was."

What color there was in it drained quickly from her face. "She'll kill me if she finds out you're still livin'."

"I know that," Lucas said. He looked up to Zeke, and nodded.

Zeke immediately holstered the Walker, headed over to a tall chest of drawers, then opened and pulled out a small white linen bag. It jingled as he pulled it close to him.

The train rumbled with a steady heartbeat as the locomotive built up head steam to depart from St. Louis.

Zeke made his way over to the desk, set the bag on it, then went around behind Molly.

"Don't thinks about doin' anything silly, miss. Ain't no harm gonna come to you unless it need to. No ladies get hurt, you hear me?"

Molly nodded, and Zeke went about untying her hands. Then he dumped out the contents of the bag onto the desk. Twenty-five gold eagles scattered across the smooth, slick surface, almost drowning out the noise of the hesitating train.

The fear in Molly's eyes was quickly replaced with the prospect of opportunity.

Lucas stood up from behind the desk. He picked up one of the coins as he leaned forward, and offered it to Molly. "Here's the deal, Molly McKay, or whatever your real name is. All of these are yours if Zeke and I make it alive to Nashville. And if we do make it there alive, and without incident, there will be another bag waiting for you with twice as much in it. That'll make for a fresh start in a place where you don't know anybody."

Molly didn't take the coin. She stared at Lucas coldly. "I can't control what happens outside of me. Nash is out to get you, you fool."

"I know that, and I'll deal with him when the time comes. But if me or Zeke come up dead, and you're in any way involved, or didn't warn us off, well, there are two detectives on this train who will knock you out, tie you up, tether you to the back of the train, and toss you overboard. In case you think I'm bluffing, they've been paid an advance, too. Go ask them."

"What happens if I say no?"

"I ship you back to Fiona Dane, tied up in a nice package, letting her know that I'm alive, well, and on my way home to see to it that a healthy dose of justice is about to be served on a wicked, wicked man."

Molly stared at Lucas, drew in a deep breath, and flickered her green eyes. The doubt turned from dark to light as she reached out, and took the eagle from Lucas's hand. "You have a deal, Mr. Fume."

"I figured you'd see it my way," Lucas said, as he gathered up the rest of the coins and handed the bag over to Molly McKay.

FORTY-SIX

HOT, SPEEDING LEAD CRACKED THROUGH the doorjamb just above Sulley's head. Splinters showered down to the floor as Little Ling pulled the Negro and Celia away from the door. The shooter was close, the gun loud, less like thunder, more like an expected explosion. The bullet had missed Celia—she felt no new raw rip of pain—but she worried about Sulley. He was already hurt from rescuing her. A death at her expense would be hard to swallow. Too much had been lost on her account the way it was.

"How many of them was there?" the man with the tin star on his chest demanded.

"Don't know for sure," Sulley said. "I just saw shadows and heard boots runnin' after us. Got here as fast as I could, but couldn't hep bein' followed. She need that girl to tend to her in the worse way."

"Get her on the bed," Little Ling ordered. "Out of here, away from the door." Celia had never heard Little Ling's voice so tense, so full of authority.

Sulley complied by pushing past the Celestial girl, easily finding the other room. He laid Celia down on a fluffy feather bed as gently and as quickly as he could. A smile tried to form on his normally happy, chubby face, but his jowls were fractured with pain, and his dark brown skin glistened with sweat from exertion, and maybe fever. He had a worn-out look about him, like he was afflicted, consumptive, wheezing in the lungs, like he was about to topple over.

Another shot rang out distantly, on the other side of the wall. Celia wasn't sure if it was more bad men who were shooting, or if the tin star man was shooting back. Either way, she wanted it all to stop. *No more guns. No more death. No more hurting anyone. Why are the stakes so high that somebody has to die to solve a problem?*

"It'll be all right, missy, Ling promises." Little Ling fussed over her immediately, appearing next to Sulley. The Celestial girl did her best to get Celia comfortable in the bed. But that was impossible—Celia was scared. Scared that they were all going to die.

A panicked look had fixed itself on Little Ling's moon face and had not gone away since Celia had first made eye contact with the girl when they'd rushed into the room. She had missed Little Ling so much, but there was no way she could express that emotion, that thought. Not now, not yet. *Please don't let us all die.*

"We get you a bath, and some food," Little Ling continued. "I bet missy is hungry. Are you hungry?" She zeroed in on Celia's face so they were eye to eye, pushing away the sight of Sulley, who looked worried and scared, too.

Celia blinked *no.* And it was the truth. The weakness she had felt after Sulley had rescued her had spread all the way from the top of her head to the tips of her toes. She felt like she could just fade away.

"No?" Little Ling said.

Celia blinked twice again. *No.*

Pounding and a scuffle came from the other room, followed by yelling and screaming. Then another gunshot. This one echoed into the room, and Little Ling looked over her shoulder, over to Sulley, who Celia could now see standing at the open door.

"What's happening, Sully?" Little Ling asked.

"Sheriff be shootin' right at the door. I think he's been shot hisself, but he still be standin'. I don't think they was a lot of mens after us. Sheriff fired the last shot. Smoke comin' from the tip of his big gun, and he be puttin' in more bullets. Fear in his eyes, sweat on his head, blood on his arm. He leave you any more guns jus' in case they was needed?"

Little Ling shook her head.

Two more shots rang out. Quiet. No running. No hard boot steps in the hallway going one way or the other. Then one more shot, crackling like thunder, a storm overhead, instead of distant like before. Celia could smell gunpowder over the fresh wind that had dried the sheets she was lying on.

Quiet followed again—quickly broken by the sudden slam of the door.

"I'm gonna see to the sheriff," Sulley said. "The gunfight looks to be over."

"He's all righty, then, Sulley? Sheriff Keane is all righty?" Little Ling asked.

"Look like he be as right as he can be. Took a bit of lead. Skin's as white as them sheets. He look weak. Like he needs my help." Sulley vanished out the door then, leaving Celia alone with the Celestial girl.

Little Ling nodded, and let out a long sigh of relief. "See, Missy, I tell you everything be all righty, and it is. Now we gotta get you scrubbed up and built back up. You looky sad, like you wilted while you was away from me."

I did. But I fear the weakness I feel is something bad. I don't think you can save me this time. It feels bad. Dark. Like it's eating me up from the inside out.

Of course, Celia knew that Ling couldn't hear her, or understand her fears. She was relieved, too, that the fighting seemed to be over. But there would be more men coming after her. She was sure of that.

"You be safe now, I promise, missy." Little Ling forced a smile.

Celia could hear Sulley and the tin star, Sheriff Keane, talking in low murmured voices. Their words were lost to her ears, but they didn't seem dire, like there was any more of a threat. Maybe Little Ling was right. Maybe everything would be all right now.

"I get you a bath now, missy. Food that you can swallow will be on the way up from a fine kitchen. I tell them to be ready with a nice soup. Before long, you be fit as a fiddle." Little Ling smiled. "I heard that in the mercantile when I was looking for new things. Wanted to say it. I thought of you. I want to sing you happy songs so you'll smile, at least on the inside."

Celia blinked once. *Yes. That would be nice. Tell me stories of your homeland, of the Valley of the Sleeping Dragon.*

And it was as if Little Ling heard Celia. She started to hum a happy song as she went about wiping the dirt and grime from Celia's face. It wasn't long, just a few bars into the singsong song, that sleep overtook her, and Celia drifted off into a deep, dreamless slumber, certain that she was safe, and nothing could hurt her.

If it did, she wouldn't know it.

FORTY-SEVEN

LUCAS AND ZEKE STEPPED OFF THE TRAIN side by side. By the time the train had stopped and allowed them to disembark, it was midmorning, offering soft, diffused light that pushed through thin clouds overhead.

The summer sky provided a slight welcoming breeze, and no apparent threats at all. Decent weather was one thing to be glad of. That, and there had been no sign of Kingsley Nash, or any other attempts at capturing or killing either of them since leaving St. Louis.

It was highly possible that Nash wasn't on the train at all, but had just been another ploy, another lie, enlisted by the talented Molly McKay. Regardless, her attack, and her revelation that Nash was on their trail, had put them on a higher form of alert than they might have been.

Lucas knew that his increased attention to his surroundings because of Molly may have warded off a less-than-skilled assassin from making an attempt at him or Zeke.

Molly, fully dressed in the fine outfit she had worn when she'd boarded with Lucas in Leavenworth, stood before Lucas with an expectant look on her face.

"Well," Molly said in full Irish brogue. "Here we are and you've got a debt to pay. Ain't it the way we agreed on things?"

Lucas nodded. "I promised you coins, and I shall deliver. You can come with me to the bank."

Zeke stood solidly next to Lucas, staring out over the crowds of people coming and going from the train. He was dressed to the nines, too, drawing stares and hateful glares from passersby dressed in less expensive rags. The Negro didn't seem to notice—or care. Of course, the undue attention to Zeke could have been the two guns he carried, one on each hip. He had settled on the Colt Single Action Army Sheriff's models with pearl grips. They stood out against his black hands like lightning on a dark night.

"The bank? What do I have need of a bank for other than to give some strange person a chance to skim somethin' from me I done earned by keepin' me word?"

"You going to carry around a bag full of gold eagles all over this town?" Lucas asked. "What kind of attention do you think that'll attract? This is your chance to start over, Molly, have a proper shot at life. A bank's a good place to start."

"What do I know about a proper life?"

Lucas stared at the girl, and knew she was probably right. He had pondered, in the darkness of the berth, what would lead a girl as beautiful as Molly to sell her body, to make a living the way she did, and he had not come up with an answer. He wasn't sure that he really wanted to know. "All right, have it your way. A deal's a deal. I'll get you the bag, and it's yours to do with as you please. We have business to tend to, and little time to get to it."

Lucas looked up at Zeke, who'd flinched, then craned forward like he was trying to see something far away.

"What's the matter?" Lucas asked.

"Not sure, but I think I mighta seen that Nash fella."

Lucas followed Zeke's gaze, but his line of sight was lower—he couldn't see through the throngs of people on the train station platform. "Coming or going?"

"Going," Zeke said. "But I can't be shore that it was him.

Never got too good a look at the fella in the first place. And whens I did, well, I wanted to look the other way, 'cause all I wanted to do was pick him up and squeeze the life out of 'im."

"Been easier for both of us if you had."

"He gone," Zeke said.

Lucas sighed, then turned his attention back to Molly McKay. "You know what, on second thought, I think you need to stay with us. Once we settle things here, and I have Nash where I want him, if it comes to that, then I'll pay up."

"That wasn't the deal."

Lucas allowed a smile to grow on his face as he looked up and down her curvaceous body. "Then we'll have to re-negotiate, won't we?"

They took rooms on the other side of town, as far away from the Maxwell House Hotel as possible. Night had fallen over Nashville, and Lucas, Zeke, and Molly were safely tucked away from prying eyes with the hopes of finding solace and rest for the night.

Two rooms had been taken, one at the top of the hotel for Lucas and Molly, a suite with three separate rooms that had spared no expense on luxury, and the other in the basement for Zeke, a small broom closet with a cot that was the only allowable space for a Negro to rest. No matter the cost, or amount of effort from Lucas to bribe the desk clerk, there was no way he could arrange for a room for Zeke next to his.

Molly was locked in the bedroom, given time for comfort after dinner, while Lucas and Zeke sat in the parlor in soft chairs that looked over a sleeping city, relaxing as well, after the trip and ride to the hotel.

"That shore was a fine meal," Zeke said. "Ain't never had a bird called peasant b'fore. It had a funny taste to it that's still sittin' on my tongue."

"Tasted like chicken to me." Lucas stood up, walked to the floor-to-ceiling window, and looked out into the darkness. "I'd hoped to never come back here," he said. There was no mistaking the melancholy in his voice.

"Ain't no cause the way I see it," Zeke said. "You coulda

jus' left me be. I don't wanna be here, neither. They's bad air here. My gut hurts with a warnin' of terrible things to come."

"It's probably just the pheasant."

"Don't think so, Mistuh Lucas, don't think so at all. They's shadows lurkin' about that are whisperin' in my ears. They say things I can't quite understand, but it ain't a good feelin', I can tells you that much. You shoulda jus' left me in Kansas under that tree."

Lucas stiffened and turned to Zeke; blood rushed to his face, and he clenched his fists to restrain himself. "You didn't leave me in the river after we escaped prison. You took me to Libertyville, hid me among your own, saw to it that I had some time to heal, to get back up on my feet and fight. I'm a free man because of you, Zeke Henry, and I aim to see that's as true for you as it is for me if it's the last thing I do in my life. I'm not going to tell you again. I owe you a debt, and I pay my debts. Always have, always will.

"From the moment I walked away from St. Louis, I was free to do whatever I wanted to. You will have that same choice when it comes time to leave Nashville. I promise you that.

"But, you're right, I could have left you in Kansas and gone on with my life, had a great adventure bouncing from one whorehouse to the next, all over the West. I've thought about it. Thought it would be a great and interesting journey, humping my way to the ocean without regard for anything but my own pleasures. There's surely enough money in my bank account to piss away for that cause. But just the thought of it leaves me empty.

"What happened between us didn't happen because one of us was less than the other. What happened between us was because of the right and wrong choices each of us made. It makes no difference to me that you're a Negro, that we're so different. You saved my life. Now, it's my turn to save yours. It's as simple as that, Zeke. On my honor, it's as simple as that."

Zeke stood up, his eyes red, but void of visible tears. "I jus' done what I was supposed to."

"It was enough, and I'm grateful for it," Lucas said. "So, enough of this idea of me leaving you behind. It's not going to happen."

Zeke nodded. "Okay, then, I suppose I understand what you say. But I shore wish you would tell me what you're waitin' on."

"News, Zeke. Seems like I'm always waiting on word to find out where all of the parts of my plans are." Lucas stepped back, hesitated with his words. "There's going to be a trial, Zeke. A big trial with a lot of people about. It's going to be noisy and ugly, and a lot of things that I don't know about are going to happen. I've put as many things in place as I can to make sure it goes our way, but I can't be sure that you'll walk away free. Just your presence there could put you in grave danger. You could go back to prison, or they could lynch you right there. You're still in danger. I can't completely protect you. I want you to know that there're still risks to be faced here. More so, really, than any other place we've traveled."

Zeke nodded, and hung his head low. "If you say we need to be here, then that's all that matters to me, I guess. I'll trust your plottin'. But I still say it'd been easier for me to just keep walkin' as far away from here as I could get. Been better for everybody."

"Not Celia," Lucas said. It was the second time he used her name, and the impact on Zeke was not hard to mistake. The big Negro was shocked to hear it.

"What you mean, Celia, Mistuh Lucas? Jus' the thought of her make my stomach even more jittery than it already is. I can't tell you how awful it was the last time I saw her. I thought she was dead—and I ran." The tears streamed down his face. "I had to leave her. But they caught me anyway. Was waitin' on me. I took a beatin' then like no other. I wished many a time that they'd just kilt me right then and there. I don't know why they didn't just kill us both, but they didn't. The sufferin's been sadder than anythin' I could ever dream up."

Lucas nodded solemnly, but made no move to console Zeke. The Negro looked like a giant little boy who had just lost his mother. "I know, and I'm sorry I haven't told you," Lucas said, "but I had her taken away from the place she was in."

"Took her? What's you mean 'took her.'" Zeke wiped the tears from his eyes.

"I had her kidnapped. It was easy. No one was expecting it. They just parked her outside and left her there like she was a log waiting to be thrown on the fire. Little Ling has been nursing her back to health. But there was trouble."

"I don't like the sound of trouble," Zeke said.

"I was expecting it. That they'd search for her once word got to Washington that she'd come up missing, but I wasn't expecting a battle, so many men. Last I heard, Little Ling and Celia got separated. I'm sorry, Zeke, I don't know their fate. That's the news I'm waiting on."

"They was coming here?" the Negro asked. "Celia was coming here?"

"She has to be here, Zeke. It's the only way she can be free, too."

"She gonna be at this trial?"

"Yes, the trial against her father."

Fear settled on Zeke's face. If he could have gone pale, he would've been whiter than a tuft of cotton. He started to say something, but was stopped by a soft tap at the door quickly followed by two loud ones.

Lucas put up his index finger. "Wait," he said to Zeke, then hurried to the door. "No room service tonight," he said.

"I bring flowers," a muffled voice said from the other side of the door.

Lucas opened the door, and came face to face with Sheriff Keane. He pulled the man inside the hotel room without saying another word, closed the door, and locked it tight.

"What the hell happened to you?" Lucas asked.

Keane looked haggard, like he had been run through the mill twenty times. His right arm was bandaged and in a sling. "Took some lead, but I came away better than the other fellas," he said with a rasp in his voice.

"Where at?"

"At the hotel. But everythin's fine now. I got men at all the doors and on the roof."

"Ling and Celia are there?"

Keane nodded, then looked to the floor. "Yeah, but she's not good, Lucas. Not good at all. I'm not sure how much time she's got left."

FORTY-EIGHT

LANCASTER BARLOW KNEW THAT MORNING
had arrived. He could tell by the movement and actions
above. Sunlight had never found a way into the subterranean
jail cell, and the senator was convinced that the key had been
thrown away, that he'd been forgotten, the pursuit of justice
lost to him forever. Water and gruel had been provided for
sustenance, but there had been no offer of a bath or a shave
since he had arrived. He could hardly stand the smell of his
own stink. But with the scurry, movement, and smell of
breakfast food drifting down from overhead, he could only
hope that today would be the day when he was vindicated.
Or at the very least, offered a pot of water to bathe from.

It wasn't long before footsteps made their way down the
long hallway. Barlow rushed to the cell door in anticipation of
food, of good news. He had not lost hope, even though it was
difficult to hold on to. John was out and about, free to come
and go as he pleased, though there was concern since the last
visit, because he had announced that he had escaped, that he
wasn't going back to the prison. That could have changed
things. It was possible that he could never see his son again.

The footsteps drew nearer, and a shadow plunged down the corridor. Whoever it was, he was carrying a torch of some kind.

Nervous, Barlow began to pace back and forth in the tight cell. The smell of food was getting stronger. Bacon. There was no denying the smell of bacon. The senator's mouth watered at the very thought of digesting meat of any kind.

His back was turned to the door when the footsteps stopped. "There you are," a vaguely familiar voice said.

Barlow turned around, and faced the man staring back at him through the bars. "Do I know you?"

"Look a little closer." The man was holding a torch in one hand, and a plate in the other.

The flickering flame hurt Barlow's eyes as he squinted.

"Your son calls me Fetch," the man said. "But my real name is Jonah Fletcher."

Senator Barlow stepped to the door, and pictured the odd little man that John shared a cell with. When he had first seen him, Fetch was very thin with a tangle of dirty gray hair, and a face withered, emaciated. Even now, he was old and wrinkled, but there had been a major change in his appearance. First off, he was scrubbed clean from head to toe, and his hair was cut neat, combed back, and shiny from a healthy dose of pomade. His hair looked like metal of some kind, like he was wearing an armor helmet, getting ready to go into battle. And he was dressed in a fine, respectable suit; one void of moth holes, though it was not new. The little old man looked comfortable in the clothes—and he wore spectacles, eyeglasses, whereas before, he hadn't.

"You are Fetch?" Barlow asked. "Did you escape prison, too?"

"Oh, no, I was never serving a sentence. I was only there to aid your son. I could come and go as I pleased, but I had to act the part of a man's keeper. It was quite a relief from my regular work."

"Like him—he walked through the bars like he was invisible."

"It was easier for me, and we had to work to get him in

and out. That only happened a handful of times. Very risky, it was, for me and him, to walk about like a normal man."

"There is nothing normal about John."

"You don't have to tell me that."

Barlow pressed close to the door, eyeing the bacon on the plate. "That's for me?"

"It is." Fetch slipped a piece of the fried meat through the bars, and the senator grabbed it away like an owl snatching up a baby bunny off the ground in the spring.

He gobbled down the bacon and looked expectantly to Fetch. "Then how'd you come to be with my son?"

"I volunteered to help him. It was going to be impossible for him to fend for himself inside the walls of the prison. The warden gave me permission to come and go, but under very strict guidelines. I am an old man, and I have little at home, so most of the time I just stayed inside with your son. It was easier. I grew to like it there, being with him. Getting him out came at a cost, paid to the guards, but they are easily bribed, and your son has a way with words, with getting people to do what he wants."

"That has always been the case." The senator pointed at the bacon on the plate. "Another piece, please."

"Oh, certainly. I beg your pardon. You must be starved."

Lancaster Barlow nodded like a vagrant child, as Fetch handed him another slice of bacon.

The senator gobbled it down just like the first. He swallowed hard, then wiped his lips and licked his fingers clean of any lingering grease. "What do you mean 'volunteered?' "

"Ah, well, I was his lawyer, you know."

"You're a lawyer?"

"Yes, yes, most days. I'm afraid to say I did your son little good. But the deck was stacked mightily against him. Quite like it is for you at the moment. But it seemed to work out all right for him."

Barlow pressed his face against the bars. "He's an escaped convict. How can that be all right? He's on the run, not free. Why, he'll be hanged if they catch him. And you seem nonchalant, like he is in fine shape."

"You underestimate the talents of your son, sir. At this very moment, I would suggest that John Barlow is quite comfortable, spending his time in a very nice room at a very nice hotel, being catered to like one of the wealthiest men in the world. He is just fine, I assure you of that. And you will be, too."

The senator stood back and drew in a deep breath. The air was filled with the wonderful smell of bacon. It had somehow managed to overtake the ghastly aroma of his piss and shit, and that of other prisoners that flowed down the wall from the cells above. "And how can you be so sure of that?" he asked.

"Because," Fetch said, "I am your lawyer, and I am here to get you out of jail."

FORTY-NINE

LUCAS RAN HIS FINGER UP MOLLY MCKAY'S naked back, and stopped just short of her hair. He pulled back then, tucked his arm to his side, and rolled over and faced the other side of the room. A sudden numb feeling coursed through him, followed by a burst of sadness that surprised him only because of the timing of it.

Night was slowly easing into day. A distant robin chirped somewhere beyond. The sound was lonely, a city bird calling out to others of its kind. So far, none had answered back.

The window was cracked to help keep the room as cool as possible. Light was muted, gray and soft, peeking in through the crack of the draperies, allowing Lucas to see the mess of clothes left in a trail to the bed. His Colt was in the middle of the floor. He had been reckless, careless, leaving a weapon lying about in a room with a woman who had already tried to kill him once. But he had woken up alive, aroused by Molly McKay's presence next to him. Not afraid, though he probably should have been.

The day that was growing, rushing toward him, called for courage and confidence. There was no place for fear or doubt. Yet he felt it—or something like it. He wasn't sure what the numbness was, though it was starting to dawn on him slowly. The gnawing feeling was more than being back in Nashville, and all that entailed, though it was related to his past. Lucas was as sure of this as he was that the day that was coming was going to be long and dangerous.

"What was her name?" Molly McKay whispered. Her Irish lilt was welcome, but the question was unexpected. He thought she was still asleep.

Lucas rolled back over to see Molly lying on her back casually, staring at the ceiling. He wasn't ready for another go around. Not yet. Tiny beads of pleasure-induced perspiration huddled at the base of her throat, leftovers from their recent roll.

It was a pleasure to see her body in the soft light, but Lucas looked away from her ample breasts and the perfectness of her alabaster skin, and found her green eyes, curiously brimmed with emotion. "What do you mean?" he asked.

"I might be young, not as experienced at being with a man as some women I have known," Molly said, "but it doesn't take long to figure out if a man is with you when he does it, or with another woman. You ain't been with me from the start."

"That bothers you?"

"It's your dollar."

Lucas exhaled deeply, and rolled over onto his back so he didn't have to look into Molly's eyes any longer. He could still see her hair in the periphery, even when he tried to find the same spot she was staring at. There was no escaping the numbness. "I've been trying to avoid it since I left St. Louis. I've been focused on seeing Zeke through this plan I've orchestrated, a plan that only by luck and misfortune has brought me back to the place that I never wanted to return. If Joe Straut were still alive, I wouldn't be here."

"Where would you be?"

"Most likely where I'm at now."

"In bed with a whore?" Molly said.

Lucas didn't answer. Silence eased between them for a long second, then Molly broke it, pushing forward with her concerns—though Lucas was not sure why she was so interested.

"She was here?" Molly asked. "This love of yours that you won't cut loose?"

"Our lives were here. Everywhere about us. I knew it might be hard coming back, but I felt the stir of grief, of missing her long before I stepped foot off the train at the Nashville station. It was you that done it, brought my heart up to my throat. I should've sent you back, said no to Fiona Dane, that it'd have to be another girl, or no girl at all. That would've saved me a lot of trouble now that I know what you were sent to do. But I couldn't bear sending you back. Not even after you tried to kill me."

"Just doin' what I was paid for."

"I'm glad I've got deep pockets."

"That you do." Molly laid her hand on Lucas's chest gently. Her touch was warm, easy. "And I'm glad of it, too. Glad that you didn't kill me in return."

"I could have never hurt you."

"Because of her?"

Lucas nodded. "Because of Charlotte."

"You loved her?"

"Since I was a boy, since the first time I saw her standing in the lane that led up to our house, holding her mother's hand, the light dimmed by the oak canopy, her bright red hair ablaze like I had never seen before, or since."

"Until you saw me."

"Until I saw you. Your hair is red like hers. Not the same shade, lighter, and you look nothing like her, not really. But there's something you share, a spirit, I haven't been able to put my finger on it."

"Umm," Molly said, suggestively. "You'll have to try harder."

"Maybe I will."

Molly rolled over on her side, and stared at Lucas. "Nash and this Barlow, they mean to kill you. But they'll torture you first. I know enough about Nash to know that he enjoys the sight of sufferin'. You can't be leadin' with grief if you're gonna face 'em down on this day, and send your Negro friend to freedom like ya say ya want to."

"He killed her," Lucas said. His voice cracked and he stiffened at the memory of Charlotte Brogan dying in his arms, pierced by a machete thrown by Barlow's Celestial valet, Bojack Wu. "And I couldn't save her."

Molly put her index finger on Lucas's lips, stopping him from saying another word. She nuzzled his neck then, and slowly trailed her other hand, the one that she had rested on his chest, down to his manhood. It didn't take much convincing, and before Lucas knew it, Molly was straddling him, joined with him, rocking slowly, pushing away his past the best way she knew how.

Lucas tapped on the door to the room in the basement. He was fully dressed, bathed, shaven, armed visibly and invisibly, and ready to get on with the day. Molly was back in the room, locked in from the outside, enjoying a long bath, and the luxury of time. Her part in the plan was over. She needed to stay out of sight, be there when Lucas returned. *If* he came back . . .

"It's time to go, Zeke," Lucas said, through the door.

No answer came, and the basement of the hotel was as quiet as it could be. Commerce had begun to commence overhead.

Hurried footsteps echoed about like a hundred drums all playing at once, and muffled voices, some shouting, some low, offering commands and gratitude, filtered downward, mixing with the mechanisms that also resided in the bowels of the hotel. A boiler for steam, generating heat and power, the wheels and cables for the Otis that carried loads up and about, along with coal, burlap bags full of unknown grains and foods, and of course, a healthy population of rats and mice.

A little mouse had run across Lucas's boot almost as soon as he had set foot on the basement floor. He'd flinched but hadn't started. He hated rodents. Rats especially, and it took all he had in him not to try to stamp on the mouse and squish it. No use spilling any blood until he really had to.

"Door be open," Zeke said, from inside the room.

Lucas pushed the door open as easily as he could, and stood at the threshold.

The room, and all of the other rooms allowable for Negro guests, was hardly larger than a broom closet. There was no way Zeke could have slept on the child-sized cot that had been provided. A mass of sheets and the pillow lay on the floor, and it was obvious that he had tried to rest there.

Zeke sat in his long johns, shirt, and pants, on the edge of the cot, his head in between his skillet-sized hands, his elbows resting on his knees. A small coal oil lamp flickered on a low flame, and made it look like Zeke took up three-quarters of the room. His shadow nearly drowned out all of the light.

"I can't do this, Mistuh Lucas. I can't go into that court-room an' see Mistuh Barlow, and all those people. I knows it be how wrongs are righted, but it might as well be a land of strange-speaking mens that I don't unnerstand. Ain't no words that can fix this wrong. Nothin' gonna make Celia like she was, ain't no kinda magic in this world that can fix that."

"You're right, Zeke, but you have to go. It's the only way to do this right. The only way you'll be able to walk as a free man wherever you go. But that's not really the reason is it?" Lucas said. "You're not just afraid of the law, are you?"

Zeke shook his head. "I never thought I'd ever see Celia alive again, Mistuh Lucas. I didn't see how no one could live like that for any length of time."

"She's the same on the inside, Zeke, if that's what you're worried about. I knew Celia as a girl, just like I knew John and Mary Catherine. She's always been the same, just like they were. She had a great capacity to love then, and I know she still does."

Zeke looked to Lucas, his eyes red. "It's my fault. I couldn't stop him from hurtin' her."

Lucas breathed regularly before he said another word,

and looked to the floor, searching for the right words. "I understand. I really do. But Celia needs to be free, too. She might not be able to walk or talk like she used to be able to. But she's lived in a prison all her own, controlled by her father, the man who put her there. You can set her free from him, Zeke. It's about Celia as much as it is about you."

Zeke matched Lucas's breath, and stood up with a sudden recognition in his eyes. "All right, you right—I can still help her. Let's go do this thing. Let's go make Celia free."

FIFTY

HARD SUMMER LIGHT BEAT DOWN FROM THE
sun even though it was young in the sky. The air was thick
with humidity, oppressive, like the world was trying to
knock Lucas and Zeke back from taking one more step forward. But nothing could stop them. Not now. The unusually
hot weather was the least of their worries.

It was a bold and calculated move to walk to the courthouse instead of sneaking in from a carriage ride, or some
other stealthy way of transporting themselves from the hotel.
The mechanics of Lucas's plot had brought them straight to
where they were: In the middle of a circus, a trial of the
century that had not only caught the locals' attention, but
the entire country's, and beyond that, the world's. Lucas had
overheard someone say that an article about Barlow and his
foul crime had appeared in a recent Paris newspaper. The
thought of such a thing made him smile.

Lucas walked with squared shoulders and assured steps.
They were protected by the eyes of a thousand onlookers.
A crowd a hundred people deep and a hundred people wide

hunkered in front of the courthouse, anxious for any news, any bit of gossip to filter out. The trial started at noon.

But as confident as Lucas was, he also knew that he and Zeke were open targets by walking down the street. A multitude of eyes had not been able to save a Union president in Ford's Theatre, nor could they save Zeke, or Lucas, for that matter. All it took was one enraged man, angry and riled by the sight of a black man who'd assumed relations with a white woman, trying to set himself free of a crime that had not taken place. There was reason enough for some madman to pull a trigger just by imagining Zeke and Celia together.

And then there was John Barlow's men to consider. Not only Kingsley Nash, but Lucas had no doubt that Barlow had his own plan, one that reached beyond the bounty hunter—especially considering the news that had come late to him from Curtis Keane, that John Barlow had escaped the prison. Walked out. Just disappeared. Lucas was not surprised, but the thought of it put another sense of risk and concern on his shoulders.

Lucas would much rather confront John Barlow out in a crowd than one on one in a dark alley somewhere unexpected. But a public showing wasn't John Barlow's style, not even with his father's freedom at stake. There was a master plan in progress at the moment, the pieces moving unseen on an invisible chessboard. Just like with Lucas. His plan was coming to an end.

He looked up to the rooftop across the street at the thought, and quickly spied one of Sheriff Keane's marksmen. His confidence had been boosted by the fact that protection had been assured from up above, and on the ground, in the crowd, along the route to the courthouse. More than a hundred deputies and special appointees had been assigned to oversee the trial, and make sure that it was a peaceful event. The sheriff was very much aware of John Barlow's capabilities, and was also concerned by a possible show of force from the Ku Klux Klan. They had promised an appearance, but so far there had been no sign of the white-sheeted men. Most likely because the court was to convene in the light of day, offering them no darkness to hide under. Still, just the rumor of the organization's presence was cause for wariness.

Zeke walked next to Lucas, silent, sweating, not so much because of the humidity and warmth, but because of the obvious fear that was painted on his face.

"It'll be fine," Lucas said. They slowed as the crowd thickened, and the advance of the carnival atmosphere was met visually as well as by the nose. The air smelled of fresh popped popcorn and sweet offerings that covered the normal odors brought on by a crowd.

"If'n you say so, Mistuh Lucas," Zeke said as a man on stilts strode by him. It was a rare moment to see Zeke have to crane his neck upward to look a man in the eye.

"I do," Lucas said.

"Shore is a lot of folks here to see how things turn out. I didn't expect such a thing. Never really seen anything like it in my life."

"Me neither," Lucas said. The crowd was getting so thick that he began to worry that they would be late to the trial.

The throng of people had closed up around the front steps of the courthouse, and it was hard to see over the fine hats the women wore, and the tall ones on the men's heads. No amount of frippery had been spared by the populace of Nashville in attendance for the event. The most fashionable dresses and suits could be seen at a glance. Lucas supposed everyone there had a secret hope of getting noticed by some newspaper reporter, perhaps getting their name mentioned in the paper, or at the very least, a description of their appearance. The trial looked to have brought out the scallywags, hucksters, and high-society folks, all packed together tighter than pork and beans in a Van Camp's can.

Just as Lucas was starting to panic, he heard a familiar voice calling out his name.

"Fume!"

Lucas's first instinct was to drop his hand to the Colt that rested on his hip, react to trouble coming his way, hoping all along that the shout was just a warning. But a quick glance to his right told him that Sheriff Keane was motioning for him, reassuring him that there was nothing to worry about.

"Over here," Keane continued, waving Lucas and Zeke over to him. He was standing in an alleyway in between a haberdashery and a milliner's shop.

Zeke saw Keane, too. "Follow me, Mistuh Lucas," he said as he pushed a path open for them to traverse. "'Xcuse me, 'xcuse me, I'm sorry, I shore am. 'Xcuse us. Don't mean no troubles, no, ma'am, I don't."

It didn't take long for them to reach Keane, but it felt like it had taken a great amount of effort.

"I was lucky to have spied you," Keane said, reaching out to shake hands with Lucas.

Lucas returned the gesture, quickly settled in, and tried to get his bearings. "I'm glad you did. I'm assuming there's an easier way into the courthouse? I was starting to get worried that we'd get trapped in this mess of folks."

"You're lucky you didn't get shot or knifed," Keane said, nodding to Zeke. "That one's hard to miss, if you ask me. Folks that can read will surely see him for what he's been made out to be."

"I tried to slouch," Zeke said.

"You'd be hard to miss on your knees, Zeke, especially in that maroon suit Lucas set you up in," Keane said. "What the hell were you thinkin', Fume? He'd glow in the dead of night." Sheriff Keane didn't look amused as he took in all of Zeke's garb.

Lucas shrugged. "Looked smart to me."

Keane acted like he was going to say something, but restrained himself. After a long second, he said, "Come on, we'd better get inside before someone figures out who you are, or we do end up bein' late. Judge Freely hates tardiness more 'an he hates liars."

The side door of the courthouse was guarded by three well-armed deputies. Each carried a rifle, six-shooters on each of their hips, and hard, unrelenting scowls on their weathered faces. They were men of Lucas's age or older—old enough to have fought in the war and know how to use the weapons they carried.

Keane pushed by the men without offering any words. Lucas and Zeke followed close behind. They were at the back of the courthouse, and a smaller crowd had formed, but there was no mistaking the words of hate being directed toward Zeke.

"Don't listen to them," Lucas said. "No matter, you know what is right and wrong. They're just taking up for their kind. Senator Barlow can do more for them than you can. He's a local son, a man that made good, so no matter what, he's going to have his supporters. That couldn't be suppressed no matter how hard I tried," Lucas said. "No amount of money can make haters stop hating."

"It be all right, Mistuh Lucas. They said you was ugly, too, so that made me feel better." Zeke forced a smile.

Lucas nodded, took the ribbing like it was intended—to break the tension.

The door slammed behind them, and the noise of the crowd softened. The hallway was long and almost immediately dark. It smelled institutional: musty, and uncertain. There were old jail cells in the basement of the courthouse, and no matter how hard he tried, Lucas couldn't shake the feeling that he was walking back into the confines of a prison. He hadn't thought he would be concerned about his own freedom, but he suddenly was. And he didn't like that sinking feeling at all.

FIFTY-ONE

CELIA COULD BARELY BREATHE. HER LUNGS felt like they were sopping wet, weighted down in her chest like lead balloons. There was a rattle caught in her throat that she was sure only she could hear. Little Ling seemed unconcerned or, if she was, she hid her feelings. All that had mattered to the Celestial girl of recent was preparing to leave again, to go to the one place Celia didn't want to go—until she heard Little Ling say these words: "Zeke be there, missy. Waiting for you. Little Ling promises you that. He be there with a smile on his face."

There was nothing to do but surrender then. No matter what she had to do or go through, there was nothing more that Celia Barlow wanted than to see Zeke Henry one more time. She gasped at the thought, drawing Little Ling back into her view.

"You okay, missy?"

One blink. *Yes*.

"Okay. It won't be long now. Sulley be here soon, then we go. You all ready, we do what we need to do, then we go get you settled. No more moving after that, okay? Just rest, talk, and watch the day come and go. No worry at all for missy."

Two blinks. *No.*

There was no way for Celia to say what she wanted to. She hadn't been able to shout gutturally like she had when she'd been scared. Her voice had left her once again. Perhaps it was the weather, hot and sticky with humidity so thick it could be seen hovering in the distance like an ever-present fog. Or maybe the loss of her voice was something else. The thing she felt deep within her, growing, eating at her, pulling her down into a darkness she feared she would never be able to escape.

What Celia wanted to say to Little Ling was this: *I will always worry about Zeke, and you, and Lucas. None of you will ever be free. Even with my brother and father in jail—if we are so lucky that they will stay there. They have fingers like shadows. There will always be men who will come to their beckoning and do their bidding. No one will be free as long as any of us Barlows are alive.*

"What do you mean no, missy?" Little Ling hovered over Celia with a desperate look of concern on her face. "You can't tell me, can you?"

Two blinks. *No.*

"Are you feeling sick?"

Celia hesitated. She didn't want to worry Little Ling unnecessarily. Two blinks.

"Scared? Are you scared?"

One blink. No hesitation. *Yes.* That was the truth of it all. Celia was scared about what was going to happen at the trial, and afterward. She was worried about what would happen to them all, because she knew her brother and father well enough to know that they would not submit to such a proceeding without a plan to control it—or escape it. At any cost. If Celia got to see Zeke she would die happy—no matter what happened. But she didn't want anyone else to get hurt because of her. There had been enough madness because she had been unable to control her heart, her feelings.

A door opened and closed in the distance, and the sound of it drew Little Ling's attention from Celia. "I be right back, missy. It's Sulley. He come to get us. It be time to go, okay?"

One blink. Two blinks. One blink. *Yes, no, yes.* Celia had no choice but to go, and she knew it.

Lancaster Barlow's ankles were confined by leg irons. A chain ran up his back to his wrists, which were pulled behind him, not allowing him to be free in any way. He had to scoot slowly to walk from the police wagon to the courthouse.

He walked with his head down, trying his best not to pay any attention to the crowd around him. Some people jeered, while others clapped and offered shouts of encouragement. But all the senator could focus on was the smell of food on the wind, and the knowledge of his son's plans, and what was going to happen next.

The thin gruel he had been fed since he'd been jailed had left him weak, near starving. Food had been such a benign presence in Washington that he had taken it for granted, never feared being without a good meal. That would never happen again.

Jonah Fletcher walked slowly next to Barlow, his hand on his elbow, guiding the senator. Fetch had relayed the plan in bits and parts, slowly, quietly, certain that it wasn't overheard. The senator worried that the plan was too dangerous, would have repercussions beyond the trial, but he was in no position to object. Not that it would have done him any good as it was. There was no arguing with John. There never had been once he settled on an idea. Even if the senator had thought to deny involvement, there was no way to communicate his opposition to his son. The plan was in motion, and John was in hiding, lying low—even though Lancaster was certain that his son was close by. For all he knew, John was in the crowd behind him, dressed in a disguise, mixed in among the onlookers, unable to be detected like the chameleon that he was—and always had been.

The senator and Fetch were surrounded by six deputies. None of whom had offered any help of any kind to the aged Barlow. They had looked at him like he was pond scum.

Ordinarily, Lancaster would have shown offense, but he'd held his tongue as he was escorted into the courthouse. He was certain of his revenge, had no doubt in his son's capabilities, and more than anything, Senator Barlow hoped that each deputy had kissed his wife good-bye when he'd left home this morning because each deputy's fate had been sealed from the moment he'd walked out the door.

FIFTY-TWO

THE SIGN ON THE DOOR SAID: NO GUNS AL-
lowed. It was a temporary sign written in fancy black ink
letters on butcher's paper, tacked next to the door that led into
the courtroom. The only exceptions granted were for Sheriff
Keane and his deputies. They were fully armed, situated at
every entrance, enforcing the new rule to groans, grunts, and
outright refusals. Those folks were kindly shown to the door.

"Sorry, Lucas, Zeke, that means the both of you," Keane
said, "unless either of you wants to become a deputy real
quick? I think I've got an extra badge or two in my pocket."

Lucas shook his head, and began to unbuckle his gun belt.
"Never had the inclination to wear a badge, Keane," Lucas
answered, handing his two Colts to an unknown deputy.
"You're under enough scrutiny the way it is for having a hand
in all of this, you don't need me pulled into that light."

Zeke stood next to Lucas, and offered nothing. He wore
no visible weapons on his hips, so there was nothing to offer
to the table full of guns. The suggestion from Keane was
more out of respect than what was apparent.

"Might be a little late for that, Lucas," Sheriff Keane

said. "*The Tennessean* has already linked our past association in the war. At least they still see spies as heroes, but they've also endorsed Lancaster Barlow for every election he's run in. Sooner or later, they're gonna have to choose a side whether they want to or not. I figure it won't go your way since you're standin' up for Zeke. Right is right, you know, as far as the press is concerned, unless it suits them for it not to be."

Once Lucas deposited his gun belt on the table, the sheriff pushed past the deputy and walked into the courtroom unhindered.

Lucas followed quickly behind Keane, relieved that he had planned ahead with another invisible set of weapons for himself and Zeke. The newspapers were the least of his concerns at the moment.

Zeke stayed at Lucas's side, almost like they were chained together, shoulder to shoulder. The Negro had remained quiet since they'd entered the courthouse, and Lucas knew that Zeke was nervous, scared by all of the proceedings going on inside the building. There was no question that this was uncertain territory for any man of color—or a white one without an education, as far as that went. One wrong word could rain down a whole lot of trouble on a simple man.

The courtroom was cavernous, three stories tall with a row of windows supporting a dome that was adorned with a trompe l'oeil mural. The mural was a painting with forced perspective that made the dome look deeper and bigger than it really was. A regiment of angels prepared for battle on one side, while ugly demons on the other side charged. Lucas supposed the mural was about finding the truth, but he held little interest in the art, or the story, that hovered over his head at the moment. His eyes immediately searched out the exits, and all of the deputies guarding them.

Keane had put normally dressed men in the room, scattered them about inconspicuously in case anything got out of hand. Their guns were hidden, and to the populace of the room, the undercover men looked like they were attending the trial for the same reasons they were.

The seats were three-quarters full, but it wouldn't take long for them all to be filled. Overflow would fill the halls all the way down the outside steps, and stretch for blocks, filling the hucksters' pockets and filling the local coffers with more coins than they had counted on. The trial was good for business in Nashville. There was some satisfaction to be had in that.

It was already warm and muggy in the courtroom, a reflection of the summer weather outside. But there was no breeze to make sitting in the courtroom bearable like there was outside. Physical comfort, though, was of little concern to Lucas. It was the outcome that he was interested in.

They all sat down in the second row, behind an empty row of seats that was blocked off with rope, saved for someone special.

Celia and Little Ling had not appeared yet—but that didn't make Lucas nervous. He hadn't expected them to be inside the courtroom yet.

Zeke had a difficult time fitting into the normal-sized chair. His knees pressed against Lucas's as he settled in, trying to get comfortable. "Sorry," he offered. Both men shrugged, and tried their best to get situated in the hard seats themselves.

Minutes passed as the courtroom filled and more people, mostly men, shuffled about, finding seats, getting comfortable themselves. Both women and men fanned themselves with one kind of instrument or another, usually held for decoration only, but in dire need in the hot room. It already felt like the inside of a Turkish steam bath.

It looked like half of Nashville had shown up for the trial.

A door just beyond the empty judge's bench opened, and the room gasped as Senator Lancaster Barlow was led into the room by a surly-looking bailiff.

Lucas's attention was drawn to the senator, a man he had known since he was a boy. Barlow was almost unrecognizable. He was tall and thin, stooped over with weakness and age, dressed in filthy clothes that resembled tramp rags, unshaven with a three-day beard, and his hair unshorn, making him look like a madman under lock and key. It was not the man Lucas had expected to see: confident, well-dressed, and commanding. "What have you done?" he asked Keane.

"What do you mean? He's been in jail just like the rest of the criminals brought in there."

"He looks like hell."

"As well he should."

"It's a mistake. He'll be pitied."

"You have little faith in Judge Freely's taste for revenge. There was nothing more that that man wanted than to be a senator, and Barlow beat him at every turn. Sometimes fairly, sometimes underhandedly by spewing lies to the newspapers. You timed this event so it would fall in Freely's court for a reason. Have some faith in your plan, Lucas," Sheriff Keane said. "It has gone off just like you hoped it would."

"Plus or minus a few folks who are dead now because of my instigations."

"You didn't commit the crime. No use blaming yourself for it. Things happen. Everything can't work out like you write it down," Keane said. His voice was low with the obvious hope that only Lucas could hear him.

"You're right. But Straut's death still stings. Hobie Lawton's, too, even though I didn't know him as well. There's a lot that can go wrong in a trial, Keane. You know that. If the senator is convicted, don't you think that he'll appeal? I do. He's got more friends in high places than either of us could ever think we do. You should have let him clean up at the very least. Your newspaper is going to have a heyday with this, draw you as some maniacal prison warden."

The sheriff shrugged. "Let 'em. I'm about done with this game anyway. I ain't goin' through another election."

The senator drew Lucas's attention as he shuffled to his seat in front of a table that faced the empty judge's bench. The opposite wall was lined with ten-shelf barrister bookcases filled to the brim with ledgers and books of all kinds.

The bailiff stood back a couple of feet behind Barlow without showing any intention of going anywhere else for the moment.

Lucas watched, too, as a lawyer, old and decrepit himself, appeared out of the same door, and made his way to the senator. He placed a simple satchel on the table in front of Barlow, and sat down next to the senator without saying a word.

Lucas had expected a team of Washington lawyers to represent Barlow, and the sight of the single, less-than-capable lawyer concerned him—but not enough to raise it to Keane.

More long minutes passed. More scuffling of feet and filling of chairs behind and above them—along with the requisite smells of a hot, closed-in crowd. It was all starting to get to Lucas, make him feel closed in like there was no escape, but the courtroom was not a jail cell or a root cellar, and he wasn't locked in with no way out. Still, he felt distantly uncomfortable. He squirmed in his seat.

A tap echoed through the room, and the bailiff walked away from the table, leaving Barlow and his lawyer to confer in whispers, as he went to the original door they had come out of. The bailiff, a middle-aged man with out-of-fashion pork-chop sideburns, grabbed the door handle, then faced the courtroom and said, "All rise!"

Everyone obeyed, and the bailiff didn't open the door until the noise died down.

Judge Jacob Freely walked into the courtroom, immediately scowled at Lancaster Barlow, then made his way to the bench and sat down heavily. He looked tired, angry, like this was the last place he wanted to be.

Freely looked to be about the same age as Lancaster Barlow, but weighed about a hundred pounds more. His black judicial robes were bursting at the seams, and the floor had protested with a loud creak when he'd stepped up onto the dais that held his seat.

The man had put on quite a bit of girth since the last time Lucas had seen him—which was a long time ago, after an election loss, licking his wounds at one of the local taverns.

The judge ignored Lucas's presence at the moment, and situated a mass of papers in front of him.

"Be seated," the bailiff instructed the crowd, and everyone

did as they were told. The motion created a quick wind that went away as quickly as it had appeared.

Judge Freely didn't seem to be in any kind of hurry, and was very exact about how he placed his papers. Once everything was in its place, he motioned for the bailiff to come over to the bench. They conferred for a long moment, with the pork-chop man checking his pocket watch more than once, all the while casting a furtive glance over to the empty seats in front of Lucas and the sheriff.

Lucas was starting to get nervous, too. "You're sure they had enough protection?" he asked, concerned about Celia and Little Ling's tardiness. They were the only missing part. All of the other players were present. Though, Lucas was still worried about John Barlow, and what he might be up to. There had been no sign, or word, of him since his escape from prison.

"Relax," Keane said, "they'll be here."

"If anything happened to them . . ."

Keane turned to Lucas. "You're in the wrong place to make threats, Lucas."

Lucas was about to recant, offer that he was frustrated and worried, but he didn't have a chance to. What they all were waiting on appeared at the door.

An audible gasp emitted from the onlookers in the courtroom as Sulley pushed a chair with big wheels attached to the back legs, and casters on the front, through the door.

The sheriff, Lucas, and Zeke stood up, all with the same intention of helping—but were immediately waved off by Little Ling. She was at the side of the chair, helping Sulley guide it inside.

Celia was barely visible. She was covered with a fancy handmade blanket, white like an angel's wing, from her neck to her feet. It was easy to see she was twisted in the bentwood wheelchair, lying sideways, with her head cocked to the right, like she was too weak to hold it upright. Her hair, once a lustrous chestnut, looked brittle and dull, though perfectly placed, and recently brushed. Her eyes were wide open, and seemed to come to life as soon as she saw Zeke.

It only took a second for the crowd to erupt in a noise that was a mixture of surprise, sadness, and disbelief.

"Order! Order in the court," Judge Freely yelled.

But the room didn't seem to hear him. Women began to sob. Some of them fainted at the sight of Celia. Men started screaming at Lancaster Barlow, pointing to him in accusation. Others just stood silent, in shock, like they were seeing something real that they hadn't believed was real until that very moment.

The senator buried his head in his hands, while his lawyer remained next to him, unaffected, like he had expected such a reaction from the crowd when Celia was carted in.

Lucas was starting to get nervous as he watched Little Ling fuss over Celia, situating the blanket, talking in her ear, obviously trying to soothe her. It was hard to tell if Celia was upset, but it was easy to see that the Celestial girl bordered on the edge of panic.

"We need to do something," Lucas said to Keane.

The sheriff shook his head, and maintained his line of vision, which was directed straight at the judge.

Lucas glanced over to Zeke then. Tears were streaming down the big Negro's face. His oversized hands gripped the rail that separated him from the seats in front of them, and Lucas feared that Zeke was either going to jump over the rail, or snap it in half with his grip. Lucas touched Zeke's wrist, and said, "We won't let anything happen to her."

Zeke looked tongue-tied, like he was a mute, too, or one of the men who was seeing something he didn't believe he ever would. It was hard to tell.

"Order! If you all don't quiet down, I will have you all removed," Judge Freely shouted. "Bailiff, quiet this crowd."

The bailiff started to walk forward toward the front of the legal stage, his hand edging to the gun on his side. Some kind of understanding must have clicked with the crowd, because they started to shush simultaneously.

Relieved, Lucas looked over his shoulder, up to the top level of the courtroom to satisfy himself that everything was going to be all right, that they were on track to get started with the trial. But everything wasn't all right. Just as he looked up, Lucas heard a series of doors slam shut, and a ruckus in the distance. Then something came flying down from the third floor. At first he thought it was paper, or a woman's handbag, but then he realized it was neither.

Lucas gasped, didn't have time to do anything but dive toward Celia once he figured out what it was that he was seeing.

The grenade landed directly behind Judge Freely and exploded on contact, just like it had been designed to do.

FIFTY-THREE

THE EXPLOSION ROCKED THE FLOOR OF THE
courtroom, but it did little damage on first glance. Like all
grenades of the type, left over from the war, it appeared to
be mostly smoke: a device to offer cover or distraction,
deadly to only those who came directly in contact with the
device, if then.

Judge Freely was knocked off the bench by the blast, and
had disappeared into the thick black cloud that hovered in
the front of the courtroom.

Screams and chaos suddenly filled the room, proving
louder than the blast originally had been.

In his overzealous desire to protect Celia, Lucas dove
over her and tumbled to the floor. He'd tried to roll, but
landed squarely on his side. Luckily, he had no gun belt on
to cause him any pain or injury. Smoke filled his nose and
burned his lungs, but he was alive, missed by any shrapnel
from the grenade. He gathered himself as quickly as he
could and bounced up into a crouch, his first concern still
Celia's health and welfare.

Chairs tipped over, and the crowd pressed out of the doors

of the three-story courtroom like horses fleeing a barn fire:
legs pumping as fast as they could, not looking behind them,
blind to what they were running toward. Gunshots rang out
distantly then, unseen, the start of a battle, or a slaughter,
Lucas wasn't sure which. The tactic at hand seemed familiar,
leaving him assured that he knew who was behind it.

Lucas rushed to Celia, who was still covered by the
blanket, unmoved from her place; she was surrounded by
Zeke, Little Ling, and Sheriff Keane.

"We need to get her out of here," Keane yelled.

"No!" Lucas answered. "No one is safe outside. Listen."

The gunshots continued. Only there were more shots
being fired. There were answers from different spots. Lucas
figured that Keane's undercover men were engaged in con-
flicts they hadn't been prepared for. At least, that's what it
sounded like.

Lucas looked around for a safe place, then pushed around
to the back of Celia's wheelchair, grabbed the handles, then
pushed the wheelchair up against the closest wall. "Zeke,
give me a hand moving some of these bookcases, and we'll
barricade her in."

"You should take her out of here," Keane yelled. A gunshot echoed down from the same spot that the grenade had
been thrown from, drawing the sheriff's attention upward.
He pulled his Colt Peacemaker from the holster, and fired
back, giving Lucas cover as he tried to drive Celia into a
safe corner.

A glance to her eyes showed that Celia was fully aware
of what was going on. Her skin was pasty white and her
brown eyes were deep with fear.

"Don't worry, Celia, I'm not going to let anything happen
to you." He gently stopped the chair, and pulled a barrister
bookcase from the wall, angling it against the seats. The
piece of furniture was heavy, but it suddenly moved with
ease as Zeke joined in.

"Don't you worry none, Celia, you be safe in here," Zeke
said.

"Ling, get in here," Lucas commanded the Celestial girl.

She was visibly shaken by the turn of events. Her eyes were glazed over with shock and fear, but she scurried to the wheelchair dutifully.

It only took Lucas and Zeke half a minute to pin Celia and Little Ling in the corner. They were reasonably protected from gunshots, but not from a fully live grenade. None of them were protected from that.

Lucas glanced through the clearing smoke, and saw Lancaster Barlow and his lawyer heading for the door that the judge and bailiff had come out of. He reached into his shirt and pulled out a .32-caliber Colt from a hidden shoulder holster he'd rigged up. He had another one on his right shoulder, too. Zeke carried the same rig. They both wore ankle holsters armed with First Model Derringers, knowing ahead of time that there would be no guns allowed in the courtroom. Neither of them had been physically searched. No one was, which was an error on Keane's part—but the sheriff had proclaimed that such a thing had never been done, and he didn't have the manpower to pull it off, not in a crowd this large. The consequences of that action were fully apparent.

The bailiff was on the floor, stunned, but not mortally injured.

Keane hit his target, and an unidentified man tumbled over the rail of the third-floor gallery and hit the floor below with a thud. There was no use in seeing if he had any life left in him. Keane followed up with a shot just to make sure the man was dead.

"Stop right there, Barlow," Lucas yelled out to Barlow and his lawyer.

Another grenade whistled down from the third floor, along with three gunshots.

The shots were haphazard, hitting the floor around Keane and Zeke, who had followed Lucas's lead, and pulled out one of his derringers. The Negro joined the sheriff, who was hunkered along the side of another bookcase. Zeke returned fire, and the gunshots from above stopped.

The grenade was another smoker, used mostly in war by the Navy. There was a small explosion, a bright orange flash.

The smoke, a stinky sulfur, was meant to be used to hide boats and their movements. This one landed a few feet from Lucas, and it knocked him backward, sending him tumbling into the judge's dais.

There had been no sign of Freely, nor had there been any time to check on his welfare. Celia was the intended target in the attack, and protecting her at all costs had been Lucas's only concern.

He was dazed by the explosion, and had not been prepared for the thickness of the smoke, the difficulty it caused him to breathe. He coughed and hacked as he tried to stand, to steady himself. The little Colt had flown out of his hand. He had no idea where it was. He wasn't quite blind, could still see fragments of light, but everything was completely out of focus. It was like being on a bad drunk and being shot at at the same time.

"Well, well, look at Lucas Fume on the floor. Just where he belongs," Lucas heard a familiar voice say. It was John Barlow, standing over him, with both of his hooks raised in the air, prepared to strike like the snake that he was.

FIFTY-FOUR

BARLOW'S METAL HOOK STRUCK LUCAS ON
the side of the face with surprising force. He crashed to the
floor unsure if his jaw was broken, in the most pain he could
ever remember feeling. His cheek was hot, like he'd been
seared with a branding iron and hit with a sledgehammer at
the same time.

He wept with the sting of smoke and pain; his vision was
blurry, and he teetered on the wrong side of consciousness.
Pain careened through his body, meeting with the recognition of fear. He was down, vulnerable, gasping for breath
like a fish out of water about to be filleted for dinner.

Lucas knew John Barlow's ways. The sadistic tactic the
handless monster liked best was to make his opponent suffer,
force him to fully digest his defeat before he finally did him
in. Killing a man quickly bore no merit. It seemed like he had
learned his ways from the Cheyenne. The Indians were said
to torture their victims for days—as a favor to them, so they
would take the fight on to the next life with them. Barlow was
not the kind of man to do a victim a favor, and he had been
torturing men long before he ventured west, an angry man

bent on revenge, retribution, and now, resurrection of his own name and presence. Barlow had always enjoyed watching living creatures suffer, especially humans. Lucas had seen it more than once, and now, it was his turn—*again*.

Lucas had the weapons to defend himself, but not the wherewithal or the strength. He could barely tell if he was alive or dead. If he were a praying man, which he was not, this would have been the time to offer up a plea to be saved or taken, whichever one was the least painful.

Distantly, he heard maniacal laughter, more gunshots, hand-to-hand fighting, fists smacking skin, pain echoing through the air, a whimper of fear underneath it all. Celia. It must have been Celia or Little Ling.

The desire to die vanished.

Suddenly, Lucas was hoisted into the air by his hair. The pain had not disappeared, but clarity returned to his vision once his feet hit the ground. He looked over his shoulder, and found himself face to face with Kingsley Nash.

"Barlow always did need someone do his fighting for him. I figured you'd be here, Nash."

"I figured you'd be dead by now." Kingsley Nash was a head taller than Lucas, and his aristrocratic tongue had not disappeared. It must not have been an act like Lucas had thought it was in Kansas. He didn't know the bounty hunter's story, and he didn't want to, either. He just wanted to kill the man. But that was out of the question at the moment. Along with the secure grip of his hair, Nash had jammed the barrel of a gun in Lucas's back.

"Lucas, Lucas, what have you gone and done now?"

Lucas blinked and John Barlow was standing in front of him.

The senator and his lawyer were huddled behind the table they had been sitting at. Zeke and Sheriff Keane were standing in front of the barrister bookcases with their hands up—held there by an unknown compatriot of Barlow's; a handkerchief covered the man's face. It appeared that the courtroom was empty. If anyone remained, they were wounded or dead. All of the doors were closed.

"You don't have much time, Barlow," Lucas said.

John Barlow shrugged. "I'll take what I came for and be on my way."

"And what is that?" Lucas asked.

"None of your damn business, Fume," Nash hissed into his ear.

"Kingsley, be nice. Once again, Lucas has brought me what I want most. Only this time, there are no traitors to spoil the victory. Joe Straut is dead from what I understand, Lucas. How does it feel to be responsible for another death? It's a wonder you have any friends at all."

"What do you want, Barlow?" Lucas said through gritted teeth.

"My sister, of course. She is in need of my care."

Gunshots erupted outside of the courtroom, drawing Barlow's attention away from Lucas. He quickly made eye contact with Nash, offering a knowing look.

"I hope you have enough men," Keane said.

Barlow exhaled and dropped his head. "Kingsley, do what you were paid to do."

Nash didn't hesitate. He pushed Lucas forward so hard that he slammed into the judge's bench, disorienting him again—but not enough to cloud his realization of what was coming next. He slid to the floor, helpless.

Nash spun around with the gun that had been jammed in Lucas's back, and fired one perfectly aimed shot. Blood splattered from the center of Sheriff Curtis Keane's head and he fell instantly to the floor, provoking a shocked look from Barlow's man employed to keep the sheriff and Zeke at bay.

The bailiff was on the floor. His eyes wide open. Death had taken him quickly. There were three bullet holes in his chest.

Barlow laughed again—but only for a second.

Zeke took advantage of the distraction the gunshot presented. With all of his might, he reared back and shoved the unknown gunman as hard as he could—his strength was the only weapon he had. Surprised by the move, the gunman was lifted off his feet and nearly propelled halfway across the legal gallery.

Nash realized what was happening and leveled his gun at Zeke—but Zeke dove into the air, throwing Nash's plan off by a second or two. When he fired the gun, he missed Zeke by inches—then tried to back away, tried to turn and run. But it was too late. Zeke crashed into Nash like a black bull trying to escape by ramming a fence. They crashed to the ground in a loud clap of thunder, so loud it made the floor shake.

A look of panic crossed John Barlow's face. He had no guns, only hooks on both hands.

Lucas willed as much strength as he could muster, jumped up, and reached inside his shirt for the other derringer.

Zeke and Nash were a bundle of rage rolling on the floor—leaving Lucas to bet on Zeke. His only other worry, unless there were more of Barlow's men up in the empty seats, was the gunman Zeke had shoved away.

The gunman had been unprepared for the assault and was just coming to his feet. The tumble had knocked the gun from the man's hand, and the hat off his head. The handkerchief had fallen away from his face, too—exposing a flow of red hair, and a pale white face. It wasn't a man at all. It was Molly McKay.

Barlow realized that Molly had been exposed a few seconds before Lucas recognized her. Barlow ran to her, grabbed her from behind, and pressed the tip of his right hook against Molly's jugular.

She didn't have time to react, time to try for the gun that was on the floor. She didn't even have time to scream.

"You move an inch, Fume, and she's a dead girl," Barlow said, shielding himself behind her.

Lucas stopped, the derringer aimed straight at Molly. He couldn't get a shot at Barlow. Out of his periphery, he saw Senator Barlow and his lawyer creeping toward the judge's chambers. "Don't think I won't shoot you, Senator Barlow. You move another inch, and I will. You just sit down right where you are."

The senator and the lawyer stopped, and sunk to the floor like they were told.

Outside, more shooting came and went; the battle for the courthouse between Keane's men and Barlow's forces raged on. Lucas hoped the number of the sheriff's men had taken Barlow by surprise. It sounded like that was the case.

Zeke reared back and punched Nash as hard as he could, bouncing the man's head off the floor. It sounded like someone had thrown a pumpkin as hard as they could against a wall.

"Let her go, John," Lucas demanded.

"Oh, Lucas," Barlow said. "You've always had a weakness for redheads. You know you're not going to let anything happen to this girl."

It was a reference to Charlotte Brogan, killed by Bojack Wu, in the battle that had set him free—but had not come without heartbreak.

Molly McKay's green eyes were stricken with fear. Lucas didn't know whether to save her, or let her die. She had betrayed him by dressing in a disguise and acting as one of Barlow's men. He knew he could never trust her, and had no idea how she had made it from the locked room in the hotel to the courthouse, but that didn't take much of a stretch of the imagination to figure out. She'd been in communication with Barlow or one of his men all along.

But Lucas couldn't let her be hurt. The red hair clouded his judgment. Regardless, Molly didn't deserve to die a senseless death.

"You're right, I'm not. But in the time it takes to make your move, I'll get a shot off," Lucas said.

"Me, too," Zeke said. He had a gun in his hand, the one that had fallen on the floor, and was standing next to Lucas. "You bes' jus' let her go now, Mistuh Barlow."

Barlow laughed. "You think I'm going to take orders from a Negro?"

"You are if you want to live," Lucas said.

"That's enough, John!" It was Lancaster Barlow. He'd stood up, and even in his ratty clothes and haggard appearance, had managed to sound and look authoritative. "Let the girl go, and put an end to this. Enough people have died, and for what end? I will be on the run just like you if this scheme of yours goes off as planned. My reputation and career as a senator are ruined. I will be removed from office. I have had enough of this! People have died without just cause. I would have been better off to have faced a trial with a real lawyer at my side."

"A trial!" John Barlow seethed. "There was never a need for a trial. There was no crime committed."

"Yes, there was, John," Senator Barlow said. "I beat Celia unmercifully. I should have never struck her, but I did—and then I didn't stop."

"For a just cause!" John Barlow yelled. "For kissing and embracing that Negro."

"That is Celia's choice, John, just like it was Mary Catherine's choice to become a nun."

Lucas didn't move, and neither had John Barlow. His hook was still pressed against Molly's throat.

"That's madness," John Barlow said.

"No, this is madness. The floor is littered with blood and death," Lancaster Barlow said, stepping away from the table and Jonah Fletcher. "I have caused a great amount of pain by my one regrettable action, not only to my family, but to many others that I don't even know. I never thought it would come to this, not even at your hand. If only I had done the right thing."

"It didn't have to come to this, Father," Barlow said. "Celia has been silenced. No one would have ever known what you did. You fell victim to a silly Lucas Fume plan. It's your idiocy that's caused this. Not anything else."

"She can communicate," Lucas said. "Distinguish between *yes* and *no*. Justice will be served. She can tell what happened in her own way."

"Not if she's dead," Barlow said.

A shiver ran up Lucas's spine, and he made direct eye contact with Molly, then dropped his head. It was a risk, hoping that she understood his direction, but it was all he had left.

He had to save Celia.

He had to stop John Barlow.

It was that simple.

Regardless of their past, regardless of what had happened between them, revenge was the last thing Lucas felt in the tip of his trigger finger or in the bottom of his heart.

Molly suddenly dropped sideways to the floor, leaving John Barlow exposed. Lucas didn't hesitate. He trusted his aim and pulled the trigger.

FIFTY-FIVE

THE ROOM WAS LIGHT AND AIRY. IT HAD ONLY taken Celia a few days to feel comfortable, to relax, and believe Little Ling when she said nothing else was going to change. This was home.

Home. It was hard to believe after all that had happened. Her brother was dead, and her father was waiting on a new trial, moved to a federal prison and heavily protected. She knew she would never see him again, and that was fine with her. Enough was enough.

Little Ling had done her best to get her to eat, to make her favorite things, but Celia's appetite was nonexistent. She could barely swallow.

The doctor had come and gone, a gentle-looking man with a soft touch and soft eyes that had trouble not telling the truth. The rims of his eyes were always red, like he was overworked or tired, but the truth of it was that no matter how hard he worked he could do nothing to save Celia. She had heard him say so in a deep whisper outside the open door. People always misjudged her capabilities, but all of her remaining senses had heightened since the incident, though there were things she wished to have never heard. But there was no going back.

She was waiting on Zeke. He was supposed to be there anytime.

Little Ling padded into the room with a happy smile on her moon face. She immediately started straightening up the covers around Celia, then fussing with her hair. "We want missy to look nice for Mr. Zeke."

Is he here? Celia strained her ears but heard nothing. The house they were in was out away from the city, nestled alongside a meadow. At night, the whip-poor-wills sang her to sleep.

Little Ling nodded her head. "Coming up the road with Mr. Lucas."

Celia relaxed. If she could have smiled, she would have. One blink. *Yes.* That was her only way to show happiness.

The window was open, and a soft breeze fluttered the curtains. Horses approached, then stopped.

"I be right back," Little Ling said, then hurried out of the room.

Celia was alone—scared, excited, sad, if it was possible to be all three. A burst of energy flooded through her body, and she almost thought she could will herself to sit up. But she knew that was impossible. Just like she knew that the energy would not last. The darkness and weakness would return sooner than she wanted. There was no denying her fate.

Footsteps approached, and Lucas Fume stopped at the door. "Well, I'll be, look there, it's Celia Barlow." A wide smile crossed his face, then he walked to the bed, took her hand, raised it gently, and kissed it. "Pretty as ever."

You always were a rascal, Lucas Fume. My life might have turned out different if I could have loved you. But your heart was taken and every woman in Bledsoe County knew it.

Celia blinked twice. *No.*

"Well," Lucas said, "I disagree with that assessment." He had obviously been schooled by Little Ling on how to read her words.

Celia stared at Lucas, tried to look past him, but there was no one with him.

Lucas had not let go of her hand. "I must apologize for what happened between John and I, Celia. I had no choice. No choice in any of it really. I wanted nothing more than for Zeke to be free, and you to be all right. I didn't count on so many people getting hurt. Zeke's a free man, Celia. Free as I am. He's been exonerated of all charges against him. That's where we've been this last couple of days, trying to set things right."

That's wonderful news. Thank you. It's okay. One blink. *Yes.*

"Zeke's here. Do you want me to stay?"

Two blinks. *No.*

Lucas smiled, then laid her hand down as gently as he could. "You'll never want for anything, Celia. I've made sure of that. Little Ling will stay with you as long as you need her."

She believed him, didn't know what to say, or how to express what she felt, what she wanted to say. So, she just stared at Lucas.

He continued to smile, and backed out of the room.

Celia drew in a deep breath, heard her chest rattle slightly, distantly. She ignored it.

Footsteps approached. She blinked her eyes and Zeke was standing in the doorway. He nearly had to duck, and he filled the frame completely. A mouse couldn't have wiggled in if it had wanted to.

Aren't you a sight? Zeke was dressed in new clothes: a comfortable summer wool that fit him like a glove. It looked like the most expensive Sunday Goin' to Meetin' Suit she'd ever seen. He held a bouquet of summer flowers, mostly white daisies with some yellow violets mixed in, and wore a smile as wide as the Mississippi River.

"These is for you, Miss Celia," Zeke said. "Ling say she'd bring a vase, come shortly." He stepped in the room, and bit his lip. He looked tongue-tied, like a teenager come to call who'd never done it before.

Celia knew better.

Zeke laid the flowers on the sink, then walked over to the side of the bed. He was still smiling, but now his lip was quivering. He leaned down and kissed Celia's forehead, then pulled away quickly.

Two blinks. *No.*

Panic flashed across Zeke's face. "You don't want no kiss, Miss Celia?"

One blink. *Yes.*

The panic disappeared, and the smile returned to Zeke's face. He leaned down slowly and brushed his lips against Celia's.

She held her breath, wanted more than anything to reach up and meet his lips, but that was impossible. Responding was impossible. But she couldn't help but feel alive, electric— like this was a dream come true.

Lucas sat on the big bay gelding in front of the house, ready to leave. Molly McKay, dressed in a dark green riding dress, sat next to him on a smaller chestnut mare.

"You sure you won't reconsider, and go with us, Zeke?"

"No, suh," Zeke said. "I'm not leavin' Miss Celia ever again."

Little Ling stood by Zeke's side. "He gonna be fine, Mr. Lucas. Lots of work to keep him busy on a place like this." She smiled widely, and looked up at Zeke with approving eyes.

"All right," Lucas said. "You ever change your mind, you know how to get ahold of me."

"I does," Zeke answered. "I sure does."

Lucas sighed, and stared at Zeke. Everything that needed to be said between the two men had been said. All that remained was the parting. "We best go then. You ready, Molly?"

"I am," she said. Her voice was softer, and her demeanor more tame than it had been previously.

"Well, I'm not saying good-bye to either of you," Lucas said. "We'll meet again. I'm sure of it." He nodded at Zeke, and Zeke nodded back, just as Lucas nickered the horse.

Molly did the same, and met Lucas head to head as they rode down the lane.

Lucas looked over his shoulder to see Zeke and Little Ling waving. He couldn't wave back. He had to go now, or he never would. At least not until something happened to Celia, and Lucas didn't want to wait for that.

He turned to Molly. "So, Miss McKay, where do you want to go?"

"Not back to Kansas, I can tell you that."

"New York City?"

"No. I always dreamed of seeing Paris. How's that? Paris, France. That's where I want to go." Molly McKay looked like a little girl asking for a Christmas present.

"Why not?" Lucas said. "Paris, it is. Let's go." He kneed the gelding, and said, "Let's go to Paris, Miss McKay." Then he rode away without looking back.

ABOUT THE AUTHOR

Larry D. Sweazy (larrydsweazy.com) is a two-time WWA Spur award winner, a two-time, back-to-back winner of the Will Rogers Medallion Award, a Best Books of Indiana award–winner, and the inaugural winner of the 2013 Elmer Kelton Book Award. He was also nominated for a Short Mystery Fiction Society (SMFS) Derringer award in 2007. Larry has published over sixty nonfiction articles and short stories, and is the author of the Josiah Wolfe, Texas Ranger Western series (Berkley), the Lucas Fume Western series (Berkley), and a thriller set in Indiana, *The Devil's Bones* (Five Star). A new mystery series from Seventh Street Books will debut in 2015.

He lives in Indiana with his wife, Rose.

Don't miss the best
Westerns from Berkley

· ·

LYLE BRANDT
PETER BRANDVOLD
JACK BALLAS
J. LEE BUTTS
JORY SHERMAN
DUSTY RICHARDS

· ·

penguin.com

M10G0610